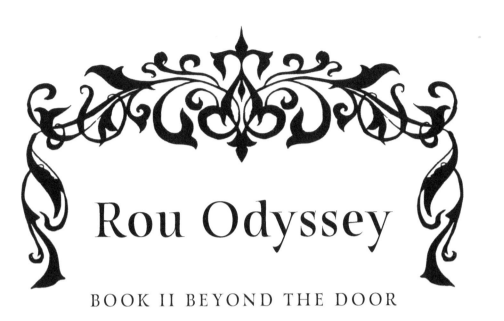

Rou Odyssey

BOOK II BEYOND THE DOOR

Kaiva Rose

MERCURY FALCON PRESS

Fargo, North Dakota

Kaiva Rose / Mercury Falcon Press
Printed in the United States of America 2021.
www.RouOdyssey.Com

Concept & Design by Kaiva Rose
Cover & Illustrations by Irina Kuzmina
Character Illustrations by Savannah Le
Layout Design by Kaiva Rose & Douglas Williams
Dragon Line Illustration by Madelyn Kolenda

Rou Odyssey : Beyond the Door/ Kaiva Rose. -- 1st ed.
ISBN: 9781732791145

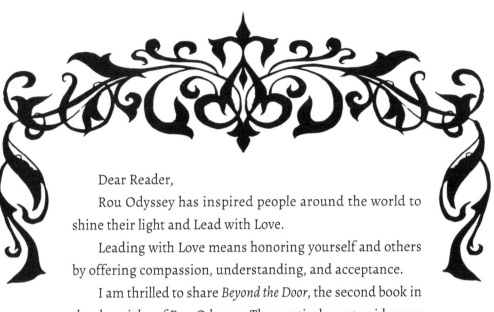

Dear Reader,

Rou Odyssey has inspired people around the world to shine their light and Lead with Love.

Leading with Love means honoring yourself and others by offering compassion, understanding, and acceptance.

I am thrilled to share *Beyond the Door*, the second book in the chronicles of Rou Odyssey. The mystical quest guides you into realms inspired by ancient wisdom and lost history. It is my humble hope to empower people with foundational truths in order to liberate them from the drama of the mundane world. I invite you to take the time to deepen your self-discovery throughout the next books in the series. You will be able to gain an understanding of the elements, planets, and chakra system should you choose to do so. Or, if you please, just simply immerse yourself into the magical worlds for the fantastical experience they offer!

May you always reflect the light of divine into the universe. You are essential to the world!

Welcome to the realm of Rou Odyssey, where the pure-hearted lead the way and rise above the Evils in the most peculiar and magical ways.

Blessings,
Kaiva Rose

In dedication to all those who live love and beam light into this world on a daily basis, may you always feel the support and blessings all around you.

I am sincerely grateful for all the support I have received from my family and community after releasing book one, *Look Beyond*. After six years of developing the Rou Odyssey screenplay series, then adapting them into books, I was finally able to share my passion with the world. Thank you to everyone who celebrated with me!

Special thanks to the talented Phoebe Darqueling for her expertise in the editing process. To the extraordinary artists Irina Kuzmina and Savanah Le for bringing life to my vision and believing in my passion!

To my parents and my sister, thank you for encouraging me through all my wild ventures. Blessings to my grandmother Mary Lou, whose devotion and compassion have taught me the power of faith.

To the reader, may you experience the blessings and love all around you.

Contents

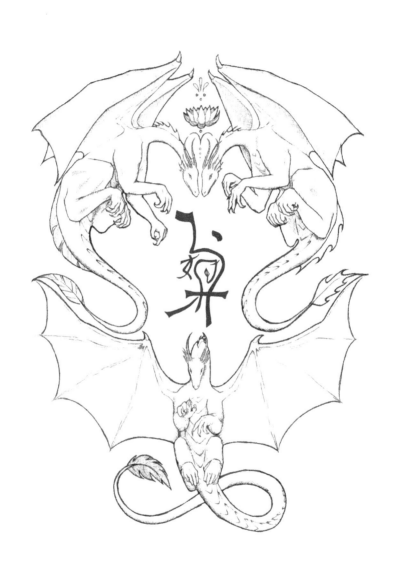

"No act of kindness, no matter how small, is ever wasted."

— AESOP

To Live or Die

S TONES CRUMBLED FROM the walls, breaking the silence as the sunlight flared to shatter the darkness. Percilla blinked away the burst of light before she whirled around to survey the area. She stood alone inside an archaic basin packed with dense sands. In the distance, a staircase led downward.

"Hello?" she called out. "Matik? Frida?"

Trudging to the edge of the hollow, her movements became strained by the sands, sinking with each step. She straightened her posture and mindfully slid her legs inch by subtle inch through the sludge, but they only sank deeper and perhaps faster. Unable to unroot herself from the heavy, seizing mixture, she paused to remind herself, "The only way is truth." Tranquilly sealing her eyelids, she let out a deep exhalation. "There is no truth in fear."

Percilla fluttered her eyes open, meeting the piercing gaze of the moss-covered eagle monument set at the edge of the basin. Rocks fragmented from its wings as they spread and it came to life. All of her instincts screamed at her to get out of there, that the eagle was coming for her. She tried to barrel toward the staircase, but the ground below her completely gave way.

Percilla recited a spell as she free-fell, enveloping her in an orb. She hung in midair while the sands continued to plummet all around her. Relief washed over her until she glanced down. "Matik!"

Her loyal companion was trapped within a glass chamber, struggling to breathe as it filled with water. Swiftly, she descended inside her orb to the base of the container.

Touching her fingertips to the glass, she concentrated, and ripples of energy spread across the surface. Matik tread at the top of the chamber, and, casting his gaze down to connect with Percilla's, he sucked in a giant breath. Percilla thrust her hands through the glass as if it were nothing more than a soap bubble, and he dove to meet her. His firm clasp wrapped around her forearms, and in one strong tug, Percilla pulled Matik through the enchanted glass. Careening backward with nothing to soften her fall, Percilla's head thumped against a boulder. She lay still for a moment, hoping to relieve the ache spreading across her skull. Then, the ground rumbled beneath her, reminding her the mission wasn't over yet.

What was once the interior of an ancient monument became nothing but a memory as it snapped into place to form a new pyramidal structure. The sound of crumbling stone at her back sent her wheeling around, and she was met with a monumental granite warrior coming to life. It heaved its sword into the air above Percilla, dropping pebbles in its wake. A white laser beam blasted through the stone being, shattering it into a million pieces.

Frida brought down her wand. "Nothing to fear, love. Keep on," she urged. Percilla clicked open a gold case, revealing a compass with an illuminated, violet arrow. It flickered as she slowly rotated the device.

A wall of vines whipped at her, but the nimble Matik grabbed Percilla by the waist to move her to safety. He kept the vines at a distance with slices from his sword. Realigning herself, Percilla watched the flickering arrow until it blazed to show the way forward.

"We got it," Percilla announced. The whole area quivered. The networks of vines trembled upon the shattering, monumental walls, and the ground beneath them split between the earth-covered stones. Ear-piercing screeches rose up over the din. Frida cupped her hand around her ear.

"Are we ready, then? I'll cover you from up there," the sorceress said, readying her wand.

Matik gazed at the moss-encrusted statues set upon the plaza before them. "Those look like they're waiting for us. Come with me, Percilla."

"That was not the plan, Matik. She must go her own way." Frida pointed her wand up, propelling herself to the top of the canopy.

Percilla nodded to her companions. "I've got my way," she assured them, even though the throbbing in her head seemed unbearable.

"Then let's move." Matik lifted himself up into a myriad of swinging vines.

The moment they'd gone, the ground shattered beneath Percilla. She managed to stay on her feet but slid down the mossy surface as it sloped. Three rings of sigils spun in the air at the base of the incline, aligning for a moment before the center opened and shot fire upward.

Percilla dropped to her seat in order to slow her descent, digging her fingers into the moss, which merely broke away. She could feel the heat of the flames rising up. Fear shook her entire being. Then, the incline of the stone earth dropped away completely, leaving her to plummet through the air. Closing her eyes, she reached inside her jacket, praying the Eye of Rou would do something to help, but then her body was abruptly suspended in midair above the peak of the flames. Sweat dripped down her face and into the fires.

Percilla craned her neck to see Frida pointing her wand. "Use your magic!" she hollered.

"I know." Percilla aimed her palm at the fire. "*Tra Tas.*" She elevated herself to the solid earth. The shrieks from the treetops grew louder, and Percilla turned her gaze up to her great-aunt.

A swarm of white monkeys swung through the canopy, heading straight for Frida. "Look out!"

"Don't you worry about me, darling. Go!"

Leaping from solid stone to the sloppy jungle floor, Percilla's boots sank into the muck. As if her throbbing skull or the incessantly transforming topography weren't enough to keep Percilla at a level of anxiety she'd never known before, panic coursed through her while her feet were sucked downward. She had no time to worry, only time to think of what she could do.

"*Atavis-na*," she recited. Instantly, her body levitated from the mud. Her lips turned up into a brief smile before dropping with concern.

"Can I run like this?" she yelled.

Frida replied from high up in the tree canopy. "Oh, very good, darling. Yes, you can." She flipped open her magical umbrella to ward off an onslaught of albino monkeys with its blinding light. Her radiant blue eyes peeked around the umbrella. "You'd better run quickly!" She pointed her finger to guide Percilla's attention to the lion statue coming to life behind her.

"This is not what I expected." Percilla ripped her attention away from the roaring lion with its sharp canines. She dashed across the air with the compass clenched in her hand. Gazing at the violet arrow, she yelled at the top of her lungs. "Keep going straight!"

Other statues had chased her on this mission, but the lion was faster than the rest. Every time its heavy stone paws met the ground, the earth rumbled so intensely she could feel it without even being on its surface.

"*Ansa... Opis?* ...Not it. Okay, I got this." Percilla hovered her palm before her forehead.

"Try '*Epis Ansa Ois*,'" Frida called from above. Her voice was somewhat muffled by the force field cascading from the umbrella over her head, her only protection from the swarm of angry primates that surrounded her.

Percilla spun around and aimed her magic at the stone beast, shouting, "*Epis Ansa Ois!*" A wall of white light spread up and down, separating her from the lion. It crashed into the wall, roaring and thrashing its mighty body to get beyond.

Satisfaction welled up inside her, but it morphed into fear just as quickly. A vine grabbed her by the legs and hoisted her upside down, dragging her up a giant tree. Then, the ground below split apart, and the vine lowered her into the gap.

Her mind was blank, but it couldn't be blank; there was no time for absent minds in the world of magic. Percilla choked, searching for words in her pounding brain and striving to pull something from her lessons. Pressing her fingers over the snapped pocket of her shoulder holster, she found a tinge of relief to feel the key was safe. And with that same breath, her fear settled. This mission wasn't over yet. Her head dipped past the threshold of the gash in the cold, wet earth.

"*Gaz an—*"

Before she could finish her spell, a sharp yank came from the other end of the vine. She rushed upward and was soon swinging safely above the gap.

"You okay?" Matik asked, heaving the vine up into the tree.

"Thank you, but I almost—" She lost her words as the branches swung around their trunks in an attempt to knock the duo out. In unison, they leapt over a branch charging for them.

"Let's go." Matik grabbed onto a vine, then tugged at Percilla's hand. She resisted and released his clasp when a buzz upon the brim of her burgundy top hat stole her attention. With a quick nod, she held her palms out to conjure a spell. An opaque light coalesced before her, forming a bridge leading past three colossal trees with leaves the size of her. She squinted at the bridge's end.

Tibs the bee took off from her hat and landed on the pocket of her shoulder holster. Lifting the flap, Percilla produced the golden key and gazed through its faceted, white gemstone.

She saw the pearly bridge, now glowing with a violet aura that led her all the way to a gold pyramid tucked high up in the branches and leaves. Tibs flew off in the direction of the pyramid, and Percilla followed, jumping over and ducking under the ever-shifting branches infiltrating the bridge. Matik chased after her, swinging from vine to vine.

Frida stood inside her glowing umbrella shield in the canopy right where the white bridge ended. The crowd of monkeys glared at her with piercing red eyes and stacked upon each other to beat upon her shield.

Percilla paused a safe distance away. She could hear her great-aunt's voice recite in her head, "Always assess the situation before using magic." Clutching the golden key, she tuned in to her surroundings and felt a subtle shift in her energy.

"Get down!" Matik shouted as a mossy branch swung toward Percilla's chest.

She dropped to her belly but never took her eyes from the area where the pyramid resided. The monkeys grew in number, swinging in from everywhere to block the path. Percilla wondered if they could see the pyramid or if they were just set on killing them. The gemstone on the key was supposed to be the only way to see the door. The bloodthirsty primates must be the guardians of this portal.

Matik dropped from the vines and hurled himself at the mass of monkeys gathering before Percilla. "Run!" he yelled.

She leapt to her feet and made a run for the golden face of the pyramid.

Inside her umbrella shield, Frida readied her wand. An ominous light pulsed from it, catching Percilla's eye as it grew bigger and bigger. Matik swooped down in front of her.

"What are you doing?" Frida shrieked. Matik was already slashing the monkeys, which only grew in number, diving in from all around them. Percilla followed Matik along the path he cut, but the closer they came to their destination, the more monkeys pounced on them from above, filling the gap in Matik's guard.

Frida dashed to her grand-niece's side, shielding her with the magical umbrella and gaining them safe passage the rest of the way to the door. The sorceress yanked Matik under the safety of the force field along the way. "Matik, you need to be more aware. I could have rid us of these primates entirely."

The symbol of Rou pulsed upon the face of the pyramid, illuminating a keyhole. "At least we made it." Percilla thrust the key in and turned it. The wall split open and revealed a calm pool of pure water. The three companions stepped through the portal one by one.

CHAPTER 2

Reckless Gathering

HUNDREDS OF CONTRAPTIONS roared across the dusty plain. Their wheels and treads kicked up clouds that mingled with the plumes of steam rising from their engines. A massive miasma of dust and steam engulfed the area where thousands of people gathered. The Rhino Engine of the Wonkt Train broke through the opaque barrier, the red lights of its eyes glowing as it howled to a stop.

A petite set of lace-up boots dropped to the dry earth followed by two sets made of worn leather. Deena, the feisty captain of the Wonkt Train, snapped her fingers as she maneuvered the gold-framed goggles from her mass of maroon curls and over her sharp, green eyes. A lanky man called Calvin tightened his goggles as the big fella, Jance, dusted off the lenses already strapped over his eyes. They traversed the area with confidence, ducking under flying contraptions floating in midair and covered with acrobats performing stunts. Music blared from a band high up on a floating stage draped with long curtains from where stilt-walkers emerged, donning clown costumes. Jance was so distracted by the spectacle, he nearly walked into a circle of fire breathers. They spit fuel at the center of the circle, and all the fires coalesced for an instant before rising to form a sigil.

"Look out there, big fella!" Deena shouted a moment before Jance was singed. The captain and her crew offered a holler of approval at the feat, then continued through the thick veil of dust and steam.

Deena clapped her hands, and as she spread them, the thick air parted before her. They now had a clear path all the way to a vibrant, multicolored, three-tiered tent held up by giant blue eagles. Plumes of rainbow-hued smoke rose from it and mingled with the dense, brown air. The captain waved her men along as the heavy veil of dust and steam returned to engulf them.

Deena reminded her companions, "You two grab us some drinks while I find the area we gatherin'." Then she swept the curtain open and entered.

Inside, crowds of eccentric characters from all over the world were gathered to share in the Dawookrunk party and sip a concoction whipped up by their renowned alchemist. The cacophony coming from the brass band at its center was hardly a match for the voices blending together with laughter and cheer.

The captain made her way to where the dancers gathered around the musicians, and the guys went in the direction of the bar. Vogle stood behind it, beautiful as ever, pouring a sparkling lime-green beverage between two copper cups. Deena removed her goggles and held a purple monocle over her eye. She scanned the room once before tapping a bare-breasted, burly man dressed in a leather vest with shimmering details. He looked down on her.

"Name's Deena. Can ya help me up so I can find my friends?" She pointed to herself and then up.

The man bent his knee for her to step on and offered her a hand so she could climb to his shoulders. Deena placed one foot on the man's brawny shoulder and the other upon his leather top hat for balance. Once more, she lifted the monocle to her eye and gazed over the room. A smile spread across her face when she found a small circle of mushrooms growing at the far corner of the tent. She climbed back down the human ladder and flipped a small linen pouch at him for his service.

"Blessed Reckless, my friend." She nodded to him before heading over to the fellas at the bar.

Vogle cracked open a sparkling gold orb like an egg and poured it over three crystal shot glasses. "There ya go, friends. Blessed Reckless," she said with a wink.

Deena sidled up beside Jance and Calvin, and the three of them lifted their glasses. "Blessed Reckless."

"May Rou keep on blessin'," Calvin said. The crew clinked their glasses together before downing the concoction.

"Ooweee! Now that is one fine potion." Jance doffed his hat to Vogle.

Within seconds, the crew shrank down to the size of ants. They each retrieved a copper wire with a tiny seven-pronged plug from their belts and connected them to the inside of their jackets. This instantly awoke the wing apparatuses on their boots and propelled them into the air. Deena took gliding steps, pointing straight at the mushroom circle. The fellas followed along, weaving in and out of the giant human bodies moving about the tent.

The three stepped through the ring of mushrooms and into a magical realm. Their feet met with green earth, and their lungs filled with fresh, crisp air.

"Welcome, friends. Welcome to the greatest place outside of Rou," Symon said with a whimsical bow before offering his open arms.

Jance embraced the ringmaster. "I still think we need ta get one of these simulators on the Wonkt Train."

"Jance, you know this ain't somethin' that can be replicated." Deena gave Symon a firm squeeze of her own. "Greetin's Symon, blessed Reckless to ya."

"Come along, the others have all arrived." Symon ushered them through the thick foliage.

Beyond it lay an ancient temple structure laced with vines. Inside, Maz, leader of Denton warriors, and Azurina, captain of the Panya airships, sat together on golden lotus seats ringing an elevated quartz basin filled with water. Seeing the party arrive, Azurina stood up and tapped her gold-heeled boot on the earth. An illuminated sigil appeared in the dirt, and a cobra materialized within the glow. It slithered onto the edge of the basin, then transformed into San, the wise elder and chieftain of Hazan. Glaring down into the pool, he fanned his fingers around his cobra staff and clenched it tightly.

Maz's impatience raised the tension of the group as he spoke first. "Glad you all found the place. Let's begin, then."

"Maz is right, we can't waste another moment," Azurina said, returning her gaze to the water inside the quartz basin. She pressed her finger to an apparatus at her ear, and a projection appeared. The light revealed the Dignitaries' elephant contraption en route for the sea's edge right near the Reckless.

"Now, why they comin' here?" Deena asked.

Maz lit a fire within his fingers and tossed it into the quartz basin. The flames spread to fill the repository. "Doesn't matter. They need a lesson from the Reckless. Let's set them ablaze, ladies and gents." Inside the flames, the projection continued.

Symon snapped, "Burning them isn't going to solve anything." He ushered Deena and her crew forward. "Please, welcome Wonkt to the circle and at least let them take their seats."

Those gathered bowed to welcome the Wonkt crew.

"Apologies for spoiling y'all's time. Azurina's right; we can't waste any more," Deena confirmed while everyone took their seats.

"I've been watching this for long enough. I can't remain here any longer." Maz hastily gathered his leather satchel and swung it over his chest. "I'm taking the Denton to torch these Evils. I'll be back shortly."

"Maz, stop," Symon interjected. "We don't know what the Digs are doing. You can't torch them until we know for certain what we are dealing with."

"I do not understand. Why would they come to the Reckless? Do they not realize who we all are?" Azurina asked.

"They absolutely know to never mess with the Reckless. Unless..." San pounded the end of his golden staff against the ground, igniting the garnet eyes on its cobra head as he drew symbols and shapes in the dirt. He whispered a chant to lift them from the earth, making them three-dimensional objects floating in the space before them. Tapping his staff again, the seven floating orbs began circling an eighth, larger orb. Each took on a color of the rainbow as they transfigured into celestial bodies. The Sun, Moon, and five planets blazed vibrantly, but not the faint, blue planet.

"Well, that's no surprise. We already know the Digs got control of the Gangleton Vortex," Deena said. "But how and why they're pulling that kinda power, I don't understand." She moved closer to the planets as they rotated around the Sun.

"That is why we have gathered here today. Not to watch the Dignitaries approach the Reckless Gathering, but to discuss—"

"The Digs ain't headin' ta the Reckless. They're goin' ta Evanstide!" Shru shouted as he rushed into the temple.

Azurina shot to her feet. "What's he doing here?"

"Aw, cool ya's. I'm one of ya guys now." Shru moved to the center of the group.

Symon pushed the orbs together to form a green, gaseous planet pulsing with toxic light. "And our time's up."

"Monzu?" Azurina touched the emeralds set into her metal chest piece, setting them aglow. "How?"

Symon faced the group. "Monzu has made contact and now has a connection with the Digs."

San pulled all of their attention as he spoke up. "The infiltration happened many rotations ago. I noticed Earth's vibration had begun to shift. There was no way to see it was Monzu, but now you confirm my worst suspicion."

"Even more of a reason to burn them to the ground and end this! Denton never fears the Digs, no matter who they're working with." Maz shoved on his white, leather helm and lifted his conch shell, ready to rally his tribe.

Azurina probed Shru with her gaze. "If this fool is actually telling the truth, and the Digs are heading for Evanstide, Maz's right. We have to stop them."

"We can't act rashly," San cautioned. "There are too many variables to consider. My people of Hazan have never fallen to the Dignitaries. They have come to our location numerous times and never once found us or our vortex. We do not waste our energy on them."

"We cannot intervene with Evanstide just yet," Symon confirmed. "We need a bigger plan of action."

"Ain't that a truth?" Deena acknowledged. "Our people of Nevuk are already on high alert, but this is a new development. Anyone hear from the Zovox folk?"

Glimmers of light flickered in the air as they swirled together, then flared. From the burst of light, an androgynous being in fitted indigo clothing laced in gemstones on gold chains appeared. It blinked its azure and white, almond-shaped eyes before speaking. "Rou has kept this planet safe from Monzu for as long as it's existed. The Sages will not let them pillage and kill it."

"Well, it's about time you say something." Maz stomped back to rejoin the group.

"Alikai, you are right, but at what cost?" Azurina tapped the button on her goggles, and the projection on the fire changed. The Earth was bombarded by meteors, followed by a sped-up scene of it flooding, freezing, and thawing. New life grew, then thrived as monuments rose. The meteors returned, cracking open the skin of the Earth and allowing its molten core to ooze from volcanoes. The cycle began anew. "I don't see any humans surviving what the Sages use to cleanse and protect the Earth."

"We all have our part. And our part is to protect our vortex and our people, and to honor our sworn duty," San said.

"Humans do and will survive, though not all," Alikai reminded them. "Those who have lost touch and have forgotten their truth will not, but that is the path they've chosen."

Symon interjected. "We can't make assumptions. Until we have word from the Sages that it is time to unite, we have time to rescue the lost. Though, we do need a better plan for how to stop the Dignitaries."

The flames in the basin rose higher as the image inside resolved into three silhouettes. They walked away from the Dignitaries' elephant contraption and neared an unnatural swirl in the shallow water. An octopus-shaped submarine emerged, pulling itself onto the sandy shoreline with its tentacles.

"You all figure out that plan. *I'm* taking Denton to set the Digs ablaze. When they come back from Evanstide, they'll have to meet our fury. I hope you will all join us." Maz bowed and stomped out of the temple.

CHAPTER 3

Fates Revealed

PERCILLA STEPPED ONTO the marble floor surrounding the pool where the Sages of Rou waited for the party. Valti, the beautiful Speaker of the Timeless Ones, stood at the front of the group. The remaining three Sages, Reenz, Phadela, and Casmir, sat cross-legged on golden lotus seats behind her. All were adorned with beautiful gemstone headpieces accenting their sparkling and flowing garments of silk. The nature surrounding them was a glorious reflection of their regal nature. The vines, flowers, and other plants radiated a peaceful serenity.

"You never mentioned bloodthirsty monkeys," Frida said, stepping through the doorway.

"You know better than I, Frida, not all details are encouraging," Valti replied. "Welcome back. We haven't much time." She waved her hand across the room, and three more lotuses bloomed beneath their feet.

Matik slumped into the seat. "Obviously, we hardly had a moment to breathe in that chamber without being taken out by some unforeseen threat."

Valti spoke with a softness as she caressed Percilla's throbbing skull, dulling the ache. "The magic in that chamber is meant to confuse the unwanted and guide the worthy. We gave you everything you needed to succeed, didn't we?"

The pain in Percilla's head may have receded, but that didn't change her opinion. "It wasn't exactly how you said it was going to be either," she admonished. "You said we were going into a chamber to retrieve a hidden door, and we would only need our magic, the compass, and the key."

"And you didn't need anything else, did you?"

She was right. They hadn't needed anything else, but the fact was that Percilla had never practiced her magic when danger threatened. Although, she did rather enjoy using it, and if she was to be honest with herself, she had plenty of time to practice her magic beforehand.

"You wouldn't have died in the chamber. And Percilla just admitted to herself she had fun."

"Maybe a tiny bit. Only because I've never been so powerful, but...ugh, still not flying on it. Maybe if I had a bag of tricks like Frida or at least a wand I could be more useful?"

Phadela spoke up. "There is not enough time to train you, and most of those things Frida uses she fashioned for herself." Frida lifted her chin at the compliment and gave a slight nod.

"You three each possess valuable strengths." Valti took a deep breath before she spoke again, as if what would follow required all her strength. "Now, let's move on to why we needed you to retrieve the door. We promised its sanctity will aid you on your quest to unite the Eyes of Rou. Though as you may know, the Dignitaries are gaining more power over our people. They have discovered how to manipulate the Earth's sacred vortexes."

Valti pointed at the pool, and water gently spouted up as a geyser. It reached to the ceiling, forming a wall of translucent water.

In the pure waters of the temple, murky clouds encroached upon the image of a mighty king and his royal retinue. The orange gemstones of the man's crown beamed through the inky veil encircling him. Standing in the silence of the sinister invasion, the soldiers drew closer to their king, hoisting their iridescent spears.

A heartbeat later, the malice burst into a tempest. Demons pounced out from the electrical green webs crackling to life and robust lightning struck from all sides to roil the king. The gems in his crown emitted a formidable, glorious energy to dispel the Evils, but he could only hold them at bay until his strength faded. The volatility of the currents inside the web flared.

The knights thrust their enchanted spears at the baleful apparitions lurking in the void. The Evils swallowed the magic from the blades and grew stronger, devouring all the resistance from the king and his men. The royal soldiers closed in around their leader, protecting him with their lives. One by one, the soldiers were consumed, dissolving into the electrical current of the ominous green web.

The king stood alone with only his mighty sword to protect him. A billowing mass of malevolence coalesced into an incorporeal entity, then morphed into an enormous scorpion. It plunged its stinger directly into the king's chest, releasing an oozing, lucent liquid into his body. The man fell instantly, his skin blistered, and his body shriveled as the light disappeared from his crown.

Percilla and the others stared on with shock and sadness until the image faded. The wall of water splashed back into the pool and vanished.

Valti broke the silence, the weight of her heart in her voice. "This great king of Evanstide lost his life to the Dignitaries. They have summoned a power more treacherous than we had feared anyone would ever see."

"This sort of magic has not been cultivated since the last apocalypse," Reenz said, adding to the air of urgency and worry building in the room.

"The vortex energy was to guide and keep the communities strong." Phadela pressed her palms together before her chest. "The crystals in them each serve as a source of wisdom and power for our people."

"Each community was to utilize these vortexes to maintain the strength amongst them," Casmir explained.

"Unfortunately, once Gangleton submitted, the Dignitaries gained access to their vortex, slowly gaining knowledge of the rest," Reenz said.

Valti stared intently at Percilla, Frida, and Matik, willing them to understand the gravity of their meeting. "Not all the vortexes have been found by the Dignitaries."

Frida scrambled to her feet. "So you want us to go?" she asked in disbelief. "Into this horrific wrath of the Dignitaries? Or should I just clear the air and tell my dear companions whose power we are really dealing with? That energy that killed the king was obviously more than just the idiotic Dignitaries. That was Monzu, wasn't it?"

Percilla shot a glance to Matik, who looked just as confused as her.

"Yes," Valti solemnly replied. "The Dignitaries are giving Monzu more power over this Earth with every vortex they claim."

"Who's Monzu?" Percilla interjected.

"Not who, what." Valti lifted her hand, presenting a live model of the Solar System rising from her palm. Using her fingers to navigate, she touched a planet that looked like a fiery green gas ball. "This is Monzu. The contaminator of the universe, the one that pillages every planet in order to claim the rare minerals for its own use. Many times, its beings have tried to come to Earth, but they are unable to survive here on this planet, for its composition is too dense. However, they have been able to connect with humans and contaminate their minds to serve them."

"That's next level," Matik said in shock.

Percilla's voice quivered as she confirmed. "So this Monzu is more powerful because of the Dignitaries?"

"Yes, and the Dignitaries are more powerful because of Monzu, which is merely using them to steal the rare minerals from Earth and gain access to the other celestial bodies in order to control them as well."

"What happens if it gets the minerals?"

"The same thing that happened to every other planet." She touched the lifeless planets floating in the universe in the center of her hand.

Frida shook her head. She glanced at Matik and Percilla before setting herself down upon the lotus seat.

Percilla's mind wandered to Evanstide's fallen king and the Evils she had already faced thus far on her long journey. Then, her eyes flicked to the Timeless Ones as Matik asked the question that permeated her own mind. "When will you, the Sages of Rou, serve your people?"

They met his intense stare with calm and collected faces.

Percilla cleared her throat loudly to dispel the tension. "Why don't we all go together?" This task was hers by fate and lineage, but she also couldn't understand the Sages' inaction in the face of such threats.

"This isn't our choice," Casmir said. "This is the fate of Rou. This is the fate of all of us."

Frida sternly asked, "Then why don't you get off your thrones and get out there and fight?"

Phadela sighed. "If you think for one moment our fate is easy, you would be mistaken. Every day we see our people suffering. Yet every day we must keep strong for them. We are the ones who protect Rou."

"Our presence may seem small here in this physical plane," Valti said. "Soon, you will come to see there is more than the eye's reality."

"I think this fight is beyond my power," Frida concluded, then clasped her petite purse shut and stood.

Matik rose to stand by Frida. "If that great king couldn't survive, how are we supposed to?"

Percilla was taken aback by her companions' refusals. In truth, she felt the same, but she'd never known either of them to be unsure of their abilities.

"I don't think we can survive this battle without the help of the Sages," Percilla said.

"We understand your concerns," Valti replied, "but you must trust us. You will be well prepared." She gestured at the gold pyramid, spinning it around to the triangular face showing the opening. "That is why you have retrieved the door."

"*Prepared?* You just told us your little chamber wouldn't have killed us, and I almost died numerous times. And now I find out Monzu is amping up the power of the Digs, which was already too wild for me to handle."

"I think you all need time to contemplate this mission. But understand that the time you spend thinking is time others are suffering." Valti dismissed them with a wave of her hands. As the others began to clear the temple space, Valti said, "Percilla, stay please."

Percilla settled into the lotus, wondering what Valti would have to say that she would not say to everyone else. Matik and Frida glanced back for a moment, watching Percilla until they turned the corner.

"You have already been a great leader for our people, Percilla," Valti said. "You've shown courage, strength—"

Percilla cut her off. "If you're trying to get me to say 'yes' by showering me with compliments...it's kind of working. But you can stop." She took a long breath, looking directly into Valti's eyes. "This isn't a rash decision to make."

"This is true." The Timeless One nodded, then called back the water-wall with a flick of her finger. Images took shape once more.

Percilla saw Vahn dressed in Dignitary attire, standing before a queen in a throne room with the Dignitaries behind him. It was already a shock to see Vahn outside of Gangleton, and here he was bowing before a queen no less. From the royal woman's expression, Percilla sensed she was troubled by something. She signaled Vahn to step forward, and he knelt before her throne.

"This is a glimpse of the future. Vahn is at present being manipulated by the Dignitaries and will soon take the hand of Queen Aurora, daughter to the great king you just witnessed fall," Valti said.

"Whoa, whoa, whoa!" Percilla cried in disbelief. "What? Vahn. My Vahn, from Gangleton, is going to take the hand of a queen? And he's hanging out with the Digs?"

"To his knowledge, he is a prince," Valti replied. Percilla's heart sank, and her throat clenched as the pressure behind her eyes built. The Sage continued. "And with this bond to the queen, the Dignitaries will take over another vortex and gain even more power."

"Why don't you tell her not to marry him? Why don't you do something?" Percilla shouted in frustration, blinking back tears.

Valti placed a hand between Percilla's shoulder blades. "Now you see why your courage and strength are needed."

Calmness settled into her mind at the touch, but she still didn't understand. "Why can't anyone else do it? Why can't you use some sort of magic or mind control?"

Valti caught her eye. "Maybe you have an idea of what sort of magic or mind control to use?"

"You're the Sages, the mighty guardians of Rou." Percilla tossed her hands in the air.

When Valti spoke again, it was a declaration of the utmost importance. "That's right. Of *Rou*. We are not able to leave here. The world outside of Rou is not our domain."

"Then why do you want us to fix it?"

"We feel all, we see all, and we cannot escape any of it." Valti sighed in sadness. "I have seen apocalypse after apocalypse. Watched humans time and time again fall to their demise. And you're right, why should we care?"

"You're that old?" Percilla asked in awe, confronted with a being unlike any she had ever met. Frida appeared young and yet was beyond age, but Valti was something different. Percilla felt it in the flow of her words, as though they were the flow of time itself.

"I've never been born, and I'll never die," Valti said. "But each time another growth cycle begins on Earth, I get another chance to evolve."

"Why didn't you tell us that from the beginning?"

"Because you should do your part to help no matter what another is willing or not willing to do. If everyone only did what the other one did, how would anything get done? People need a leader to get in and do the work."

Percilla dropped her head, closing her eyes to seal in the tears. "I'm sorry. I can't hold the weight of the world on my shoulders. I hardly even know how to use the magic I've been taught."

"Fair enough. This is a lot to take in. I shouldn't expect you to make your decision so quickly. Forgive me," Valti replied, her gentle voice full of understanding. "Let's meet in the morning and decide the fate of the world."

CHAPTER 4

Beyond The Veil

THE FULL MOON'S usual dance upon the sea was disturbed by angry waters fragmenting the shimmering brilliance. Steam burst from an unnatural maelstrom, further agitating the once peaceful tides. The Dignitaries' octopus submarine descended, sending out blasts of burning hot vapor and blinding lights. Water spun through its propellers as its eight metal tentacles sped them through the fantastical underwater world.

Franc stepped forward to gaze through the window at the illuminated depths. The multitude of colorful fish scales and deep sea surfaces glinted in the light of the submarine, exposing a wonderland of humanity's long-lost objects.

Fiercely racing gears, pistons, and levers creaked and groaned as the metal monstrosity's engines roared into the ocean's abyss. Drendle pushed a blinking button on the control panel, releasing a viscous layer to cover the octopus. The noises ceased as the thirsty joints were replenished and protected with a slimy ichor created through a mix of dark, warped alchemy and magic born of Evils. Mechanical gadgets blinked and shone ghastly lights from the white metal exterior, where golden ingots joined by flexible copper wires brought fluidity to the contraption's progress in the salty waters. With each movement of the submarine's tentacles propelling it deeper into the depths, clouds of hot steam and bubbles erupted, creating a murky veil in the otherwise calm waters.

At last, a faint, peach glow pulsed in the distance, though it was hardly visible through the turbid mixture of liquids surrounding the submarine. Ons unrolled the parchment map upon the control panel and pointed to an area marked "Evanstide." Franc grinned at the living illustration of their octopus nearing the kingdom. The light from below peeked through the waving seaweed like moonlight through the trees.

The submarine's destination lay at the very bottom of the sea, safely hidden away from anyone not aware of its existence. At the very edge of the forest of seaweed, surrounded by a moat of jagged coral, an iridescent orange dome danced with fractals of magical energy. It responded to the ocean's ever-moving touch, radiating a peaceful and vibrant energy amid the turquoise water. It stood tall, not dissimilar from the dome that enveloped Gangleton, but formed from a wholly different spell source. Also unlike in Gangleton, one that did not act as a blinder to the people within. The diamond shield let them see the beauty that surrounded them, and they were not afraid. Though if they had looked to their beloved ocean now, they should have been.

Aurora tried to mask her melancholy as she made her way over to the crowd of subjects. The young queen had to get through this day without breaking. Her people needed her.

Bells chimed throughout the dome, enlivening the extravagant kingdom. Guards in silver armor holding sharp crystal lances at their sides stood watch from the spiraling pearl and shimmering carnelian stone towers. They offered salutes to Aurora as she passed; a symbol of honor.

Aurora's vibrant, indigo hair was elegantly styled, framing her pearlescent black skin. Though she was only in her twenties, there was a regalness about her that was beyond age. Spotlit by the Moon, her silk gown and cape glittered with each stride as if it were woven from stars.

"Are you faring well, my queen?" a familiar and kind voice asked from Aurora's right.

She hadn't even noticed her most trusted advisor Pith had caught up to her. "I'm fine."

At the sound of the chimes, the finely adorned people of Evanstide poured from each of the ornate structures. Their elegant silken attire was woven with utmost precision, and each person had decorated their garments with unique golden accessories laced with radiant carnelians, pearls, and other precious crystals. Each of them sparkled in the light of the pearl lanterns hanging above the spiraling lapis streets.

"You are allowed to show your emotion," Pith said gently. "The people will understand your pain. You lost your father."

"Yes, but they lost their king. Their very strong king who had a plan." She sighed in frustration and slowed her steps. "I'm sorry, I didn't mean to snap at you. I'm just... I feel as though the ocean is going to break through the dome and carry me away with it."

Together, they passed in silence through the extraordinary coral and sea plant gardens that showcased the magnificent statues of great leaders made from precious stones. Gentle tides touched their toes when they entered the center of the city where the water from pristine terraced pools trickled over the pathways.

Pith placed his hand on Aurora's arm, and they came to a stop in the middle of the trail. "My queen." He leaned in and whispered, "Aurora, your people are here for you. I am here for you. We will mourn the loss of Divinu, but never doubt your ability to rule in his absence. You come from greatness. Remember how powerful you are, how strong."

She smiled and took his hand. "Thank you, Pith. I'm not sure I'd be able to get through this without you by my side."

He bowed. "I live to serve you, my queen. I shall always be here in your time of need."

The crowd of people solemnly gathered among the pools, their attention turned to the Moon shining through the dome's soft, peach glow. Pale light beamed into the kingdom, illuminating Aurora and cloaking her in its silvery aura as she made her way through the populace. The queen strode along the gemstone pathway leading to the royal pool, and her people bowed, bending a knee to the wet ground without a moment's thought. They were so loyal to her, yet she was so uncertain. If she could hardly hold back her tears and keep her poise, how could she be their queen?

Aurora kept her eyes on the Moon, her beacon of strength. She paused for a moment before ascending to her final destination. The tears she'd been trying to hold back dribbled down her cheeks. As she continued her ascent, she glanced at the people entering into the pools. Her people. They cried with her, giving her sympathetic smiles and nods of understanding. Warmth filled Aurora, and she repeated Pith's words in her mind.

She was strong.
She was powerful.
She could rule Evanstide.
They were all going to be just fine.

CHAPTER 5

Vision of Truth

A GENTLE BREEZE SWEPT the mists from an expansive valley of cascading waterfalls. Sunlight danced through the water vapors, casting rainbows across the sky. Inhaling a deep, full breath of the moist air, Percilla closed her eyes as the final tears fell down her cheeks. She rested in her soft bed placed high upon the thick arboreal canopy, letting her eyelids droop from the weight of the day. The subtle sounds of falling water, the scent of fresh jasmine growing all around her bed, and the soothing energy from the trees eased her anxiety and cleared her mind from all the pressure and expectations put upon her this day.

She remained unsure whether she should leave Rou in an attempt to save everyone she loved or to remain safe within its protection. All she could do now was gather her strength to make the right decision. The emotional, physical, and mental exhaustion of the day needed to wear off before she could honestly make her choice. As Percilla settled in to rest, Tibs flew from the brim of her hat to land upon the space between her eyebrows. The subtle vibration of her little companion sent Percilla into a deep sleep.

Geometric shapes rotated and shifted inside of a tunnel stretching out into infinity. Percilla tentatively assessed her placement in the familiar kaleidoscopic portal. Flickering up from the ground in front of her, wisps of light manifested into blue flames blockading her from what lay beyond. A white figure appeared within the blaze. Percilla hesitated to near the fire until she realized it emitted no heat. The illuminated figure pulsed brighter, taking on a familiar silhouette that wore an all-too-familiar hat.

From the flames, she heard a sympathetic voice. "Percilla, love, you mustn't waste any more time."

"Victoria?" Percilla thrust herself through the flames to the other side. Nobody was there. Turning around to face the blaze again, Percilla found the white figure still pulsing with life inside the flickering shades of indigo.

"Yes, my sweet darling. I am here as my spirit body now. I've had to let go of my physical body, for the Dignitaries were relentless and horrible to me."

Percilla tilted her head and touched the magical fire as tears rolled down her cheeks in an endless stream.

"It's okay, love. I am fine. I am free now."

"I tried... I didn't know how... I couldn't save you!" Percilla gushed out the words through her tightened throat.

"There is nothing you could have done. Please, wipe that from your mind. There are more important things at hand. I am

merely a drop in the bucket of existence, and when the time is right, I will embody again," Victoria assured her. "I must urge you to continue, my love. For you three are the only ones to make it back to Rou to receive the message from the Sages."

"Why me? Why am I the only one who can do this? There are other people living happily in Rou. If the Sages can't leave here, what about them?"

"They are not fully embodied yet, my dear. They have never left Rou, nor have they existed in the outer realms. The dimensions outside of Rou are extremely dense, and one must have training to survive in them. Those beings will be released from Rou just like our ancestors were when the Earth has begun a new growth cycle."

"What can I do? What am I supposed to do? I am just a girl from a small village half-trained in magic. I don't have the ability to take on the Digs, especially as they are friends of Monzu!"

Tibs flew from her hat and buzzed all around her face.

"The little one is right, Percilla. Once upon a time, you were a rebellious young lady from a small village who walked to her own drum. And thank goodness you were a feisty little one to contend with. I wouldn't have allowed you to be so if I didn't see how it made you a leader and an inspiration for others," Victoria said, flickering brighter.

A slight smile bloomed across Percilla's face. She had never been so praised by anyone for her rebellious ways. The smile quickly faded as her grandmother's white shimmer disappeared, and the fire dissolved into thin air.

"Victoria?"

Percilla looked all around, but nothing moved except for the geometric shapes rotating into a new order. When they snapped into place, the gates to Rou appeared at the end of the tunnel just like they had when she opened the Eye of Rou. The portal all around her dissolved into twinkling stars and radiant planets guiding her toward the magnificent entrance to Rou.

A current of energy swept her forward. Weightlessly, Percilla watched the celestials pass, each shining in their own way. A tiny green orb in the distance grew immensely as she neared the gates of Rou. She'd seen this before, but she couldn't remember where until she felt its sinister energy. She tried to change directions, but she had no control over where she flew. Percilla stopped her futile struggle, though whether the current pulled her to the vibrant gates of Rou or to Monzu, she could not tell. Once still, she noticed a white aura encasing her being and a golden dragon guardian sweeping across the sky. Her awareness shifted from fear to strength as she felt the protection from Rou.

"There is no truth in fear," she murmured.

As she flew forward with intention and ease, Monzu stopped its advance as it touched the portal around her.

Below her, Vahn stood at the gates of Rou and waved. As she touched the ground, he was instantly right before her eyes.

"Percilla, my dear friend! I've been waiting for you."

"Vahn? You escaped?"

His eyes were ablaze with a green, gaseous swirl. This person felt foreign to her even though she recognized him.

Vahn's voice and smile were different, and she had no sense of Vahn in this person standing before her. Percilla turned to run, only to find the portal stretching into an endless void and her feet unable to move.

"Don't go," the Vahn creature said in a deep, ominous tone.

Percilla was ready to give in to despair when her hands began glimmering with magic. She faced him again, but instead of her friend, she found a bleak, shadowy figure rising out of Vahn's body. Beyond the apparition, Monzu pulsed in sync with the toxic green of its eyes.

Vahn's lifeless body lay on the ground before the gates. Frozen in space, Percilla tried to yell out to him, but she couldn't force the words from her mouth.

The demonic spirit loomed nearer. She shook her body, trying to free herself and move out of harm's way, but nothing could shift her. Tears poured from her eyes and floated on the air before her as she choked for breath, for words, for movement. All was lost.

Percilla shook violently and gasped desperately for air. Her eyes shot open, meeting Matik's gaze of utter fear upon her. He cradled her upper body, which was sopping wet with sweat. Percilla froze as she recalled everything that transpired in the dream.

"What happened?" Matik asked.

Percilla sank into his strong yet gentle care. "I don't know. I was in the portal again. It was so real...Victoria's spirit, Monzu, and Vahn."

Matik held her tighter. "You're safe now. It was all just a dream. I was afraid you'd been poisoned or something. You were shaking out of control, and your breathing was so erratic. But everything is okay now."

Percilla's mind raced with the horrors she had witnessed, especially that of her dear friend. Unable to bear the images in her mind's eye a second longer, she pushed herself out of Matik's arms. "Vahn isn't okay. Monzu is using his body because of the Dignitaries...because of me. He was supposed to come with me. We were leaving Gangleton together, but they forced him into their control. I should have gone back for him. I should have saved him with the Eye of Rou. I should have learnt magic from him. I could have saved him, and we'd have come to Rou together. No one else could have saved him in Gangleton. This is all my fault."

"Percilla, there is nothing you could have done. You had to uphold your oath to return the Eye to Rou. You did everything you could have," Matik said gently running his hand up and down her back to comfort her.

Percilla stood. "No, I didn't. I didn't. I took refuge in your and Frida's care when I should have been stronger on my own."

"You couldn't have fought the Digs on your own; nobody has that power. We are a team for a reason," Matik reminded her.

"We are a team, but I made a promise that I need to keep. And if you want to join me, I'm going to save my best friend. Victoria is dead because of the Digs, and I won't let them take the only other person that ever loved me in Gangleton."

Matik dropped his head toward his empty lap before raising it to Percilla with a look of sadness. It lasted but a moment before his brows lifted. "You're right. We have to save the ones we love. And I will always be at your side, Percilla."

CHAPTER 6

Royal Offerings

HUES OF ORANGE tinted the white hull of the octopus contraption approaching the illuminated dome of Evanstide. A torrent of bubbles gasped from the rear of the submarine as it pushed fully through the gel-like seal. From water to air, the octopus contraption's legs became docile as treads on its underbelly took over. It moved toward the tall gates built into a reinforced wall of sand and sea-stone. Guards patrolling the top of the wall peered down to see what had passed through the barrier.

When they spotted the contraption, one called out to it. "Cease your advance and speak your intent!"

A short moment of nothing passed; only the sound of the contraption's engines coming to idle filled the silence. The watchmen readied their weapons while one stood by, prepared to sound the alarm bell. A small device like a gramophone popped out from the top of the hull, and a voice resounded through the dome.

"We, the Dignitaries of Gangleton, have come to offer our aid to Queen Aurora of Evanstide in these dark and troubled times."

The patrolmen exchanged skeptical glances.

"Time is of the essence. Open your gates to us."

One watchman hesitantly nodded to the other, then spoke. "Show yourself." He pulled a reflective glass from inside his jacket. The surface rippled, then a curious, brown eye appeared upon the translucent area. It roved around, taking in the new arrival suspiciously.

Gears clicked and pistons wheezed as a circular door slid open atop the octopus. An extravagant, purple top hat emerged from the opening, followed by the rest of the astute captain.

"Greetings! I am Dignitary Franc of Gangleton. As stated before, our business is urgent. As you well know, darkness lurks in the seas, as it does in the rest of the world."

The eye upon the glass blinked once, then disappeared. The massive doors of the gate slowly split apart, allowing them to enter. Steam billowed from the sides of the octopus contraption as it crept forward through the gates.

The octopus docked at a sea-stone plank, its roaring engines whirring to a halt. A wheeled hatch on the machine's side creaked open, revealing none other than the amenable Dignitary Drendle. He stepped out onto the plank and marveled at the sights. The gangly Lyken followed, accompanied by the ferocious Nylz, whose hat was singed at the edge. Ons came next, sliding a blue lens over his monocle. Finally, the exalted Franc and newest addition, Vahn, promenaded from the interior to gaze upon the place they had so longed to see. All, even Vahn, were dressed in the Dignitaries' usual dark purple attire, each with a signature striped pant.

"Evanstide," Drendle said with some relief as he stared up at the kingdom's spiral towers.

"Our long sought-after companion." Ons leaned on his cane and slid another lens over his eye as he looked around.

Lyken lifted his boot out of a puddle with a disgusted twitch of his lip. "It's wet."

"I told you to put on your other boots," Nylz sneered. "You know I'm always right. You should just do what I say."

Lyken whirled around and flicked Nylz's hat. "Do you know your hat is burnt?" he said with a cackle. "Told you not to set it next to—"

"Enough. Be on your best behavior," Franc commanded. "The queen is in mourning."

The Dignitaries flounced down the glistening pathways en route to the gathering area. Vahn remained silent and close behind with a vacant expression. They eased their way through the crowd until they could finally see what, or rather whom, everyone was so intently watching. Franc motioned at the Dignitaries to be still.

Queen Aurora stood inside the uppermost pool, looking down over the rest of the people of Evanstide and holding a vial of luminous, orange liquid in her hand. Franc's eyes narrowed, curious as to what they had stumbled upon. She stepped closer and waited.

Aurora addressed the crowd in a loud, solemn voice. "Together, we can keep our kingdom strong." Her curious gaze lingered on Franc for just a moment, then moved on. "As one, we can be the strength that Divinu was. We must live in my father's, your king's, essence and spirit. As we offer his soul to the eternal waters, let us think of his glory. May his mighty powers live on through us."

Aurora tipped her hand and poured the vial into the water. The luminous liquid mingled with the water, then began to spread, gradually expanding into the other pools. It flowed down into the aqueducts, distributing the sacredness throughout the entire kingdom. In that moment, the sea glowed with a mystical aura, then it vanished back into the clear blue.

Having seen enough of the memorial service, Franc's eyes wandered up the winding road before them. The carnelian pathways that paved the gathering area spiraled out from the pools, leading up the hill to the palace. It was high above the sacred waters, seated atop a prominent reef of white coral. The radiant underwater castle shone with the light of the Moon twinkling across its organic curves and carved turrets.

Franc tilted her head, and the Dignitaries followed her lead. They walked up to the top of that hill at a brisk pace, ignoring the staring villagers they passed. The royal guards eyed the Dignitaries with suspicion, ready to strike at a moment's notice. Paying no heed to the sentries, Franc walked up the steps and entered the palace. The rest of the Dignitaries followed close behind. The royal sentinels fell in line, never taking their eyes off the mysterious group.

Inside the palace, even Franc was taken aback for a moment at the elaborate display of Evanstide's wealth. Pillars of carnelian and lapis supported a dazzling ceiling of gold. The marble floor was inlaid with pearl and ruby designs depicting mystical moon and star symbols. Masterwork sculptures of coral lined the halls. Grand, golden doors at the far end of the foyer concluded the sight as they remained closed, hiding what lay beyond the regal ramp.

The sentries surrounded them as a mysterious man cloaked in fine garments approached. A shimmering, orange crystal engraved with the symbol of the Moon hung around his neck. The guards cleared a path for him as he neared.

He scrutinized the group as if reading a book. "Welcome to Evanstide. Who are you, and what brings you to our kingdom?"

"Thank you," Franc replied with a short bow, which the rest of the Dignitaries immediately repeated. "We are the Dignitaries of Gangleton, here to offer our condolences to the queen."

"Gangleton." He thought to himself for a moment. "You are in the lineage of Rou?"

"True bloods," Franc said, clasping her palm over a gemstone ring to hide its green pulses of light from view.

The cloaked man nodded to the guards. All but two obediently returned to their positions outside the palace. The others led the man and the Dignitaries to the golden doors.

"Queen Aurora was leading a ceremony for her people at the pools. She is just now returning and may need a moment. So if you will follow me, I will take you inside to where you can wait for her to invite you into her throne room."

"Are you family to the queen?" Franc asked curiously following the man ever so closely as they crossed through the doorway.

"Ah. Forgive me for not introducing myself. I am Pith, council to the queen." The man politely turned around to regard the visitors.

Franc smiled as her eyes widened and pupils narrowed, their gaze focused on Pith's striking brown eyes. At the moment of eye contact, Pith's pupils dilated. Her obscured ring throbbed with a force only Franc and Pith could feel. "Greetings, Pith."

The lids of Pith's eyes drooped. "Pleasure to meet you..."

"Franc."

"Franc. Would you care for anything?" Pith asked as his pupils shrank down to their normal size. "I imagine your travels have been long."

Franc looked beyond Pith's pupils, penetrating the very depths of his mind until once again they dilated. "We're fine. Your relationship to the queen must be quite intimate."

"I do my best to advise our queen. She is wise beyond her years, but still young."

"We need your help in advising the queen during these vile times."

"Of course, I am here to serve the kingdom," Pith replied in a slow drawl.

"We have come to save your kingdom."

As Franc finished speaking, the next set of golden doors were pulled open from within by two guardsmen. The scent of amber and rose drifted out from the queen's quarters along with the gentle sounds of a fountain. The two guardsmen stood aside and bowed.

"The queen is ready to see you now."

Pith nodded to the sentry as he led the Dignitaries inside. An enormous balcony overlooked the gathering area and its many sacred pools. Pure, shimmering water flowed from the kingdom's aqueducts into the palace's channels on either side of a purple carpet that led to an exquisite throne made of gold, gemstones, and white velvet.

Queen Aurora sat upon her throne, shining with a brilliance that matched the grandeur of the throne room itself. Pith scampered to his queen's side, greeting her with a hushed voice. Franc knelt before Aurora, and the rest of the Dignitaries followed suit, awaiting her royal acknowledgment.

The queen spoke with a serene, almost motherly voice. "Dignitaries of Gangleton, thank you for coming. What news have you for me?"

"Your Majesty, we are honored to be in your presence," Franc replied as she straightened to her full height. "Your loss is all too close to home for us."

"These are the treacherous times we live in," Nylz said.

The rest of the Dignitaries rose as Franc continued, "Everyone is out for themselves. Our dear community of Gangleton has suffered the same dire fate as Evanstide."

"An awful battle to witness," Lyken added with feigned grief. Tears welled up in the corners of his eyes.

Aurora's face turned into a solemn frown. "Tragic to think our bond to Rou wasn't kept in their hearts."

"Fear eats away at them," Nylz said.

Aurora perked up at the mention of fear. "The only witness of the battle spoke of dark clouds surrounding them and no fair warning of attack. Why was there a call from Rou? Our pools lit up; it was an omen. My father went to the mainland to witness the state of the world."

"Omen," Franc staggered, clasping her palms together before her mouth while she carefully crafted the sentiments of her next lie. "Gangleton had one as well. Right before our Keeper of the Eye met her demise."

"Is Rou under attack?" Aurora asked.

Ons cleared his throat, adjusted his monocle, and stepped forward to speak. "We have been monitoring the vortex activity inside of Gangleton's monument, and it seems the Earth is speaking in profound ways."

"What does that mean for us? For Rou?" Aurora demanded.

Ons sighed heavily. "Unfortunately, we cannot translate this into meaning yet. But with your help we can."

Franc spoke up, forcing herself to hide a smile behind a mask of deceit. "We would like to form a sacred contract with you. We want you and your people to be safe from any further attack."

Lyken feigned an expression of anguish. "Vagabonds disguised as Keepers of the Eye of Rou have been terrorizing the Rou communities." He placed his spindly fingers over his heart.

"We would like to offer you a warrior and guardian, a prince," Nylz interjected confidently.

Franc turned to Vahn, who met her gaze with a silent nod. She led Vahn to Aurora and held her arms out as if to present him as a gift. "To seal our bond in blood. To unite our kingdoms for Rou."

"A prince?" Aurora asked with surprise.

"Our purest blood." Nylz raised her arms to frame Vahn from the other side.

Aurora gently shook her head, then replied with a voice heavy with exhaustion. "I must speak honestly. I was not expecting you to bring me a wedding proposal. My kingdom has just lost their beloved king. I do not know if it is time for me to choose a suitor." She looked to Pith, who placed his hand on her shoulder and nodded his approval. "However, I am also not in the right state of mind to make such a decision. And so, if you will bid me this Moon-time, I will come to my right mind and decide. Until then, please enjoy the bounty of our kingdom. May our home be yours."

Franc could no longer hold back her smile, releasing a twisted grin as she glanced devilishly at Pith and Vahn. "Gladly."

CHAPTER 7

Written in Time

E MPOWERED BY HER own will yet disheartened by the gravity of her fate, Percilla silently prayed the Sages had a new idea for how to save the world. However, Matik's presence did bolster courage. He proudly strode across the magical bridge she'd created, his strength and confidence reminding Percilla she would always have protection. Percilla slowed when they reached the edge of the Sages' island. From behind, Matik wove his fingers into hers and with a gentle squeeze led them forward. Stepping over the ancient runes which glimmered in response, they entered the divine space of the Timeless.

Outside the sanctuary, the Sages ringed a quartz basin filled with pure, sparkling water. Phadela held her palm over the pool before pulling a golden glyph from its depths and placing it on a blank area on the wall. The other Sages followed with different symbols.

Valti left the ring to greet Percilla with a smile. "Blessings, you're earlier than we'd expected."

"I suppose it shouldn't surprise me that you knew we were coming." Matik peered at the Sages as they placed their glyphs upon the walls.

"Your journey was written in time." Valti pointed to the symbols.

Percilla squinted at the engravings. "I can't read that."

Valti ran her hand over a symbol on the wall, and it illumined at her touch. "I wouldn't expect you to be able to. This is the language of the Timeless."

Matik stepped forward to touch a symbol. "Does it say we will win against Monzu?"

The Sage smiled as she gestured at the pair to enter the temple. "Follow me."

The pyramid door floated above the pool at the center. "This portal that you retrieved," Valti said. "It only could have been claimed by those who will avert Monzu's destruction of the Earth."

"Has anyone else tried?" Matik asked archly.

"Nobody else from your growth cycle has made it to Rou." Valti stepped around a smaller quartz basin and conjured three symbols. Two of them floated toward Percilla and Matik. They landed directly on their foreheads, sparkling there for but a moment before sinking into their skin. The third symbol lifted into the air and vanished. "You are the chosen ones. And together with Frida, you will defend our Earth."

"So we are going to win? Is that written in time?" Matik asked.

Valti placed her palms upon their foreheads. "We hope so." Her energy flowed into Percilla's center, refreshing her spirit and relieving her anxiety.

"I'm ready," Percilla said solemnly. "My best friend is in horrible danger, and my grandmother is gone. I don't know how we are going to fight Monzu, exactly, but I will not stand by while it or its minions destroy us."

A smile bloomed across Valti's face as she nodded to Percilla, then she looked to Matik. "Are you ready to accept your mission?"

"Wherever Percilla goes, I will always be by her side."

"Then let's gather the final member of your party and see if she is ready to save the world."

Rhythmic puffs of blue smoke emitted from the confines of a fluffy nimbus hovering over an eclectic island, a treasure trove floating high above Rou. Frida puffed her pipe, and a sparkling blue dragon manifested to circle the island. A sensation on her forehead made her jerk to attention. Sweeping her finger across it did nothing to change the touch of warmth settling into her skin. Frida pulled a mirror from inside the nimbus and fixated on the delicate lines of the warm, pulsing glyph set between her brows. "A seal of protection? Well then, I guess we've decided." The sorceress lifted a spyglass to her eye, confirming her conclusion as she peered at the Temple of the Timeless.

Valti's voice floated through the air. "Will you accept?"

"Where Percilla goes, I go. I just need time to ready my things," Frida silently replied before rising to stand above the island. With her petite purse open and ready beside her, she snapped her fingers to bring her little musicians to life along with all her other belongings. The spirited, life-sized marching band blasted brass music for Frida's pleasure while she joyfully prepared everything for travel. From trunks to tea sets, parasols to gramophones, vases to vials, everything danced and gracefully floated over to her magical bag. One by one, each shrank and disappeared inside. An unrhythmic banging stole Frida's attention and abruptly halted her enthusiastic preparations. She glanced from side to side, but the dissonance ceased to exist as if never there. Finished with packing the lot of eccentric objects, the marching band silenced, then shrank back to their ornamental size. When all was tucked away safely into her bag, Frida breathed a deep sigh of satisfaction.

The knocking came once again to startle Frida. Instantly, she spun around to find a woodpecker sitting upon the pyramid door. "Good day. You're just in time. I guess I'll just take the door to meet the others then?" Frida examined the key in the hole, wondering why the white gemstone had such a similar look to the many gemstones that she collected on her island.

Frida grabbed her purse, then turned the knob and bid the woodpecker adieu. Stepping through the portal, to her great surprise, she found an all too familiar shoreline and cherry tree. "What is this? Fridanda?"

She scanned the island for a particular gemstone formation in the shape of a ring. Once in her sights, she jumped into its center and cast a spell.

The sands moved away like a secret hatch entrance and revealed a worn trunk hidden beneath the shore.

"I'm home!" Frida exclaimed, bursting into a little jig on the beach.

As she danced, Matik and Percilla too walked through the golden door.

"Hey!" Percilla shouted. "You don't get to retire yet. We have to save the world."

Matik looked all around with an amused expression on his face. "So this is the great Fridanda?"

"It is!" Frida answered, bringing a stop to her dance. "Isn't it wonderful?

"Valti is waiting for us, Frida," Percilla said.

"But we've only just arrived."

"We all accepted the mission together, remember?" Matik reminded her.

"Oh, fine, fine. Let's get this over with, then."

At that, Frida dashed out of the door, returning to Rou and her island in the sky, where she found Valti awaiting her return.

"It's good to feel you so happy," Valti said with a smile.

Matik and Percilla followed Frida back through the door. Valti shut the door from afar with a short wave of her hand. With another flick of her wrist, Valti summoned a cloud with a seashell plate resting atop it and acting like an altar. The plate held seven keys on golden chains, each adorned with a colored gemstone.

"This is our gift to you. They will guide you to the Keepers," Valti explained. "Each Eye of Rou can only be found by using the door and the key with the matching gemstone."

"So this other one leads to Fridanda?" Frida asked, motioning at the key already inserted into the door. "Why do we have a key to Fridanda?"

"In time, you will understand. But for now, think of it as the key that leads you home."

"Which one leads to Evanstide?" Percilla asked. "We should go there first."

"I cannot tell you this," Valti replied. "The journey must be taken in the order I give you. You cannot stray from the path."

"But Evanstide is obviously the most important! The Digs are there. We have to stop them before they get to the vortex or hurt the people and their queen."

"Trust me, I know," answered Valti. "But you must go in this order. It will be for your safety and the rest. There is an alignment that must be connected by this order."

With that, Valti began to hand out the keys. "One. Two," she said as she passed the keys with red and orange gemstones to Matik. "Three. Four." The keys with yellow and green gemstones went to Frida. Valti held up the fifth key, the one with a blue stone. "This leads to the Eye of Gangleton. You will not need to use it now, as the Keeper of that Eye stands among you, but its order must be remembered."

Frida nodded along, considering all the possibilities now open to them.

"Six. Seven," Valti continued, gifting the indigo and violet keys to Percilla. Finally, she took the white key from the door and handed it to Percilla as well. "Eight. This is the order you must keep."

"Why is Percilla in charge of Fridanda?" Frida asked, flustered.

"In time you will understand and probably thank me," Valti answered. "Your purpose is to unite with the Keepers of the Eyes, all of them."

"We unite with them and then...?" Percilla said, eager to hasten their arrival to Evanstide.

"You tell them you are uniting, and each one will offer you more information about the alignment. They will have what you need. The Keepers of the Eyes will always know."

Percilla regarded the keys in her hands with skepticism. "I didn't know."

"You did. You just haven't realized it yet."

The Timeless Sage disappeared as she spoke her final words.

Frida eyed the pearlescent key and wrinkled her brow. "Percilla, you can give me the key to Fridanda," she said nonchalantly.

"No," Percilla replied as she placed each of her three keys around her neck. "I promise, if you want to go there, and it's right for all of us, I will open the door."

"Mmm. Trickery," Frida huffed, pulling her own keys' chains over her head.

"Let's get started," Matik said. "I've got number one. You ladies ready?"

They nodded to one another, as ready as they would ever be. Matik inserted his first key into the keyhole and turned the knob.

CHAPTER 8

Leveraging Unity

ONS AND FRANC prowled around the exterior edges of Evanstide's pools within a hushed exchange, glaring into the waters. Franc waved to a few curious people as Ons plunged a meter device into the pool. He took a small vial from the holster at his breast and collected a sample, then observed the apparatus. The arrow on the gauge was swinging around. The alchemist's crooked smile grew with every spin of the arrow. Beyond thrilled, he let out a wheezing laugh. It was only a matter of time until they learnt how to access the power of the vortex.

Out of the corner of his eye, Ons saw a few teenagers staring directly at him and Franc. The lead Dignitary said nothing, but the smile plastered on her face was unsettling, even to Ons.

Sliding a robust monocle apparatus over his eye, Ons spoke to his audience. "Do not worry, Evanstiders, we will keep you safe. I am merely measuring the levels of your sacred pools for your well-being."

A young woman standing at the front of the group spoke up. "I heard you all have iffy motives. Word on our streets is you're carrying some dark magic."

"Young lady," Franc snapped, "we are here on behalf of Rou. I'd be wary of who you believe."

"You're lying." A young man stepped forward to speak up. "Your energy speaks louder than your words."

Franc clasped her hands behind her back, and Ons could see the subtle green glow of her ring. The alchemist smiled, knowing all would be well, and went about scanning the wavelengths of energy in the pools. The areas with a higher density were most likely located right above the vortex. These people were much more aware than the people of Gangleton, and the sooner Franc took control, the sooner the monument could be built. Franc spoke to the kids in an enchanting voice, and soon they would forget what they'd seen and heard.

Ons peered over his shoulder to watch the intruders walk away from the area, then excitedly shared his discoveries with Franc. "Without a doubt, it is under these pools." He shoved the apparatus into Franc's face.

"Mmmhmm," Franc agreed, dunking her hand into another pool and rubbing the water between her fingers. "The queen herself said they lit up as an omen." There was a faint, peach glow lingering along the top of the water, a remnant from Aurora's earlier ceremony.

"Celebrations must stop immediately." Franc glared around the pools. "These people..."

"They must be numbed, yes. I've already come to that conclusion myself."

"That should be easy."

"The real question is, how can we utilize the vortex?" Ons wondered aloud. Evanstide was very different from Gangleton, after all. His keen technological mind could not help but conceive of new, inventive ways to harness the energy at will.

"Just like we have before," Franc replied curtly.

Ons knew Franc would provide him with everything he needed. This was why he liked her; she gave him access to everything in his wildest dreams. His mind teemed with visions as he stared at the area before him. He sorted through his mental blueprints, wondering which one would sit best here.

"You think she will let us build a tower, or better yet, a henge around a tower?" Ons asked with a sense of excitement he'd not felt since building Gangleton's tower.

Franc smirked and pulled Ons's monocle from his breast pocket, putting it to her eye as she gazed around the pools. "We are going to be part-owners soon. You just conceive of a way to use the energy, and let me do the rest." She placed the lens back into Ons's pocket, and they shared mutually devious grins.

Franc departed for the palace. Ons slid a new lens into place and clicked several rounds before locating the rendering of the henge around the tower. He then pressed a button, merging the pools and the plans into one image, then pressed it again to capture it for later. Ons let out another wheezing laugh as he safely lifted the imprint out of the apparatus and tucked it gently into his holster. Just looking around the pools was elating; he wanted to begin now.

He hastened after Franc. "No time to waste."

Pith waited for them just inside the palace entrance. "Greetings."

"Good day," Franc replied. "How is the queen?"

"In good spirits given the circumstances," Pith said wistfully, rubbing between his eyes.

Franc tilted her head, eyeing Pith intensely. "Would you mind telling us a bit about the kingdom?"

"Perhaps you can take us on a little tour?" Ons added, tapping his cane against the floor.

Pith removed his hand from his head. "That would be my pleasure. Certainly a nice distraction from this awful headache of mine."

"Happy to be of service. We were wondering specifically, what is the status of the caverns?" Ons had particular interest in what he was sure was the key to harnessing Evanstide's vortex energies. "You see, in Gangleton we have a cavern of blue crystals that makes up our vortex."

Pith stared at nothing for a moment, no doubt pondering something trivial, before asking, "What would you like to know about the cavern?"

"Has anyone ever entered it?" Franc asked. "Or seen inside of it?"

"There is no reason to disturb it," Pith replied, his sensibility momentarily getting the better of Franc's magic. "If you wish to experience the vortex, please, bathe in our pools with the rest of our community. The cavern is better left alone."

"So, it *is* below the pools?" Ons asked pointedly.

Pith's eyes narrowed, and he squared his shoulders. "You can feel the vortex in the pools. I, however, cannot disclose their exact location," he replied bluntly. "Surely you understand."

Ons raised his eyebrows and rolled his eyes slightly at his associate.

Franc closed the distance between her and the advisor. "If anyone came to Gangleton, I would surely take the same measures. Your vortex is similar to Gangleton's; one can feel its energy by simply standing in the community plaza. No need to be inside the caverns."

Pith's pupils dilated, and his movements halted before Franc's powerful stare.

"Though...we *are* part of the kingdom now," Franc said deviously. "You can disclose to us where the caverns are."

Pith replied in a slow, dull voice. "The caverns are under the pools."

"I knew it!" Ons exclaimed.

"Is there anything else you wish to see in our kingdom? Perhaps the coral gardens?" Pith asked.

"Personally, I would like to try the pools now that you've spoken of them," Ons said.

"Thank you, Pith, you've been quite helpful." Franc stepped back and released the advisor from her gaze.

Pith gave his head a slight shake as if clearing away a daze. Then, he bowed his head and smiled. "My pleasure. May the waters of Evanstide bring you joy."

He turned to leave and resume his duties, but before he could step away, Franc called to him yet again.

"Yes?" Pith asked.

"Will you encourage the queen to make her decision? Times are getting more and more dangerous by the minute," Franc said, her voice dreadfully calm, each word precise like a razor.

"Prince Vahn's people miss him dearly, and we would like to know that his presence and time are being honored," Ons added.

"Of course, we value your presence," Pith replied. "I shall see if I can't persuade her to make the right decision for the betterment of our kingdom."

From her throne, Aurora stared out a large, circular window at the extravagant kingdom. Her usual joyful disposition was crushed under the weight of her duty, and not even the view could buoy her spirits. She hadn't even had time to mourn for the loss of her father or come to terms with what it meant for her before the Dignitaries came bearing further dreadful news.

The sound of the heavy doors swinging open drew her attention.

"Greetings," Pith said as he bowed to the queen.

"I'm lost, Pith," Aurora replied, not masking the anxiety in her voice. "What am I to do? My people have just lost their powerful king, and now those same Evils are lurking right outside our barriers. I don't know how to protect them."

"My queen, this is why Rou has sent you allies. And a new king."

"Do you truly trust these Dignitaries?" Aurora gazed out the window at Franc and Ons exiting her palace.

"What makes you doubt their intentions?"

"There is something in their energy," Aurora said, her mind and heart telling her not to take them at their word. "Something of an almost dark nature."

"I understand," Pith replied. "I had my concerns as well, but after spending more time with them, I have come to find their truth."

Aurora perked up with genuine interest. "Is that so? Then what of this prince? He is quite intriguing. Did you spend time with him yet?"

"No, but he is their great prince. Apparently, he treats his people like they are his brothers and sisters. He is very good to them, and they love and respect him a great deal. Franc told me the people were devastated to hear he would no longer be in their presence, though they understand that what he is doing will make both kingdoms stronger in the face of such growing uncertainty and troubled times." The entire time he spoke, his hands continuously rolled over one another, and his gaze was unfocused.

"Is that so?" Aurora replied, trying to understand her aide's peculiar gestures.

"Yes. She said to have him come to Evanstide was a sacrifice they had to make for the safety of their people. Uniting your blood and your kingdoms will bring security throughout the land."

"Are you feeling all right?"

Pith's hands clenched together before dropping to his sides, where they found his garments to fiddle with. His eyes seemed to float in their sockets. The silence between them made him more agitated, his head darting left and right. "My queen, my well-being should be the least of your concerns. Though in truth, my head does ache."

"Perhaps you need rest. Before you do so, would you please send for Dazell? I would like to have her read the energy of these Dignitaries."

Pith frowned at his queen's response. "Dazell is not that easy to locate. There is no time to waste, my queen. Who will protect our kingdom if we do not make this alliance?"

"Pith, I did not ask for your opinion," Aurora snapped. "I asked you to bring me Dazell so I can make the best decision for my kingdom. The power of our vortex has kept Evanstide connected and protected since our dawning. Now, I wish to speak with our Keeper. What is wrong with that precaution?"

"Things are different now. Our vortex can only protect us for so long. Didn't you hear the Dignitaries' warning?" Pith's voice echoed loud enough to draw the attention of the palace guards.

Aurora blinked at him in shock, then her startlement was replaced by anger. "What has gotten into you? Why do you act as if I have no power beneath my feet? I might not be Divinu, but I am strong enough to use my power if and when the time comes."

"You are not acting in accordance with the danger beyond these walls," Pith said, passion gathering in his voice as he resumed his fidgeting. His eyes were still wandering in their sockets as he turned his head to the right and began to speak. "Did you forget what happened to your father? Our great king? He was cut down in mere moments." His head rolled back to meet Aurora's gaze.

"You have spoken out of turn," Aurora replied stiffly.

"I am only trying to counsel you to make good decisions. For yourself, for me, and all the people of Evanstide," Pith insisted as he dropped to his knees before the queen, taking her hand. "We depend on you. Your marriage to Prince Vahn is more than just a bond between two people. It is a union between two great kingdoms against the Evils that lurk outside our gates."

He bowed low. "I only wish to save our people. I hope that is your wish as well, my queen."

Pith stalked out of the throne room, his cloak sweeping behind him as he left an exasperated Aurora alone with her thoughts.

CHAPTER 9

Earth Alliance

PERCILLA, MATIK, AND Frida emerged from the mystical door and stepped into a vast, barren desert. Mesas of solid red rock decorated the landscape, eroded at the hands of time and fierce desert elements. This land was quite like the Barrens they had traveled through for so long and come to know so well, and yet, the place was distinctly different. There was a wealth of rich color in this land, but it was also a silent, empty place.

When they were all clear of the pyramid door, it became invisible to the eye. Percilla took the compass from inside her jacket to make sure it led them back to it. As the arrow pointed at the area from which they had just emerged, she gazed through the gemstone end of one of her keys, and the door was clearly visible.

Returning her sights to where they'd arrived, Percilla saw no Keeper of the Eye, nor anyone for that matter. The only sign that life had ever existed in this deserted land was a megalithic pyramid standing alone above the red earth, carved from the same rock of the mesas. It stood taller even than them, blocking the heavy light of the afternoon sun. Hundreds of steps led up to the pyramid's zenith, where a monumental garnet crystal gleamed radiantly. At the base of the pyramid, symbols were scattered across a sheet of pure, smooth bedrock. The pattern reminded Percilla of the runes on the Sages' temple in Rou.

"Hello?" Percilla walked in the empty desert, peering around for any sign of anything or anyone.

"Do you know where we are?" Matik asked, following behind her.

"No, but I'm sure someone here does," Percilla replied, turning back to Matik as she swept her body around in a slow circle. "We just have to find them."

Frida turned to the pyramid, her gaze narrowed and eyebrows perked with curiosity. "There is an energy present." She pointed up toward the garnet.

With his sword hand firmly on the hilt of his Rou blade, Matik nimbly stepped onto the pyramid's engraved grounds. He made no sound and took each step with the utmost caution, ready for whatever dangers lay ahead. Even so, the slightest brush of Matik's heels against the carved symbols caused flashes of scarlet light to shimmer across them.

"Watch your step," Frida shouted.

Matik never had a chance to react. Cobras slithered out from the runes, their bodies materializing in between the flashes of red light. They moved toward the pyramid, passing between and over Matik's feet to reach the bottom steps to

stack themselves on top of each other in a rigid line. At least a few hundred cobras formed a serpentine wall, standing tall and wide enough to block anyone who dared set foot in the pyramid. The snakes hissed and flicked their tongues, focusing their unblinking stares on the trio.

Matik had unsheathed his blade, ready for battle. A monstrous cobra rose from a symbol at the center of the engravings, as tall as a man. It posed before him without fear of his blade.

The cobra spoke in a slick, imposing voice. "Do not test me, boy." It flicked its forked tongue at Matik with each serpentine syllable. "I've eaten larger things than you in one bite." The cobra unhinged its maw to show the intruder a row of fangs that glimmered in the pyramid's flashing crimson lights.

Matik swallowed hard, but tightened the grip on his Rou blade as he boldly replied, "And I've killed larger snakes than you in one slice."

A sound like a low, sharp laugh came from within the cobra's throat as it leaned closer to Matik. It flicked its tongue, tauntingly sweeping it across the warrior's nose. The creature blazed bright red, shining with a menacing aura as magic filled the air. The ground at Matik's feet turned into clay cobras that slithered up his legs. He fought to get free, but the clay immediately hardened back to stone at his slightest movement, encasing his legs and rising to cover the rest of his body.

Frida bellowed the magic words, "*Ha Mic Ta*," filling the air with a counterspell as light blue sparkles glittered all around him.

"You think you have power here?" the cobra hissed. Its aura intensified, shining brighter as if to display its dominance. Without hesitation, it slithered over to Frida.

"I do not fear you," Frida said, staunch and sure of her own magic.

"Why have you disssssturbed Hazan?" the cobra asked, unable to hide its surprise at their steadfast bravery.

Percilla stepped forward. "Are you the Keeper of the Eye of Rou? The portal brought us here from Rou."

It slithered over to her. Once again, its red glare intensified as if it were resonating with the word "Rou."

"You're not from Rou," the cobra accused. Its tongue flicked, and its eyes examined Percilla with a curiosity that matched her own.

The ground at her feet turned to clay and began to rise up her legs, wrapping itself around her body just as it had Matik, but faster now in the intense presence of the cobra's red aura.

"*Ha Mic Ta!*" Frida shouted, casting her counterspell again and stopping the clay at Percilla's hips.

The cobra's eyes flashed with anger. "Why have you disssturbed—"

"Rou wanted to bring you a sssssurprise," Frida taunted.

"I do not recognize you. You are not from Rou," the cobra replied, maintaining an air of nobility. With a stubborn flick of its tongue, the clay began to rise around all three of them even faster than before.

"*Ha Mic Ta*," Frida said calmly. She looked deep into the snake's eyes, and a faint light connected them. "Rou has sent us to bring you a message."

The cobra looked stunned as it returned her gaze. "Who are you?" the snake asked with a genuine curiosity and confusion.

"Frida. I am in the lineage of the Keeper of the Eye of Rou of Gangleton. As is she." Her voice held a slight tinge of bragging as she gestured at Percilla.

Pleased by those words, the cobra nodded before lifting its head straight into the air. A faraway wind howled through the desert as the serpent's crimson scales stretched and melded together into human skin. From its long body, arms and legs emerged, replacing its tail on the stone ground. Its head slowly changed, shifting into the countenance of an old and wise man. Ornate fabrics, precious gemstones, and gold materialized from the scarlet glow onto the cobra's changing form. His auburn hair draped around his sharp facial features, which held no hint of the serpent he had just been. His golden staff was the last thing to materialize, and it held the trio in the garnet gaze of the cobra at the top. The symbols Valti had placed on their foreheads presented themselves for a flash before fading into their skin.

"Greetings. I am San, Chieftain of Hazan. I understand your people have fallen."

"In a sense, yes," Frida replied, a note of surprise in her voice. "They were deceived."

"They wasted their energy and put all of our lives in danger," San said resentfully.

"Um. No," Percilla scoffed. "They were deceived by Evils."

"We have never wasted a moment. Our energy is maintained and directed." San pointed to the humming garnet held at the top of the pyramid.

"You're an original person from Rou?"

"We all are," San replied, stretching his arms wide to encompass the breadth of the pyramid grounds.

Now that all danger had passed and they were freed from the hardened clay, Matik finally sheathed his Rou blade. "I thought everyone left Rou to start communities and teach wisdom."

"This is our creation for the people." San gestured again to the pyramid and its crystal. It glowed brighter and pulsed more radiantly at his words.

The midday sun reached its peak high in the sky and shone down onto the pyramid with a sudden, bright beam. Struck by the sunlight, the garnet peak shimmered and flashed with a burst of potent energy. Acting as a conductor, the crystal dispersed scarlet light, which flowed down the pyramid like waves of crimson fire, bathing the desert and the grounds below in its vibrant color.

Once touched by the wave, the wall of snakes guarding the pyramid steps broke apart. Each individual serpent went through the same transformation as San, regaining their original human forms. They scattered and arranged themselves along the organized pattern of symbols beneath the pyramid, each aligning themselves with a specific symbol.

All at once, the community stomped their feet against the ground in a ritualistic rhythm, their ceremonial sound filling the previously silent desert. San joined the beat with a chant that resonated with the escalating hum of the pyramid's crystal. The rest of the tribe joined in, perfectly in tune with one another and the garnet. They moved their bodies in a practiced sequence. Light flashed through the symbols beneath their feet until the whole area became illuminated. The sounds built to a final, deafening climax, followed by a sudden pause.

The runes on the pyramid grounds blazed with the energy of the garnet. All members of the tribe lifted their right foot and with immense, channeled intention, they stomped upon the earth, shaking the ground below them. Then they followed suit with their left foot. Finally, their arms and heads dropped back as they raised their chests skyward, ending their ritual.

The scarlet light shot up from beneath the tribe's feet and into the sky. It expanded in all directions like a shockwave of energy sprawling across the expansive landscape. The drifting trails of light faded into the distance like the tails of far-off comets, and the tribe simultaneously returned to their cobra forms. They slithered back into their symbols, leaving only the traces of their echoing hissing on the party's ears.

"This is how we extend our energy to the world," San explained to the thoroughly impressed trio. "We do not waste our bodies."

"You have obviously been the most honorable in your loyalty to Rou," Frida remarked.

"For what reason has Rou has sent *you?*"

"To unite," Percilla said boldly, stepping forward and presenting San with her keys of Rou to prove her truth. She motioned to Matik, and he too held up the keys he was given, the red one blazing from being so near to its origin.

The chieftain hummed, contemplating their sudden arrival. "When all the colors reach the sky, we open the Eye."

"What?"

"That is what we were told before leaving Rou."

San reached toward a symbol on the pyramid grounds. A ball of energy that rippled like water emerged from it. He then used his golden cobra staff to draw symbols in the solid bedrock at their feet. First, he drew a large circle, soon joined by smaller circles of various sizes orbiting around it. Upon count and close inspection, Percilla realized the surrounding circles San drew were representations of the Sun, Moon, Mercury, Venus, Mars, Jupiter, and Saturn. San then reached into his garments and produced a small, leather satchel from within. He pulled out a handful of white powder and lightly shook it in over a symbol on the ground.

The colorful representations of the Solar System rose out from the earth in a mystic projection. The planets rotated around the Sun and eventually aligned with specific locations on the Earth, which beamed with bright lights that matched the various colors of the celestials with which they aligned.

San indicated the red point with his staff. "Our Eye of Rou brought my people here. We are connected to Saturn." He used his staff to point out the glowing red planet. "When Saturn's force pulls the energy of the vortex, it is too powerful for my people to embody. No ritual can occur because the force of the vortex is being pulled up. So we get out of the way and let it reach the sky—"

"And you open the Eye," Frida said, beating San to the punch.

Matik scratched his chin. "Then what?"

"We go inside." San answered with a deep mystery building in his eyes as he pointed to the pyramid.

"So to 'unite' means all the vortex energy must reach the planets?" Percilla asked, still examining the alignment of the stars and planets in the magic projection.

"*Alli min*," San said, and the illuminated spots on the projection of Earth connected into a beam of light with their orbiting stars and planets. "Unite."

"What is a vortex?" Matik asked.

San laughed heartily and replied, "Okay, let me show you." With a clap of the old man's hands, the miniature Solar System vanished back into the dirt. Motioning for Percilla, Frida, and Matik to follow, he mounted the steps of the pyramid, leading the way to its peak and the crystal awaiting their arrival.

CHAPTER 10

Crowning Ruse

T HE TROMBONES SOUNDED, echoing across the kingdom of Evanstide, to commence the marital celebration.
The royal parade promenaded out from the palace to the lower
terraces and down into the plaza. Joy filled the area for the first
time in weeks as the people gathered to honor the queen's communion. Embroidered banners of orange and blue hung between glorious flower and coral arrangements decorating the
uppermost terrace. At the parade's center, warriors of special
esteem carried a gilded and finely embellished litter on their
shoulders.

All Evanstide paraded through the kingdom in the direction
of the ceremonial pagoda at the edge of the pools. The platinum
structure was surrounded by a moat and laced in vines and
exotic flowers of rich hues. It held an essence more ancient than
Evanstide within it. Young and old citizens alike sang together
and paired their song with the tapping of their fanciful heels.
Some particularly curious young children snuck their way to

the litter and tried to peek inside, but they were too short to see over the large figures of the royal guard.

The parade continued until at last it came to a halt at the single cherrywood bridge leading to the pagoda. The musicians transitioned to a distinctly aristocratic tune, signaling the warriors carrying the litter to stop.

From inside the coral maze just beyond the pagoda, the Dignitaries watched and waited for the litter's arrival. Franc's face stretched into an uncontrollable grin as the sentries dropped to one knee and a single stair descended from the litter.

Queen Aurora stepped out, dazzling all those gathered. Her regal beauty was complemented by the finest silk that flowed over her figure like water. Delicate crystals sparkled across the fabric, glittering in the sun.

Striding out from behind the coral wall, Vahn revealed himself to his bride. His sky-blue suit was fit for a king, with stripes of blue and purple on his legs and a metallic raven emblem sewn onto the back of his jacket. "Look at her. A real queen to be my wife." Vahn's eyes shimmered with a flicker of light.

"You are a prince, Vahn. Who else would be your wife?" Franc locked his gaze.

"Only a queen. Queen Aurora," Vahn replied as his pupils enlarged, then contracted. Franc left Vahn's side to join the rest of the Dignitaries as Aurora approached. He bowed deeply until she arrived.

Soon, all of Evanstide gathered before the Dignitaries and the queen. The music reached an imperial crescendo, then was replaced by wedding music. A cheer rang out from the crowd as Aurora and Vahn joined each other inside the ancient monument.

At Franc's nudging, Drendle scurried across the bridge to Vahn's side with a ceremonial tray. He carried an extravagant platinum crown fitted with beautiful blue crystals that blinked with their own soft light. Pith followed soon after with a sword that bore a large carnelian at the center of its hilt. The royal advisor knelt before his queen and offered her the blade. With a solemn nod, she accepted the sword.

Vahn knelt before Aurora, and time seemed to stand still in the silence. He peeked upward and saw a flash of sadness wash over Aurora's expression as she examined the sword in her hands. But like all emotions, the sadness quickly passed and was replaced by an expression of royal determination and responsibility. Aurora held the sword up high, then slowly lowered its flat edge to Vahn's head. She silently recited the words that bound her to the man before her. Lifting the sword from the top of his head, she bowed to the new King of Evanstide. With a deep breath, she offered the blade to Vahn, who stood and graciously accepted it before sheathing it at his side.

The now-king and Dignitary turned to Drendle and took the crown from the tray. Its soft glow pulsed more intensely in Vahn's hands as he gently placed the crown atop her head.

Within the depths of Aurora's eyes, the same blue light blinked to life.

Another cheer rang out from the crowd enhanced by the wedding music, this one even louder and more excited than before. The words "Blessed be the queen!" and "Blessed be the king!" traveled from person to person in the cacophony of celebration.

But amidst the crowd, disapproving eyes watched the ceremony with a furious intensity. Dazell, a sorceress with an appearance that was both keen and wise, stood unnoticed. She'd pulled her hood low to conceal her from the rest of Evanstide's citizens. Her gaze traveled along a coral aqueduct running beside the pagoda, one positioned directly next to the Dignitaries. Even from this great distance, the Keeper of Evanstide's Eye made out the duplicitous grin plastered on Franc's devious face.

Dazell's scowl of disapproval changed to a mischievous smirk as a spark of trickery entered her thoughts. With a snap of her fingers and the magic word *"Tiluma,"* a spell entered the water and shot out at the Dignitaries.

Franc shrieked. She and her cohorts were drenched and knocked to the ground. All who watched could not help but laugh at the spectacle, Aurora herself quickly turning to hide a chuckle. Franc stumbled to her feet, glaring over the crowd, hunting for the trickster who caused this unforgivable disturbance.

Dazell pulled her hood closer and slipped back into the safety of the shadows.

CHAPTER 11

Source of Life

*S*TREAMS OF RADIANT crimson light flowed out from the garnet at Hazan's apex, welcoming the chieftain and his guests with its calming force. San paused before a sigil blazing with the same energy while Percilla, Matik, and Frida gazed over the vista, awestruck. After an assortment of knocks of the chieftain's staff against the rarely trodden ground, a hum of magic rumbled from deep within the Earth. The Hazan sigil flashed on the stone, which slowly dropped into the ground. Beyond the entrance flanked by statues, a dark tunnel led downward into a mysterious luminescence.

Percilla's eyes widened as the magic inside the pyramid caressed her body like a gentle breeze. At first glance, she had thought this megalithic structure was lifeless, but this was not the case. The vortex inside was full of life.

Frida whispered to herself as she opened her palm, igniting a magical flame. Exchanging a quick nod with Percilla, the sorceress cradled her fire as she stepped into the tunnel. "Well, shall we? I've never been into one of these. Heard about them plenty, though."

San smiled at her eagerness. "Come along."

They walked into the darkness until San came to another sealed doorway, this one carved with runic symbols of cobras slithering amongst stars. Crimson light pierced the thin cracks of the doorway, bathing them in its soft radiance. San recited words of magic before the ancient stone, and in the silence of the tunnel, Percilla swore she heard something whisper back. The doorway slid open, revealing a cathedral of brilliant, glistening gems. Throughout the expansive cavern, monumental garnet walls shimmered with a mystical life force.

"If you want to understand the frequency of a vortex, you must experience the wisdom at its core. For it is the focal point, harnessing the power of precious minerals of this Earth," San said with reverence for the hallowed ground they walked upon.

"What an honor," Frida said, her mouth agape. Slowly moving around the cavern, the sorceress stretched her arms above her and exhaled, then circled her palms back to her side. "I can't believe I've never been in one of these. How enchanting." She eagerly climbed onto a flat slab of crystal protruding from the floor and sat down. Crossing her legs in front of her, she closed her eyes and quietly hummed mystical tones that gently echoed off the garnet walls.

Tibs buzzed away from Percilla's hat and flew to the center of the temple. Her spirit guide only flew away when she was meant to follow, so she fell in step behind the bee. They wove through the tall, garnet uprights that radiated out from a central point, and Percilla felt the intense gravitational pull of the sacred force at the core of the cavern. Tibs buzzed all around the immense, crystalline sphere at the center before returning to her hat. Shocked by the magnitude of mystical power of the garnet before her, Percilla paused and caught San watching her with wise, old eyes. He didn't say anything to stop her, so she continued. Her eyes became fixated on the crystal, and the spiral of energy within pulled her gaze deep inside.

Images flashed; visions of the past or the future, she couldn't tell. At first, it was nearly overwhelming and confounding to look upon, like a question with no possible answer. But as her eyes focused on the images within the crystal, brief flickers of understanding began to dawn. With enough concentration, the spinning pattern was steady and consistent.

A flaming, gaseous mixture bubbled and burst through the molten earth, a crucible of destruction in which nothing could live. And yet, with the passage of time, the raging magma cooled and hardened into an empty, obsidian sphere. Cracks formed on that black, barren rock as the force of time pressed the stone against itself. Crashing tides of clear, pristine water pushed through the crevices and expanded to cover the Earth in a sea of blue.

More time passed. The sunlight cascaded from the sky, the rays carrying life itself. The waters dwindled as the earth changed at the Sun's touch, and lush, green plants sprouted. Tall, leafy trees grew from patches of rich soil, accompanied by flowers in all the colors of the rainbow. Fruits and vegetables grew from every leaf and stem that covered the vibrant landscape.

A spiraling portal of magic twisted open from within the Earth. Masses of men and women emerged, scattering across the land to form thriving communities built of thatch, wood, and stone. They fed on the bounty of the Earth, drank from its pure water, and prospered in the warmth of its light. For a long time, there was peace and happiness shared by all. Then, their buildings grew so tall, they even outstripped the great trees.

But just as quickly as the men and women came, their communities fell into ruin, meteors crashed to earth, and all they'd built crumbled to nothing. All of humanity vanished, leaving behind only their broken homes, tools, and trinkets to be swallowed by the earth.

For a time, there was nothing, then once again the magma spewed through the cracks and shot out from the volcanoes to cover the Earth. The tapestry of vision repeated in Percilla's eyes for as long as she gazed into the crystalline sphere, mesmerized by the sequence of time that looped back in an endless knot.

Matik wandered along the edges, exploring the walls of the cavern and curiously observing the subtle crevices. Out of the corner of his eye, a shadow caught his attention before it disappeared behind a large upright. Intrigued, Matik followed after it. He peeked around the stone wall and discovered a tunnel leading into the depths of the pyramid. The passageway's entrance was only large enough to allow a single person to pass at one time. From what Matik could make out inside the darkness, the space within the tunnel seemed to expand into another cavern the deeper it went.

Matik turned to the chieftain and motioned at the tunnel. "Where does this go?"

San looked to Matik's discovery with a flash of uneasiness in his eyes that was quickly hidden beneath a controlled glare. "Nothing different than what lies within every vortex."

"Which is what?" Matik pressed, not satisfied with the vague answer.

"When you return to your own vortex, you are welcome to go in and see." San turned his back to punctuate the dismissal.

Percilla's attention was drawn away from the crystal and over to San and Matik's conversation. "Does it lead to other vortexes?" she asked.

"Only the Hazan are allowed in that tunnel. That is where we go when we open the eye. Until then, it must be undisturbed," San said sternly.

Matik would have turned away from the tunnel, but a burst of air rushed past him. A magnetic force pulled his focus deeper into the tunnel. Though San's tone had left no room for argument, something was telling him he must go inside. Hunching himself over to crouch through its entrance, he took delicate steps, steadily disappearing to explore the shadowy mystery.

Percilla watched him nervously, unsure why he would go against the wishes of San, but also knowing she mustn't say a word.

"I saw the growth cycle Valti spoke of," Percilla said. She could not help but wonder at what she had seen within the cavern's crystal. And what's more, she wondered what such a growth cycle might mean for her, her family, and her friends. "But I don't understand how you use it."

"When the light of the Sun hits our planet, the energy of the vortexes speak," San explained, making artful gestures with his hands to convey his meaning. "The people of Hazan perform a ritual in order to use our bodies to channel that energy into the world. Our vortex is the base for all other vortexes. We begin every cycle because our element is earth, which is the most dense frequency."

"Curious," Frida pondered aloud. "Each vortex is made of a unique gemstone, connected to a planet, and each has a different element?"

"Yes. All of the Rou communities had a destiny when we left Rou many years ago. Each one of us extends the energy of our vortex into the world. We circulate the frequency on the surface of the Earth and in the universe at large."

"Aw, Earth, the blessed connector of our Galaxy," Frida praised.

"But we aren't the first humans to live on Earth, right?" Percilla concluded, remembering what she'd seen in the garnet sphere.

"That's right. And it seems your friend was beckoned by the ancients within Hazan's vortex." San's eyes darted back toward the hidden tunnel. "I hope it was by the good ones. Come on. Let's go see if he's alive."

"Alive?" Percilla asked. She and Frida rushed past San, whose pace was far too slow for Percilla's comfort.

CHAPTER 12

Superficial Machinations

FOLLOWING THE WEDDING ceremony, the Dignitaries set out along with the royal couple to gather at the kingdom's pools and examine their current strength. The dim light of a late evening sky fell upon Evanstide, making evermore apparent the shimmering shield surrounding it. For this brief time, when all the people gathered in the pools, both the Sun and Moon were visible to them as one fell and the other rose. Scurrying through the streets at the heels of the party, a white crab shifted its color to a deep purple before delicately crawling up the coattails of Drendle's long, purple duster.

Pearl lanterns illuminated the walls and archways as Franc walked along the outer edges of the pools, scrutinizing them with an intense gaze. Nylz and Lyken entertained the royal couple, allowing Ons the time he needed to analyze Evanstide's pools. Using his copper tablet device, he probed the sacred waters for any information about their abilities. He tapped its glass screen and turned the dials on its side. Drendle peeked his head over the tainted alchemist's shoulder to watch the slow progress of the meters.

Dazell was watching too, hidden inside the safety of her home. She gazed into the magical pool as her own enchanted tools went to work. The camouflaged crab climbed onto the Dignitary's hat to eavesdrop on the information Ons gathered, watching intently with crustacean eyes. Zooming into the screen, Dazell was full of anger as her predictions proved correct. These Dignitaries were indeed attempting to impose their power upon Evanstide. With the full, disgraceful plot revealed, she opened the claws of the crab and had it snap Drendle's earlobe between its pincers. The crab leapt onto Ons's hat as Drendle shouted out in pain. He stumbled, falling face-first into the pools with a giant, undignified splash, once again soaking in Evanstide's waters. Ons paid no heed to the mischief, ignoring the shameful sight and only moving enough to keep his apparatus dry.

Dazell observed the dissonance between Drendle and the rest of the Dignitaries as he floundered about in the waters. He had a softness to him.

Drendle found himself face to face with a beautiful woman who had also been drenched by his fall. She playfully splashed

Drendle back. He wiped his face, then chuckled for a moment before getting his payback with his own huge splashes of water.

Franc glanced at Drendle's noisy shenanigans with rage burning in her eyes. "Beautiful ceremony," Franc said to Aurora.

"Besides getting all wet," Lyken seethed, sliding his hand over his damp hair.

Nylz stood behind Lyken, her eyes slowly traveling up and down her nearly dry companion. With a smirk, she swept her foot beneath Lyken's, tripping him into a nearby pool. The lanky creep let out a yelp as his long arms waved awkwardly in the air. He tottered into the pool, and Nylz bent over with laughter, struggling even to point a finger at the result of her prank.

"Truly, we couldn't be happier for you both," Ons said with strictly regulated composure.

"Thank you," Aurora replied, trying not to laugh at her kingdom's guests and their apparent inability to stay dry. Vahn's lips kept twitching, as if fighting back a grin. "I am sorry for the aqueduct's malfunction. I must say, I have never seen it occur before today."

"That is the least of our concerns," Franc replied, then stated with an authoritative air, "We'll take it as a blessing from Evanstide."

Aurora's eyes wandered over to the top pool. "Probably the spirit of my father welcoming you into our family. His way of blessing you. He did always enjoy his pranks."

Dazell could not help but pick up on the tinge of melancholy in the queen's words. Vahn must have sensed it as well because he leaned in closer, placing a hand upon Aurora's back. At least he was playing his part well.

Aurora stretched her arm out to the pools. "Have you gone into the waters yet?"

"Ever since we arrived!" Lyken shouted in frustration, dripping wet.

"Not yet," Nylz answered. "You see, we come from a dryer climate. Water is something we need to get used to."

"I understand." Aurora watched Lyken awkwardly climb his way to dry land. "Take your time. I do encourage you, though. The energy in them is magical."

"Precisely." Ons's head jolted up. "That was what Pith was telling us."

"I suppose this is where you would be able to monitor the energy levels," Aurora hesitantly replied as she stepped closer to Ons.

"Exactly my point." Ons made a quick adjustment on his device, then his enthusiasm nearly dislodged the crustacean spy atop his hat when he shoved the tablet into Aurora's hands. "I would like to run my plans for the vortex monument by you."

"Vortex monument?"

"Yes," Franc smoothly interjected. "In order to understand what's occurring, we must set up a measuring device."

"The device is multi-purpose, you see," Ons said, joy creeping into his voice at the mention of his ingenious plans. He pointed to the screen glowing before Aurora, displaying a multitude of drab, systematic meters fully filled. "One aspect of it is to monitor the pools' energy levels, and the other is to serve as a meeting area for Evanstide."

Ons flicked his finger, changing the display to a presentation of some sort of blueprint. Dazell saw the plans for a tall monument of quartz, like a tower surrounded by smaller, obsidian slabs, purposefully arranged. Below the structure, Evanstide's blessed gathering area was flattened to a single level, destroying the very sacred grounds they now stood upon. A projection of the ocean's tides showed waves flowing in and out of Evanstide as the Moon aligned with the kingdom. Spiraling vortex energies gathered on the screen, concentrating their invisible paths on the monument. As the tides fell, an orange beam of light shot up from the center of the monument. It led up to a quartz sphere of unknown purpose floating between two pillars made of obsidian that jutted up from the ocean floor.

"I tried to change as little as possible," Ons explained. Then through clenched teeth, he asked, "What do you think?"

"The pools are gone," Aurora replied with horror.

Ons pressed on, paying little heed to Aurora's emotional state. "When the Moon is full, so is the pool. I wanted the waters to be more ceremonial."

"I agree," Franc added as she grabbed Aurora by her shoulder. "Also, I love how the people can utilize the vortex energy better by walking inside the stone walls."

"The apparatus at the top is clearly a marvelous touch," Nylz added, grabbing Aurora's other shoulder and turning her to get a better view of the monument's design.

Lyken stood by, wringing his clothes and hair dry. "I like the control of the water flow."

"It's pretty," Drendle absentmindedly remarked, still playing splashing games with the woman in the pool.

"It is, isn't it?" Ons replied with satisfaction and clearly longed for appreciation.

"I..."

Dazell saw Aurora's expression change as her brows furrowed and her gaze dropped, as if searching the ground for what she was about to say. The blue crystals affixed to her crown blinked to life and glowed with a magical energy, further alerting Dazell to the machinations of the Dignitaries. The queen's expression darkened and her pupils grew wide as a cloudy haze washed over her eyes. Her lips struggled to move, quivering with short, desperate twitches.

Franc looked on with a smug smile, silently awaiting the next words to come from the queen's mouth. Aurora's voice was as blank and emotionless as a void. "I think the people will love it. When do you start building?"

"I can assemble a team immediately," Nylz replied.

Ons took his tablet from Aurora's limp grasp and put it in his pocket. "First, let's look at the caverns."

"You read my mind," Franc said, her voice filled with a calm, controlled superiority.

The haze covering Aurora's eyes gradually dispersed, allowing some sentience to return to the queen. "We've never disturbed the caverns before. I'm not sure it's a good idea—"

The stones atop her crown gleamed as her eyes were once again enveloped in a mist of dark magic.

"We won't be disturbing anything," Ons said softly as he leaned in closer to Aurora's face, speaking in a hypnotic rhythm. "We are meant to go into the caverns."

"If that is what's best," Aurora replied, her voice as weightless as a hollow puppet held up by strings. She held out her hand and Vahn was back at her side a second later.

They turned to face the pool at the apex of the gathering area, its calm waters gently trickling down into the next. Franc hustled them along, and the queen led the Dignitaries up the path, her expression empty and movements lacking the regal grace that was usually present. The Dignitaries followed close behind with Franc at the head of the pack.

Letting go of Vahn's hand, Aurora waded into the high pool's sacred waters, submerging herself up to her waist as she approached a golden panel built into an extravagant pedestal. At the queen's touch, the panel lit up. A spiraling pattern followed her finger as she drew the symbol of Evanstide. The water drained from the pool into the lower ones, which revealed a circular hatch built into the ground. Without skipping a beat, Aurora knelt and lifted the cover, exposing what lay beneath. The sound of far-off waves crashing against subterranean walls rebounded from a long stairway leading down into the murky cavern.

Fragments of light emitted from the depths, just bright enough to illuminate their path into the heart of Evanstide. With each step, the sounds of the kingdom grew quieter, leaving only the echo of distant waves to fill the cavern's enclosed air. The radiance guiding them grew brighter the farther down they delved.

They finally came to the bottom of the stone stairway, which was lit with the warm, earthy glow of orange crystals. The extravagant cavern was brimming with formations that provided a constant illumination. At the far end of the chamber, a dark tunnel led further into the cavern, which not even the light of the geodes could illuminate.

"What unique formations," Ons remarked, the crab's line of sight rising as he stared up at the cavern's carnelian ceiling.

Aurora led the Dignitaries into the center of the chamber. "Are they different from the ones under Gangleton?" she asked.

"Very different frequency." Franc touched one of the cavern's many clusters of carnelians. "I would say these have the power to draw people together," she said, wonderment exuding from her genuine, toothy smile.

"That's why we use the pools as a vortex location. Our people live in harmony when they are communal."

"Where do all these tunnels go?" Franc asked tersely.

"I've never been down here before," Aurora replied, turning herself around and looking over the cavern before settling her eyes upon the shafts. "I didn't even know there were tunnels leading away from the main chamber."

"Your father really kept some important things from you," Nylz thought aloud, the excitement in her voice alerting Dazell.

Dazell affixed her spy's crustacean body to the petite warrior to get a different viewpoint. These Dignitaries would go to great lengths, even so far as to trek into the mysteries that might lay within the tunnels.

"Only the Keeper of the Eye knows what's down here," Aurora said as she placed her hand on one of the radiant crystals.

"Aren't you the Keeper?" Nylz asked.

"No. My family are the keepers of the *kingdom*. Not the Eye."

"This is important information," Franc growled, approaching the queen. "I am shocked you would keep such things from our knowledge."

The cluster of geodes flared under Aurora's hand as she replied in a hushed voice, "You never asked me."

"I'm sure she would have told me when it was necessary," Vahn interjected, placing himself between Franc and Aurora.

Ons adjusted the dial on his belt and turned his monocle to switch the lens. "Since the news is out, perhaps you can introduce us."

"If that is what the Keeper wishes," Aurora said, her voice tinged with defiance and respect for her people. But as the blue crystals on her crown lit up once more, her words were forcibly filled with a distilled, controlled intonation. "I will take you to meet her," she said.

"Grand," Franc curtly replied, stepping away from Vahn and Aurora. "Lyken, bring the torch," she continued, turning to the dark tunnel at the far end of the chamber. "Let's see what's down there."

Dazell watched as Lyken produced a wooden torch and a vial of black powder from his coat, holding them aloft in the cavern's light. With just a small pinch of the powder, a flame arose to cast light into the tunnel's entrance. Franc, Lyken, Ons, and Nylz entered first, followed closely by Aurora and Vahn, and lastly Drendle, who was mesmerized by the many crystals littering the cavern floor.

Once they were deep enough and they only had the torchlight to see by, Aurora began to speak with a sense of bittersweet wonder in her voice. "When I was young, my mother would tell me legends of tunnels under a great kingdom. I never knew they were real."

"My grandfather was a great storyteller as well," Vahn said.

"I love fairy tales," Drendle said idly, barely paying attention to Aurora's words as he quickened his pace.

Aurora continued. "She said once upon a time, before the last apocalypse, there were many people who lived in tunnels deep inside the Earth. Guardians of ancient wisdom who dwelled under the lands where great kingdoms thrived. These tunnel dwellers painted elaborate murals telling stories of the past. Unfortunately, after the Dezireden Apocalypse, these people disappeared before they could pass on all of their wisdom. Though a few stories and symbols were preserved in murals. And a few of these murals can still be understood, for they depict the longtime alliance to the kingdoms of Rou."

Lyken held up his torch as he led the way, illuminating stone walls etched and painted with ancient glyphs detailing long-forgotten tales. Old though they were, they were also well maintained. The crash of distant waves was stronger here; the deeper down they went, the closer they came to a secret ocean entrance.

Lyken stopped short as something on the wall caught his eye, and the rest of the Dignitaries paused as the light stopped. Nylz elbowed her way forward to see what he'd found. Shining his light close to the glyphs, Lyken revealed the tip of a lizard's tail carved into the stone. Nylz followed right behind him as he ran the torch across the full length of the cavern wall to reveal the rest of a long tail, vast wings, sharp claws, and finally the face of a dragon that breathed a mural of flame across the stone. Just beyond the glyph, the tunnel's walls were charred black. And beyond that, the sounds of something hidden within the waves.

CHAPTER 13

Guardians of Rou

D AZELL GLARED AT the live vision of the Dignitaries creeping into the ancient underbelly of Evanstide and groaned. "So you've made your way into my domain, have you? First my queen and now my tunnels."

Having enough of the sight, she shifted her attention from the pool to the stairwell leading up. Though Dazell was usually calm and controlled, she couldn't help the annoyance from creeping in as she hurried through the trapdoor to the main floor of her home. A sizable pyramid dominated the center of the room. Below the golden structure, vines grew from between the stones to spread across the floor. It was clean and nearly empty, except for where the carnelian walls were carved into inlets and filled with rows of organized jars, vials, and pyramid-shaped gemstones of various colors. The sorceress grabbed two of the crystalline pyramids from high shelves, as well as a couple vials of multi-colored liquid and a glittering black jar no larger than her palm.

"If introductions are what you want, then let me introduce you," she said with a mischievous smirk.

She rushed back down the stairway and submerged the two crystalline pyramids in the pool. Magically popping the corks from the two vials, she emptied the contents of one into the pool, followed by just a splash of the other. A sparkling amalgam began naturally swirling together while she gave a big shake from the little jar, releasing black flakes into the pool.

From her cloak, Dazell produced a yellow crystal. She held it up, focusing her eyes on the flickering interior. A fire ignited in her palm that neither burned nor surprised her. It fluttered as it followed her hand down to the pool. The moment Dazell gently brought the fire to the water, the flames spread in a sacred geometric pattern around the glittery black powder and twinkling mixture. The flames shaped themselves, moving with the essence of life within them as the pattern transformed into a dragon.

"*Nagonis, Nagonis, hybin loctin Nagonis,*" Dazell chanted. The ignited flecks of powder rose out from the water and through the flames, forming an aqueous dragon that glimmered in the fires. Its wings flapped in the air before Dazell, scattering trace amounts of the sacred liquids. The elemental dragon was made of the very same waters filling Evanstide and held all the power of their vortex.

Dazell continued her chanting as the dragon listened, its eyes becoming red hot flames that seared with fiery intentions. A low growl echoed throughout her home as the dragon darted through the bottom of the pool, clearing away the remnants of the ritual that had formed it and leaving only a ripple of clear water in its place.

The vision of the Dignitaries in the cavern materialized in the sacred pool once again, and Dazell saw the Dignitary pull his torch back from the engraved walls of stone before him.

"Dragons?" Lyken shuddered, stepping back from the scorch marks that dominated the blackened tunnel.

"Extinct," Ons remarked with outright dismissal, urging Lyken forward with a light shove of his hand.

Franc held no fear for a beast which even she, with all her arcane knowledge and many travels, had never come across. "Only in fairy tales."

Two large and motionless blue flames appeared before Lyken, hovering in the air like ghosts. He stumbled forward into the tunnel as sweltering heat invaded the cold air of the cavern. He shook with fear as he held up his torch. The meager flame danced in reflected, orange swirls on the watery skin of a glittering dragon.

The dragon was colossal, its reptilian head alone larger than each of the Dignitaries, with a maw of razor-sharp teeth that could swallow them whole. Four heavy legs rested on the ground, talons scraping the charred, stone floor. Smooth wings composed of flowing, watery skin that reached all the way to the ceiling. The dragon reared up in the presence of the intruders and beat its wings, releasing a gust of wind and mist that filled the tunnel.

"Fly me home!" Lyken screeched. He turned and ran away from the great beast, his flailing limbs sending torchlight waving haphazardly in the cavern.

"Not a fairy tale!" Nylz shouted. She and the rest of the Dignitaries ran rather than battle this living relic. Only Aurora remained calm when the large being passed by her.

Heat built in the cavern as the dragon's lungs filled, and the soft light of Lyken's torch was replaced with a bright, all-consuming blossom of fire. A torrent of flame bounced off the walls of the tunnel and overwhelmed the sound of distant waves with an explosive roar.

Franc turned to face the dragon's breath, casting a spell that projected a magical barrier from her hands. *"Devis non!"*

The fire pounded against the invisible wall, slamming it like a raging gust of infernal wind. Franc's ring glowed, and the magic held until the flames were extinguished. Without hesitation the dragon charged through the barrier with the force of a tidal wave. Franc turned to flee but was thrown to the ground. She rolled through the dirt, pushed by waters thrust forward from the mighty creature.

Nylz unsheathed her blade, the ring of metal echoing off the stone. Franc came swiftly to her feet with a roar to match the dragon's.

"Run!" Franc yelled as an even more powerful blast of flames erupted from the dragon's fiery lungs, followed by, *"Optimino!"* Franc once again flew to the ground.

A raging waterfall crashed down from the tunnel's ceiling, bringing forth a freezing downpour that shielded the Dignitaries from the dragon's fire. Nylz rushed to Franc's side and reached out to grab her, but Franc only slapped her minion's hand away. The captain bolted out of the area. Nylz quickly followed close behind, and soon the two joined Lyken up ahead. The warm glow of the crystal chamber filled the tunnel's entryway with light.

The Dignitaries stumbled out of the tunnel and practically fell into the crystal chamber as Lyken yelled, "I'm outta here." Drendle and Ons darted after him through the last chamber leading to the stairwell.

Dazell scurried her crustacean body off of Nylz, who sprinted toward the exit.

Franc was the last to enter the chamber where Vahn gazed around, confused. "Where is Aurora?" he asked.

"You're the king now, boy," she replied, rushing up and out of the chamber.

Vahn glanced at the edge of the tunnel just as the dragon's fiery eyes flashed into view. Its heavy claws stomped into the chamber, sending a cloud of dirt into the air and shockwaves reverberating through the cavern's crystals. Vahn froze as the ancient beast slowly approached him.

Following behind it, Aurora emerged, unharmed by the creature. She stood beside him, and the being lowered its enormous head down to hers. Its ghostly eyes met with Aurora's, the two locking their gazes in silence.

Vahn reached for his golden sword and whispered, "What are you doing?"

"This is my kingdom," Aurora replied without a backward glance. "Dragons are our allies."

"It just tried to kill our family," he said, trying to keep himself from shouting in the dragon's presence.

The dragon appeared relaxed and reverent of Aurora. The gust of heat from its fiery breath vanished, and the cool air of the underground returned. The sound of distant waves crashed once more from somewhere far away. The dragon lowered itself to the ground, bowing to Aurora before returning to the darkened tunnel from whence it came.

Back in her home, Dazell held her hand above the pool, obscuring the vision of the cavern as it shattered into a ripple across the water's surface. "I am sorry I failed you, Aurora! I nearly had them burnt!" she moaned, throwing her hands in the air.

Undoubtedly, Dazell was about to be paid a visit by these distasteful people, and she marched upstairs with no time to waste. She flicked her wand as she turned in a circle, leaving faint, spiral trails of glittering dust behind her. The entire room shifted in appearance, save for the large, golden pyramid in the center of the room. The clutter-free room was replaced with the wild jumble of a sorceress's shack. Papers filled with hastily transcribed, coded writing were thrown about the vine-covered floor. Jars, vials, and crystals were haphazardly set about in disorganized piles. Multitudes of instruments cluttered up a corner of the room. Where the trapdoor had once stood, there was a bubbling cauldron instead. From inside the cauldron, two kangaroos came bouncing out into the room. The curious, young creatures knocked over a table and sent even more papers flying all over the place.

"That's right, my little darlings," Dazell said to the kangaroos. "Have a good time. Play, make a mess of things."

Dazell placed her wand over the golden pyramid and cast a spell. *"Eptida Le."* The pyramid shrank down to miniature size, and she carefully placed it inside a pouch and secured it safely inside a pocket hanging on her holster. Closing her eyes, Dazell recited a spell. Instantly, her body shrank and her face shifted to that of a young girl. She lifted her wand, tapping it to her long cloak and transforming it into a green cape. Her dress, stockings, and shoes morphed to suit her youthful identity. Leaving her kangaroos to their play, Dazell raised her green hood over her now strawberry-blond hair and opened the door to her home.

"Oh, right. Can't forget you," she said to a French horn set beside her doorway. She grabbed the brass instrument and set out onto the busy streets of Evanstide.

CHAPTER 14

The Ancient Ones

MATIK TOOK A deep breath to center himself and release the tension crawling inside his body. Exhaling, he confidently yet cautiously stepped onto the new pathway in the tunnel system made of obsidian. He retrieved a circular, metal case from his vest pocket. When he snapped it open, a flame flickered to life inside.

The path led deeper into the darkness, which seemed to swallow what little light he had created. To remain oriented, Matik walked close to the wall. He ran his hand over the vitreous surface, smooth like glass yet solid as any stone. Every step Matik took into the cavern scattered dust, making it obvious to the warrior that no one had stepped foot into this place for a long time.

Never deterred by the untrodden, he held the flame closer to examine the cavern's walls. As he slid his hand across the stone, something with a fine grain stuck to it, and he found it covered in a thick, black soot. To his surprise, the stone wall gleamed under his light and was not carved from obsidian at all. This area had once been charred by fire. Below the sooty surface, a red, crystalline wall inlaid with gold glyphs glittered in the light.

His flame danced in an unnatural current of air, then went out. A sudden change in the darkness caught Matik's eye, pulling his attention to another tunnel within the cavern. A burst of light flickered off the walls before going dark again.

The erratic bursts of light beckoned the warrior forward into a tight corridor. He re-ignited his apparatus, then proceeded. The ceiling grew taller the deeper he went, making the heavy air easier to breathe. He exited the narrow passage through an ornately carved archway, and the other side was distinctly different. The runes below his feet and along the walls came to life with an ominous, scarlet glow. This must be the place the Hazan lived when they went into their runes outside the pyramid. The thought was comforting, but he continued to be cautious as his curiosity led him farther into the enchanting tunnel.

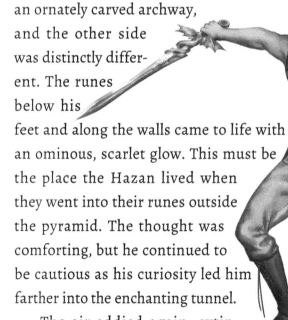

The air eddied again, extinguishing his light. This time, flames licked the walls ahead of him. The source was close enough for him to feel the heat and hear the sounds of the creature that had released it. Matik reignited his light and lifted his Rou blade from its sheath in preparation for what lay beyond the next bend.

A gust from behind Matik launched him off his feet. His weapon slipped from his grasp and was carried away as if held by a person. At the curve in the tunnel, a set of glowing eyes the size of a human's floated in the air. They blinked closed just as Matik's blade bobbed around the bend.

"Come back!" Matik jumped to his feet and chased after his sword. When he reached the curve in the tunnel, he smashed into an invisible wall. Pain spread across his body. A light flared against his eyelids, and he opened them to find shimmering runes spreading across the now-visible wall. Energy pulsed through the glyphs wherever his body made contact. On the other side of the wall, his sword levitated above an illuminated quartz basin filled with crystal clear water.

Matik slammed his fist against the obstruction. "Give it back." The second time he hit the barrier, a scaly foot with sharp claws stepped out from behind an upright, blocking the area on the other side of the basin. A mighty dragon, nearly the height of the arched ceiling, stepped forward, its red scales shimmering from the light inside the water basin.

With his eyes frozen open, Matik slowly pushed himself away from the wall. It dissolved as he did so, leaving nothing to separate him from the approaching dragon. Though he knew on some level he should flee the wrath of this being, he couldn't take his eyes off his sword.

"Matik!" Percilla yelled from behind him.

San held Matik in his gaze as he led Percilla and Frida to his side, shaming the young man for disobeying his request. "You have gone too far, Matik. You are never to disturb the ancient ones."

The dragon bowed to San as he did the same, sharing some sort of wordless connection. After a long moment, they lifted their heads, and San smiled. He faced the group of three. "It is time for you to leave. The ancient ones have nothing more to offer you."

"*Offer* us?" Matik said "They *took* my sword."

"It belongs to them now." He raised his hands to usher the group out of the tunnel.

"But it was a gift," Matik challenged.

"That's very kind of you. They appreciate it," the chieftain said as he walked away.

Matik watched him for a moment, then turned back to the sword and lunged for it, the golden runes on the invisible wall shimmering once more.

"You can't enter there," San said from a distance.

Matik gazed longingly upon his Rou blade for a second, then it vanished into thin air. He withdrew his fury at that sight; whatever cryptic reason they needed the sword was likely far beyond his understanding, as most of this journey had been so far. He jogged after his companions to catch up.

"Who are the ancients? Why did they want my sword?" Matik asked when he'd caught up to San.

The chieftain kept his pace steady and looked directly ahead. "You gave them your sword. I thought it was a gift?" His eyes sparkled, and a slight smile curved his lips. "The ancients are the ancients. Have your people really forgotten everything?"

Matik's Rou blade manifested before him. Relieved to see his prized sword return to him, the warrior tried to grab it from the air, but it moved away as if taunting him.

"It wasn't intentional," Frida chimed in. "We were forced to forget. Everything that would have reminded us was destroyed or kept hidden."

"So it be. So it be. What color is your Eye of Rou?" San inquired.

"Blue," Percilla said.

"Aw, Mercury, well, you're still doing your part. You've communicated with me and are going to communicate with the others. So you're still aligned with the rest. That's good."

The chieftain chuckled as Matik made another mad grab for his blade, but it continued to elude him. They neared the curve leading back to the main cavern, where the garnet crystals beamed far brighter than before. The ground beneath their feet surged with light as the earth started to shake. The light was erratic, with brief blackouts interrupting the shimmering, red radiance. Tibs leapt from Percilla's hat, hovering in front of her face for a moment before darting toward the exit. She was about to follow, but the earth began to quake more fiercely.

San's face went blank as he closed his eyes, then they darted open. With utter terror, he said, "They've come. Follow this tunnel. I'll meet you outside. We have to protect our vortex."

He shifted into his cobra form and vanished into a sigil upon the wall.

Fear quivered in Percilla's voice. "They've found us." Tibs returned, meeting her eyes and buzzing erratically. "What? You're not making this better, Tibs."

"We have to face our fears, Percilla," Frida said, resting a hand on each of her young companions. "Together, we can win. We must believe in our strength. Rou is on our side."

Matik's sword stopped its weaving, inviting him to finally take it out of the air. With the enchanted blade in hand and a final look to his companions, he ushered them forward, racing through the cavern and to the stairs leading out of the pyramid.

CHAPTER 15

Musical Surprise

SPIRITED MUSICAL HARMONIES filled the streets of Evanstide as the young children gathered inside the coral walls of an outdoor schoolhouse to rehearse. The squeal of an instrument pierced Dazell's ears, followed by another uncontrolled burst of bass from a tuba. She in her now-youthful appearance skipped over to the coral structure with her French horn in hand. Pausing outside, she raised her hands to face the entry.

"Rut Num Gilda."

Inside the coral walls, a large group of children no older than fifteen gathered with their instruments and blasted sounds into the air. Skipping into the classroom, Dazell waved to the petite lady undulating her hands wildly through the air and tapping her bare feet.

The woman halted her dance, causing all the shells upon her dress to clap together. She pushed her glasses up, enlarging her eyes. "Gilda, why are you late?"

Dazell smiled at the success of her spell. Responding to her new name and bursting with excitement, she said, "Ms. Lampker, you'd never believe what news I have! The Gangleton Dignitaries want us to rehearse at the pools right now. Queen Aurora said we were supposed to bless them today, and we are late."

"Oh, dear." Ms. Lampker shuffled through her miniature pocketbook. Dazell silently recited a spell as the woman did so. "My goodness, how could I have forgotten such an honor?" Ms. Lampker hopped down from her platform. "Quickly, children, parade formation! One-two-three. One-two-three."

The schoolteacher stepped into her sparkling, orange shoes. All of the children, including Dazell, marched in a line behind Ms. Lampker, whose spirited movements ignited the sounds of her little musicians.

Franc watched Pith shamefully walking away from her to exit the gathering pools. "I can't believe he assumed knowledge of the Keeper was insignificant."

Ons rolled his eyes. "He isn't one of us."

"We need him to be," Franc barked.

Furious, she gazed over Ons's shoulder at the erratic sounds intruding upon their conversation and seeming to come from everywhere. Concluding their council, she nodded to the other Dignitaries to leave, and tried to make a hasty retreat herself.

However, that quickly became impossible. Children, blasting their instruments, flooded the four pathways leading away from the pools, blocking any chance of an exit. The wild woman leading the little rascals approached Franc to stand right before her.

Franc's eyes widened as the children surrounded them. Unsure how to respond, which was never her nature, Franc turned her snarl into a forced smile. Each of her companions followed suit with an equally confused snarl-smile upon their faces. Except for Drendle, whose excitement at the hoopla was shamefully earnest. The glee was plastered upon his face, accompanied by the clapping and shuffling of his feet. This imbecile needed another brainwashing. He was just not at the others' level yet.

Drendle grabbed the hand of a woman in the crowd of adults gathering to join in the impromptu celebration. He twirled her around and dipped her. Franc shook her head and glared at him. Annoyed by the blaring music, she slammed her hands over her ears and closed her eyes to collect herself. As the air entered her nostrils, something in its energy made her feel light. Her body couldn't help but move to the music even though she sternly braced herself against it. Dancing was nothing she had ever openly engaged in, nor was it something she had intended to do.

"Magic," she whispered to herself. She covered her nose to avoid breathing in any more of the spell. A bony hand with long fingers grabbed hers and swung her into a twirl.

When she glowered at the person holding her hand, Lyken's expression mirrored her shock. Unable to control himself, he spun her again. Franc ripped her hand from his and turned to the other Dignitaries with a fire raging in her eyes just as she was rear-ended by Nylz's bottom. A moment later, Ons threw Nylz into the air and caught her.

Franc ignited a glow inside her palm. It flickered, then grew and slithered across her body, coating it with a faint shield of protection. Scanning the area to find the culprit of this magic, Franc's teeth ground together at the sight of the spirited ringleader with her sparkly, orange shoes. She thought she was so sneaky.

"*Yarrow On,*" Franc recited, pointing her palm at the joyful woman. The conductor froze as dark magic silently churned around her. In the next instant, she was hurled forward to the stone earth, holding her throat.

The music ceased as the children's eyes fell upon their beloved teacher. One young girl in a green cape ran to the bandleader's aid. Franc glared at the children with her fists clenched. All the dancing stopped, the joy wiped clear of the once spirited celebration. A crowd quickly gathered around the fallen woman, and the girl in the green cape blocked her from Franc's view.

A shout from behind Franc shifted her gaze to Ons, who was behind her holding his beloved apparatus. He tapped its lifeless screen and turned its useless knobs. Ons nearly started sobbing before his eyes met with Franc's wrath.

He quickly composed himself and looked Franc square in the eyes. "I'll meet you in the octopus. We'll have a slight delay due to this unexpected...dance party."

Alarms sounded throughout the kingdom while the guards rushed down to the gathering pools. Queen Aurora watched the scene below in shock and confusion from her windowsill. She couldn't tell what had happened, only heard the sound of her own sentries clamoring through the halls.

Pith burst into the queen's chambers, forcing his breath through his mouth. After releasing an airy mumble, he managed to fully enunciate one word: "Fallen." The advisor lifted his head to speak once more, but unable to catch his breath, he simply pointed toward the window.

Aurora gazed out over her kingdom once more, hoping for a chance to see anything. The crowd of people still gathered around in a circle, and the guards rushed in from every side. Aurora went directly for the doorway to get a closer look at the calamity.

But Pith grabbed her arm to stop her from going beyond him. "My queen, it is not safe for you. The Lady Lampker has been attacked. Everyone was dancing, and she was right before me. Then, it was as if black magic had taken her."

"Who did it, Pith? Why have the guards been discharged without my orders? I didn't give any order to search the kingdom. Who are they looking for?" She looked to him for answers, but he averted his eyes.

"I don't know who did this terrible deed, my queen, but I sent the guards to find them," Pith said. "The Dignitaries have warned us that Evils are coming. Franc told me to send them to the schoolhouse to search for the culprit."

Aurora held her advisor in her stern, regal gaze. "You need to remember your place, Pith. The Dignitaries are not the ones in charge here."

CHAPTER 16

Illuminate the Dark

S AN SHIFTED INTO his human form outside the pyramid. An unsettling presence permeated the area, stealing the vibrancy from the Sun. He tapped his staff upon the ground, igniting the runes and whispering magic words to beckon the cobras held within. They slithered out, their fiery glow far brighter than before.

A crash of thunder shook the earth, drawing San's attention to whatever hell had broken loose. A looming cloud billowed out from the abyss. Demonic entities took shape within the dark void, illuminated solely by the erratic strikes of lightning. The ominous force pressed closer, until the shadow-creatures broke free, swooping down to thrash at San and the cobras with their talons. They screeched, burning as they touched the red aura of the Hazan. The shock cast the beasts back into the cloud, which droned with malevolence. A torrent of energy shot down from the darkness, pushing ceaselessly upon San and Hazan's serpentine protectors. San slammed into the ground, struggling to point his staff at the pyramid and summon his magic.

"*Shalee om!*" he shouted. Red light shot from the eyes of the cobra on his staff and into the crystal at the tip of the pyramid. The force swept across the sky, clearing away the frequency emitting from the whirlpool. San stood and faced the pyramid, chanting silently and waving his staff.

The four statues around the garnet on top of the pyramid came to life. Their eyes flashed with energy as they beat upon the drums before them. The cobras shifted into their human forms amidst the rapidly manifesting tornadoes. The electrified cyclones encircled the tribe, lashing their virescent tendrils and hurling boulders at the Hazan.

San spun, casting a wall of protection all around them with another chant. The heavy stones crashed into the shield, the air around it becoming as dark as the sky above. The people of Hazan began another ritual dance to amplify the effect of the drums booming from the top of the pyramid. As they stomped, energy surged toward the Evils. The darkness rippled and thinned enough that the sunlight could shine in.

The effects of the counterattack lasted but a moment before the void thickened and sprawled across Hazan's shield. Only the red glow of their auras and the pulse of the garnet at the top of the pyramid was left behind. An elongated skull emerged from the darkness and blinked open its irradiating eyes.

Percilla, Matik, and Frida sprinted out from the pyramid. An unnatural force slammed the door shut behind them. At the sight of the magnitude of Evils all around them, Percilla tried and failed to open the door. She didn't possess the magic of Hazan.

Frida brandished her wand. "We have to help them. That is the power of Monzu."

Frida and Matik both readied themselves to fight as they raced out from the pyramid. A light shot out through the fabric of Percilla's jacket, catching her attention. She pulled out the illuminating compass in the same instant Tibs frantically buzzed in front of her face, urging her to open it. "Tibs, please!" she shouted. Observing the direction of the arrow she realized their portal was not protected by the shield of Hazan.

She cried out to her companions, but the winds were too loud for either Matik or Frida to hear her. Tibs flew off toward the portal, and Percilla followed, shielding her eyes from the sand churning in the air. She raised her hand and manifested a magic shield to protect herself from the raging winds. Tibs joined her inside to guide the way forward.

Heaving wings slammed onto Percilla's shield as a demonic beast pressed itself tight against her protection. Out from its entire being an electrified web spewed all around her. Its green glow throbbed, then blazed, cracking her shield into sections and breaking it completely. With no protection, the torrential forces of the tornado threw her backward, then raised her into the air. She closed her eyes to refocus her strength, closing out the external world and repelling the fear trying to seep into her soul.

In her mind's eye, the golden light of the temple swept across the sky, followed by the dragon guardian. Percilla inhaled a long breath, allowing it to circulate throughout her entire body and mind. Realigned with her truth, she opened her eyes to see a golden glow cast around her body. No longer afflicted by the ravaging winds, she slowly descended to the ground.

A bright light broke through the intense darkness all around her. On the other side of the nebulous shield of mystic power, Frida pointed her wand and hurried forward. Matik followed close behind. They met before the golden doorway with only the glow of Frida's magic illuminating the area around them.

A piercing red light forced its way through the darkness in front of them. San charged between the demonic figures thrashing at his shield.

"You need to go," San said. "The Hazan will return to our vortex now to protect it. I am sorry, you will not be able to go with us. We've done what we can to ward them off, but I'm afraid Monzu has come because of you and that." San pointed at the portal. "You have the blessings of Hazan. Keep uniting!" Shifting into his cobra body, he slithered into the rune and disappeared.

Matik held out the second key, the one with the orange gemstone, then slid it into the keyhole. "Here we go," Matik said to his companions. "Door number two."

Moon Delay

NIGHT'S VEIL OF darkness engulfed Evanstide as the pale light of the Moon shimmered through the dome to bless the kingdom with its soft glow. In the common gathering area, the workers sloshed in the pools, scattering the Moon's reflection across the waters. They strung ropes and chains through pulleys in order to transport slabs of stone. Lyken and Nylz watched from an elevated, coral platform as the building blocks of their vortex monument were stacked on top of one another. The workers strained in the night air, heavy with sweat and steam. Under the Dignitaries' orders, a smaller group of excavators dug away at one of their sacred pools with picks and shovels, spilling its sparkling contents onto the pure, black foundation of the monument.

As faint as it was, when the light of the Moon positioned overhead, all of the workers dropped their tools and turned their attention to the sky. The Dignitaries scanned the work site, searching for what had prompted the stoppage but unable to discern the cause. Then, the splendorous sounds of music could be heard approaching from the kingdom's streets.

An extravagant parade of musicians, dancers, and the citizens of Evanstide marched around the bend. Ceremonial, silk flags and clam shells filled with pearl torches made the parade burst with festive spirit. Soon, the crowd came to a stop just below the sacred pools, parting to make way for none other than Aurora, wearing a pearlescent gown. The song and dance continued with the workers joining in the celebration, much to the chagrin of Lyken and Nylz. They nudged each other's sides nervously.

Franc's voice crackled to life inside Nylz's earpiece. "Ons, have you failed to render your plans? Nylz, why have they stopped construction?"

"They've just stopped, and now they're back to parading and doing that whole thing," Nylz blurted, eager to assure Franc this was none of her doing.

"How can they celebrate when danger is lurking around them?" Lyken wondered aloud in disbelief.

"We need to be clearer about the importance of the monument."

Nylz looked to Lyken, who eyed the perfectly intact ceremonial pools, glowing as the people began a ritual. Their monument should be farther along by now, but it was little more than a stack of jagged, black blocks strewn around the area. Not even two pools had been excavated; everything was nearly intact.

"The work must never stop," Franc said grimly. "And it's time to make sure everyone knows it."

Nylz yanked out her earpiece as it squealed.

Lyken looked into her eyes. "What's the plan?"

Aurora made her way to the highest of the sacred pools. Her pace was heavier than usual, taking in all the black stones and equipment poised to destroy the sacred waters of her kingdom. From behind the heap of stones, Vahn offered her a slight bow, then blew her a kiss. She would have allowed tears to fall if she had not thought all this was necessary for the survival of her people. Her royal responsibility to their safety came above all else, even their most sacred of traditions.

Aurora waded into the water, submerging herself in its comforting embrace. At the center of the pool, the Moon's gentle light beamed down strongest of all, and once she reached it, she faced her subjects below. The citizens of Evanstide silently awaited the words of hope from their queen.

"As the Moon returns to silence, offering us stillness, let us release this cycle in the eternal waters in remembrance of the womb from which we come and to which we will return," Aurora said, recalling the words of her late mother and father.

Her tears would not join with the consecrated pool's waters today.

From a pouch in her gown, Aurora produced a glass vial of sparkling liquid charged by the vortex and the moonlight. With care befitting the honor, she tipped her hand, slowly releasing the vial's contents into the water. The liquids joined, creating a magical shimmer that spread to every surface, trickling all the way down to the gathering area where it touched every Evanstide citizen present for the ceremony. The people closed their eyes and meditated in the mystical caress, basking in the sacred purity of its cleansing aura. For that brief moment, their hearts were connected as one. When the emanation of the blessings had faded, everyone slowly retired to their homes for the night.

Aurora remained in the high pool, watching the waters gently descend from it and flow from basin to basin. Her father always told her to seek guidance in the waters, for they were connected to Rou and could help her find hope. She gazed at her reflection, looking to her eyes for strength before a sparkle from the blue crystals on her crown stole her attention. She couldn't help but wonder if it was trying to tell her something.

Pith's reflection appeared in the pool beside her. "My queen, the Dignitaries would like to discuss the safety of our kingdom." As he spoke, the crystals in Aurora's crown throbbed with life. Leaving the sacred space, she made her way to the base of the pools. The moonlight ceremony had brought with it memories of both happiness and despair. All six of the Dignitaries awaited her, and she greeted them as cheerfully as she could manage.

"Blessed Moontime. I didn't know you were waiting for me."

Vahn moved to stand beside his wife.

"We didn't know you were having a celebration this evening," Franc said curtly, tapping her foot against the wet ground.

"Forgive me, I forget you do not have the same ceremonies in Gangleton. In Evanstide, we celebrate the Moon," Aurora explained. Franc's irritation surprised her; she saw nothing wrong with a momentary reprieve from her citizens' hard work.

"Our ceremonies have been put on hold while our kingdom is at war," Nylz interjected, drumming her fingers on the hilt of her sword.

Vahn looked into her eyes and took her hand. "No time to celebrate when Evils are lurking at your gates."

"I am sorry to hear that," Aurora replied. "Ceremonies are what keep our people together."

"We understand," Franc said, "but times are not the same."

"Ceremonies must cease immediately in order to finish the monument," Lyken slowly instructed the queen. "We must keep your kingdom safe."

Aurora wanted to object, but instead she heard her own emotionless reply. "I understand."

"We knew you would." Franc smirked, holding back a cruel chuckle.

"Your—" Lyken stopped himself, bringing his bony hand up to slowly stroke his chin. "Our vortex must be used to fight off the Evils that threaten us all," he explained, his tone dripping with its natural pretension.

"I will do anything to help keep my people safe," Aurora said in the same lifeless tone.

"And I will always support you as your king," Vahn reminded her.

Franc's eyes lit up. "Since we are all gathered here now, why don't you take us to your Keeper of the Eye? We will be leaving for Gangleton soon and will need to meet with her beforehand."

"I'll send... Follow me," Aurora interrupted herself as she subtly tripped over her own feet to turn around. She felt the urgency sparkling around in her mind and wasted no time in leading them to Dazell's house.

CHAPTER 18

Presumptuous Guests

D AZELL SILENTLY STOOD in the dim light of her home before a painting. Its surface turned from one of brushstrokes to that of an actual landscape. Now, it was as if she were looking through a window. An extravagant ship sailed across a beautiful turquoise ocean while the midday sun shone upon the calm seas.

In awe of her creation, she paid little attention to the two kangaroos jumping and noisily playing around her. The joeys chased each other around the cauldron covering the trap door. Papers, jars, vials, and crystals lay scattered about the home in a state of disarray, but Dazell paid no heed. *"Eptic ta kai,"* Dazell said, her eyes fixed on the image in front of her.

A breeze filled the ship's sails, making them flutter as the waves slid up and down its great wooden hull. The scenery changed; on the distant horizon, beneath a blue sky filled with white clouds, a small, tropical island rippled into view like a mirage.

"You greet our guests kindly," Dazell said to her kangaroos cheerfully, briefly waving her hand to them. Then, she shrank and flew directly into the painting. Its surface wavered at her touch, bending the space around it as though she were stepping into a pool of still water. "I'll be watching you," she continued, wagging her finger at the animals. Their little mouths were agape as they tilted their heads from side to side.

Just as a knock landed against her home's wooden door, Dazell disappeared aboard the ship. Another loud knock hit the door, jiggling the many latched locks and chains keeping it closed.

"Dazell," Aurora gently called from behind the door. The wood was bent and nearly splintering from age, no longer fitting tightly into its frame. Sharp rays of light passed through its thin gaps, illuminating the room. But at the sound of Aurora's voice, that light was blocked by a group of shadows gathering in front of it.

Aurora continued knocking, intriguing the kangaroos, who quickly jumped over to investigate. They stood in front of the door, curiously awaiting the landing of the next knock to make it jiggle against its flimsy hinges.

"Dazell," Aurora called again.

One joey hesitantly tapped its knuckles against the door in reply.

"Dazell, it's Aurora. I have brought the Dignitaries."

Aurora stood with all six of the Dignitaries waiting impatiently at her back. A mist rolled through the streets, filling the air with a thick veil of tension.

Aurora was calm, having come to expect some delay from Dazell, who was not exactly the most social of people. The Dignitaries, however, were not amused. Quite displeased in fact, as evinced by the aggravated expressions on their tired faces.

"Why is she knocking back?" Nylz asked, yawning into her hand.

"Is she well?" Lyken petted the door with greasy fingers and placed his ear against it.

"Yes, I would know if she weren't," Aurora assured them. However, the knocking coming from inside her home was certainly bizarre even for Dazell. She wondered if perhaps it was some kind of prank, though it was hard to believe the Keeper of Evanstide's vortex would act so immature when confronted by the Keeper of the Kingdom.

"Then why is she knocking back?" Lyken asked again.

"This is strange," Aurora agreed, no longer sure what to make of the situation and feeling somewhat embarrassed in front of the Dignitaries.

Franc groaned, pushing everyone aside. "Let me handle this."

She joined her hands and shut her eyes. Aurora felt uneasy as the Dignitary harnessed energy within her hands to use against Dazell. She was once more taken back at the anger within Franc's voice as she shouted a curse that cast the door straight off its hinges. Splinters split from the old frame and flew off the wall. The kangaroos barked and bounced backwards into the air. Franc turned to Aurora, gesturing at the queen to guide them in. A gentle, blue light cast down over Aurora's eyes, relieving her mind of what she'd just seen.

"Dazell, forgive our intrusion," Aurora called out. She hesitantly stepped into the home, taking care not to accidentally break anything lying about the floor. "Are you well?"

The Dignitaries hastily followed her, each of them covering a different part of the room with their eyes. They examined every inch of it with their thorough stares. The two kangaroos bounced all about the domain, growling and balling their little fists, ready to box.

Franc surveyed the room, taking special interest in the various objects that made up a mess on the floor. The dignified woman scoffed. "She is your Keeper?"

Aurora was equally disturbed; the room appeared to be more like a jungle than a house. "Something must have happened to her."

"She vanished just when we arrived," Franc said skeptically.

"She is not really a people person."

Ons tapped one of the vials on the floor with his cane, observing its contents. "Or maybe she is neglecting us."

"Unfortunate," Franc snapped. Then she sniffed derisively. "Perhaps while we are away, she will come out. I have wasted quite enough time here as it is."

Franc spun around with an emphasized "hmph" and walked back out the door with the Dignitaries following close behind, leaving Aurora alone in Dazell's home. She picked up some of the fallen vials and put them back in their proper place. As she went about her cleaning, out of the corner of her eye, she swore the ship in the painting on the wall was moving.

CHAPTER 19

The Ending Calm

THE DIGNITARIES READIED their octopus machine, preparing to ignite its steam engine and take to the seas. Aurora and Vahn wished them well from a nearby coral platform.

"May our kingdoms thrive together," Franc said humbly, bowing to Aurora as Drendle spun open the wheeled hatch.

Ons saluted the couple with a proper tip of his hat. "We will be back shortly to check in."

"Give my blessings to Gangleton," Vahn happily replied. "Tell our people their prince has wed the most divine queen."

"I am sorry to see you off so soon," Aurora said.

"We have much business to attend to in the Barrens," Nylz replied, grabbing her sword's hilt with a smirk of bravado.

"No one protects it better than us," Lyken chimed in with outstretched arms. He happily removed his boots to pour out the last of the waters.

"We will keep you in our hearts and prayers," Vahn said, pressing his palm against the Gangleton emblem pinned to his jacket.

"Just oversee the construction and make sure it never stops," Ons replied, holding up his finger and spinning it around like a clock. "It's for all of our safety."

"Also, please warm up the Keeper for us," Franc said, connecting with Aurora's eyes as she spoke. "I'm sure change is hard for anyone who does not understand the dangers that lurk just beyond the walls these days." Her mouth widened into a feigned smile, and her gaze never left Aurora.

"I'm sure she was probably just not expecting us so early. She will be delighted to meet you," Aurora assured her.

"This monument is for the good of everyone. I cannot urge enough how important its completion is," Ons said, gesturing at the queen with his cane.

Vahn acknowledged to all gathered with a wide sweep of his arm. "Protection of the vortex is important to all of us."

"It must be completed by the time we return."

"I will see to it," Vahn assured him.

"This is life or death," Lyken said, placing his boot back on his foot.

"Fate or fatal." Nylz brushed her fingers against the burnt rim of her hat.

Aurora's spirits sank at the repetitive reminder. "I had no idea there was so much war outside our dome. I will do anything to protect my people from it."

"Smart." Franc smirked. "Till then."

With that, the Dignitaries boarded their octopus ship, closing its hatch tight behind them. Hot steam gushed from within the metal contraption as its engine roared to life. Its plated tentacles swayed back and forth, synchronizing with the motor and holding the vessel upright. Finally, it was steered through the golden gates, past the kingdom's magical dome, and into the sea.

Franc and Ons watched Evanstide disappear into the murky depths from a convex window. Then, they walked together over steel walkways into a control room filled with panels made up of levers, buttons, and meters. At the front, Drendle steered the submarine, navigating the ocean with a radar guidance system designed by Ons.

"The Keeper must be taken down," Franc announced with grim intent.

Ons pored over the mechanism's data presented to him on the control stations' meters. "Obviously."

"I want you to activate the queen to do it for us."

"Of course," he replied. "We wouldn't want our hands to get dirty."

Nylz laughed heartily as she walked with Lyken into the control area, clutching at her sides.

"I do not know fear," Lyken said boldly, puffing out his thin, gangly chest.

Nylz wiped away a stray tear of laughter and taunted, "You were so scared when you saw the dragon."

"No," Lyken huffed.

"Fly me home!" Nylz shouted, imitating Lyken's voice and the awkward movements of his body from the incident in the cavern. She pranced along the steel floor, her boot heels thudding. She nearly toppled over in laughter from her own impression of him. "You were like a scared little fawn!" she struggled to say in between laughs. "Your long legs flailing about!"

"Not so," Lyken insisted. "I fear nothing!"

"Oh, Lyken, it *was* funny," Franc interjected, almost laughing herself. "You were such a clown."

"Me!" Lyken shouted, turning to the rest of the Dignitaries, his face bright red. "What about the rest of you scaredy-cats?"

Nylz's laughter continued to fill the submarine, echoing off the interior of its hull as Drendle navigated it through the currents. For a good while, the vessel continued to ascend, passing a multitude of underwater creatures that set off tiny blips on the radar. The sea began to brighten. A loud, repeating beep suddenly filled the submarine.

"We're surfacing," Drendle announced.

The ocean's surface split apart, and the submarine rose to meet the air once more. Drendle peered down at the radar where he saw hundreds of blips filling the screen. He moaned, "We've got resistance."

The Dignitaries rushed over, and Franc flipped a switch, sliding open a large window panel on the front of the submarine. She pulled a spyglass from her coat and looked through it to the nearby shore.

Upon the barren shoreline, golden chariots covered the beach. They were captained by nomadic warriors holding torches and pulled by mighty rams. Fires raged across the land, filling the dim dawn of the day with intense flames. And there at the center of it all lay the Dignitaries' elephant contraption, burning to charred scrap within the grandest fire. Warriors celebrated around it, taking great pride in the destruction of the Dignitaries' favored tool.

"Denton," Franc growled. "Release the wings and raise the tentacles. We are flying out of here."

Nylz pulled a heavy lever built into one of the control panels. Lyken cranked a valve, releasing heavy puffs of steam into the open air. Ons pushed a series of buttons until the contraption's pressure was adjusted to optimal levels. Drendle pulled the gear upward, and the hull lifted out of the water and into the sky.

CHAPTER 20

Changing Tides

O NE OF DAZELL'S joeys picked up a coral vase. With a bark to alert its companion, it flung it halfway across the room. Dazell laughed at her little pets' games while lounging in the crow's nest of the painted ship. As the kangaroo lifted its arm to toss the vase back, the air before it rippled. A disembodied arm pushed through the energy disturbance, and the joey barked in shock, flinging its arms into the air and releasing the vase. It shattered, and the shards were strewn over all of the other objects thoughtlessly discarded onto the floor. Both marsupials bounced to hide behind the wardrobe, hissing with panic.

Three strangers stepped out into the room. The pair of women and the man looked around, getting their bearings. The kangaroos bobbed their heads around the wardrobe and eyed the trio with energetic curiosity. One of them bounced out and took the older woman's hat.

"Excuse me, that is mine," the eccentric woman scolded, snatching it back.

The kangaroo barked as if it understood her before reluctantly bouncing back to its hiding place.

"Where are we?" the young lady asked. She went about the room, lifting a fallen rod strung with curtains, inspecting the broken herb jars, and caressing the sprawling vines covering the walls.

The three intruders continued to gaze around the space, murmuring quietly to one another. Dazell put a small horn to her ear to better listen to their conversation. A bee flew from the young woman's hat and landed upon the picture frame, sending a blast of buzzing in her ear.

"What is this?" Dazell murmured.

The sorceress made herself invisible when the young woman came over to inspect the painting. "Since when do you care about artwork, Tibs?" she asked the bee, then rejoined the other two intruders.

"Go on. Who are you? Where did come from?" Dazell whispered as she lifted the horn to her ear and carefully examined the faces of the unfamiliar trio. "You aren't with the Digs. Are you?"

The young woman hunched over the cauldron. The older woman had her hands raised, feeling the energy of the room and revealing herself as a fellow sorceress.

Meanwhile, the kangaroos unscrewed the lid of a jar full of sticky slugs they'd nabbed from one of her many shelves. With an alerting bark, one of the joeys threw a slug right at the man's face, and it landed on his cheek with a wet splat. The slug slowly slid down to his neck, and he grimaced as he pulled off the slimy creature.

"Ugh, why did you do that?" he yelled at the marsupial, who hissed back at him and fled behind the wardrobe with more slugs in its hand.

"That's what joeys do, Matik," the sorceress nonchalantly remarked. "You're lucky they aren't punching you."

Matik's eyes widened as he hesitantly touched the slime trail on his face and brought his fingers to his nose for a reluctant sniff. He drew closer to the wall of jars, wiping their labels to read them. "This place is a circus."

"You would know," she replied.

"Sort of looks like a place where we could find the Keeper," the young woman said. "Doesn't it, Frida? There's magic in this place."

"You're right," Frida agreed quietly. "But whoever lives here must be a bit frazzled by the look of things."

Matik wiped the remainder of the slug slime from his face with his vest. "Maybe the Keeper has been taken in by the Dignitaries."

"This door does look like someone busted it off the hinges," the young woman said.

"Good observation, Percilla." Frida flicked the many broken locks on the door. "Apparently, someone was trying to keep this place secure."

"Safe to say we found the home of the Keeper?" Matik slowly poked his head out of an open window to look into the street.

Percilla peeked her head out of the front doorway. "Do you think this is Evanstide?"

"Yes. The orange gemstone on the key was the same as the king's regalia. I've known all along it was door two." Frida peered out of another window. I just hope we're not too late." She turned her attention back to the magic things thrown all about the house.

"Do you think the Digs are still here?" Matik asked, resting his hand on his sword. As the hilt tilted, Dazell could see the dragon and the symbol resembling that of Rou.

"High probability," Frida replied, dipping her finger into a solution of pink dust and aquamarine oil, then tasting it. Judging from her expression, it didn't taste half bad.

"Do you have any disguises for us in that bag of yours?" Percilla asked. "We need to find the Keeper and help the queen, right?"

"Of course I do." Frida tossed aside all the interesting curiosities she'd found and rummaged through the contents of her magical bag. Pleased with her findings, she handed two vials of a reddish color to Percilla and Matik and took out a greenish-blue for herself. All three downed the magical concoctions and morphed right before Dazell's eyes.

A few moments later, an enchanting man in a wide-brimmed, deep red hat and two geese stood in her home. The man's appearance was not only naturally alluring, but the shimmering silver threads woven into his black cloak and striped trousers were equally captivating. The geese alongside him were beautiful, black birds with rare, silver feathers showcasing their value. One had a patch of long silver feathers growing from its head like a crown. The other had a chest of silver feathers like stripes. Dazell chuckled to herself at the sight before her now.

The goose with the silver crown craned its neck to look at its body and honked. Tibs flew from the painting and settled itself into that goose's feathers.

The goose with silver stripes slapped its little feet on the floor and flapped its wings with a fit of squawking.

Dazell lifted her wand to her ear, and with a little flick, she could hear Matik's voice again. She chuckled. "Much better. I'd like to be in on your game."

"I thought it was a good idea," the man said in Frida's voice. "I'm a traveling alchemist, and you two are my most valued finds on my wondrous adventures. They'll buy it, trust me."

"Whatever, Frida," Matik groaned through his goose bill.

"Let's go greet the queen, oh great traveler," Percilla said with a goosey squawk.

"That's the spirit!" Frida exclaimed, carefully placing the disguised Percilla and Matik under her arms. "I have come from a far distant land, bringing gifts of magical geese as an offering."

Matik jostled in protest. "You're going to use me as an offering?"

"Don't worry," Frida assured him. "You are *magical* geese, not dinner geese. Golden-egg-laying geese!"

"I've gotta lay eggs too?"

"Wouldn't hurt to keep you out of the cooking pot."

Matik sighed, then let out a rather loud, frustrated squawk as the trio exited the home. "Frida, this is the last time I trust you and your tricks."

"Tricks! This is not a trick. This is a game of wits."

"Will you two stop fighting and stay focused?" Percilla scolded. "We have to be on full alert as to the whereabouts of the vortex and the Eye."

"And the Dignitaries," Matik added.

Dazell could barely hear their departing words, but she made out the most important ones. "Is that right? You are looking for me and the Dignitaries?" Dazell said to herself. Then, she passed out of the seascape and back into her home. Inspecting her domain to make for certain nothing had been stolen, she found everything mostly where it was before she'd disappeared.

"What kind of game are they playing?" Dazell wondered aloud as she trotted over to the window. She stuck her face close to the glass, peering outside just in time to see the "enchanting man" and his "two prized geese" promenading down the street in the direction of the palace. Dazell frankly did not quite know what to make of all that. Certainly though, today had been quite eventful.

From one of her desk drawers, Dazell retrieved a large magnifying apparatus and examined the area from where they'd emerged. She could make out only sparkles hanging in the air. "What in the world is this kind of magic?"

When she pushed an orange lens attachment on her hat over her eye, the pyramid door appeared. With a closer look, she found engravings from Rou carved into it. She knelt down to the floor and analyzed where the trio had stood with her magnifying glass. They'd left behind trace amounts of a red dust.

"Perhaps they are not with the Dignitaries at all," Dazell mused. "But then, who are they?"

CHAPTER 21

Perspective
of Beauty

A URORA RESTED HER delicate hands on the balcony railing as she looked out over the central gathering area. Her astonished gaze set upon what was left of the healing pools of her kingdom, and what met her eyes hardened her core. The glistening waters had been restricted to one pool at the center of the nearly completed megalithic monument. The Dignitaries claimed the monstrosity was for the good of her people, but in the back of her mind, she sensed treachery.

"I wish for them to stop working," she said.

"No. You can't. It's beautiful." Vahn beamed as he rotated the metal dial on an elaborate looking glass. His joy eased Aurora's distress, but the moment passed when her eyes shifted back to the demolition of the place she loved. Chaos swirled through every inch of her being, piercing her heart and stealing her breath. "It's ruined the pools. I...I'm not certain I've done what's right for my people after all." A flame ignited inside her mind, racing through everything that brought about this moment.

The presence of the crown upon her head felt heavier than usual, like a weight she no longer wanted to bear. Part of her motioned at the builders to stop, while in the same moment she felt herself halted by an eerie ease, an unspoken promise that everything was fine. Gasping for air, she dropped to the floor with only the clink of her jewelry hitting the floor to alert Vahn.

His gleeful fixation upon the construction shifted, and he immediately dropped to his knees beside Aurora. He took one of her hands in his, and with his other, he gently lifted her chin.

Wiping a tear from her cheek, he said, "You are so beautiful. The care you have for your people and the love of your kingdom is one of your finest qualities. Will you trust that I share your concern for our people? We are doing what's right, my darling."

A smile bloomed across his face, creating a soothing balm to the stinging anxiety inside Aurora. He wrapped her in his arms, and she let her weight fall into him. She was safe.

"You are a great queen, Aurora. That monument will keep all your kingdom safe. You mustn't stop its construction." He kissed her forehead. The blue crystals upon her crown reflected in the metal pin on his jacket. "You have to keep them building. Yes?"

"Yes, you're right," Aurora said dully, then turned her head away from Vahn's chest to look through the railing's slats at her kingdom. The sight was still nothing she'd ever think she'd be proud of nor would honor her greatness as queen, but it was the truth. Her kingdom was in danger, and this was all she could do.

"That one there," Vahn said as he pointed, drawing her attention away from the monument and over to a statue. "Who is that?"

Aurora's lips curled into a soft smile. "That is Irita, the Moon Goddess. She is the mother of our people, one of our most important gods. It is she who watches over us."

"Irita," Vahn said quietly. He rubbed his chest just below the Gangleton pin as if to relieve a pain. "We don't have any gods or goddesses in Gangleton. Just we, the Dignitaries, keep everyone safe."

"Our kingdoms are both devoted to Rou." Aurora rested her warm, soft hand on his to comfort him. "That's all the gods in one."

"Is your Keeper an original person from Rou? This Dazell woman?"

"I'm not certain. I just know she's the Keeper and always has been."

Vahn tilted his head. "And your father trusted her?"

"He did." Aurora nodded earnestly.

"And yet, he wound up dead. Perhaps you should not be so trusting of this woman."

Aurora sat up to put some distance between them, but Vahn froze her with his eyes. Her lips moved, but no sound came out. Her thoughts burned like a wildfire, then receded. She returned to the dull, obsequious disposition she'd been experiencing of late.

"I would expect you would be closer to her. Are you sure you can trust her?"

"Yes."

"Your father died a horrible death," Vahn said quietly.

"That was not her fault," she said, but her conviction waned as her mind grew murkier. Perhaps it was Dazell who killed her father. Maybe she had turned against the kingdom. But why would she do that?

"Are you certain it wasn't her fault?" Vahn leaned in closer. "I think to ensure the safety of all in your kingdom, you should be the Keeper of the Eye. Don't you?"

"You're right," she whispered.

Vahn grinned as he stood, offering Aurora a hand up. "It's really the only way to guarantee our kingdom's safety."

Aurora elegantly rose, a proud queen accepting her new purpose. "I will ask her to give the Eye to me. It's my duty now to keep us all safe."

Vahn lifted their hands above their heads in celebration of his queen's decision and loyalty to her kingdom. "We can protect it together," he promised, pulling her closer to him to seal it with a kiss.

The doors to the queen's chambers opened, and Pith entered. He bowed before them. "Excuse me, forgive my intrusion—"

"Your timing is perfect." Vahn gestured at Aurora to continue.

"Have you seen Dazell? It's quite urgent that I speak with her."

Pith rubbed his chin thoughtfully. "No, I have not, but I can find her for you of course." He intentionally looked to Vahn and gave him a nod before he continued. "Though in the meantime, you do have a traveler who wishes the honor of meeting you."

"A traveler?" Vahn asked suspiciously.

Aurora looked past Pith, her eyes alight with curiosity. "Who is this traveler?"

"An alchemist wishing to make an offering of two geese that lay golden eggs," Pith explained. "It is quite an interesting visitor, I must say."

"Golden eggs? That is odd," Aurora said with a grin. "Tell the traveler we will see him. Could be just what I need to lift my spirits."

"Anything else, my queen?"

Aurora felt Vahn's stern eyes upon her, and once she looked at him, she was instantly reminded. "Dazell," she uttered, turning toward Pith. "Tell her it's urgent. I must see her today."

Pith assured her he would find the Keeper and exited the room. Vahn held out his arm for Aurora's, and she took it, letting him lead her to the throne room to greet their eccentric guest.

CHAPTER 22

Power of Charm

SMILES WERE PLASTERED to the faces of every Gangle-
toner as they collectively raised their arms to welcome
back their beloved Dignitaries. The octopus contraption descended through the dome from above the crowd, delighting
the people within their perfectly manicured yards with joyous
music. For most citizens, this was the best day they'd had in
weeks. They donned their bright, celebratory clothing. Each
had their family's distinguishing sashes strapped across their
chests. The men proudly topped their heads with hats in vary-
ing sizes, while the women glossed their lips with rosy shades
to mark this wondrous and rare occasion.

The Dignitaries had made it to Gangleton without further
issue, but that didn't set any of them at ease. They landed and
cut a path to the Cuckoo Clock Tower.

They hid their annoyance behind fake smiles and theatrics.
Lyken pulled a rope, and a burst of glittering confetti shot out of
a petite cannon. The children laughed with glee as they tried to

catch it. Nylz wound the gramophone, sending a rush of happy music resounding throughout the dome. People danced behind the octopus all the way to the tower. Ons waved, tapping his cane against the metal deck. Franc bowed and waved her hat, her lips stretched into more of a grimace than a cheerful grin.

Drendle steered from inside, able to see everyone yet unable to share his eagerness to celebrate along with them. Even if he could, it was best he kept his focus on the road ahead. He wasn't too keen on having to steer the octopus through the streets. A blinking light on the control panel to his right drew his attention. He leaned over to answer the call, but a crowd of people appeared to his left. Best to keep both hands on the wheel and not crush anyone.

Once they reached the tower, he steered the octopus to the large, metal platform at the back. The contraption easily fit into it, and Drendle pulled it to a stop. Lowering his platform with delight, he waved to all the children gathered around to watch the spectacle.

The Dignitaries disembarked one by one and filed into the Tower. Once inside, they marched up the set of stairs that ran around the outer wall until they reached the platform near the top. A giant orb faintly glowed in the center of the structure. Ons went straight for his chair in the control booth while Franc observed the orb with her usual agitated tapping of fingers on the railing. Nylz and Lyken stayed close by her side.

Drendle was assigned to keep his eye on a control panel inside the tower, and so he kept himself safely away from Franc's wrath by cleaning it. The same kind of light that had been blinking in the octopus was now blinking there as well. He was going to mention it, but then Franc sighed heavily.

"Our speeches need to be more effective," she ranted. "How can our storage be so minuscule? This vortex is active every three days. Is it not?" She turned around to eye the other Dignitaries. "Do you know what that means?"

"You need to get me more energy," Ons asserted, stepping out of his special booth to hand Franc a copper bracelet with a round dial. "Try this out when you speak to the Gangletoners. Run your finger around the rim and watch their minds scramble," he said with a wheezing laugh.

Franc sneered, then she snatched the bracelet and shifted her gaze to Lyken and Nylz. "Well, do one of *you* know what low energy levels mean?"

"We're using more energy than we create," Nylz replied.

"No."

She frowned at Franc's quick response.

"We need the Moon vortex, which is active every night," Lyken chimed in, giving Nylz a knowing smirk.

"Yes, and?"

He blinked, not sure what else there was to say until it came to him. "We need Gangleton to be more fearful, so we have more energy."

"Every day," Nylz practically shouted in his ear.

As Franc nodded at them, Drendle glanced at the blinking light and decided he should probably speak up now. "Evanstide rang."

"Then answer."

Drendle cringed. "No, they rang. As in a while ago. We missed it."

Franc clasped her hands behind her back, then stalked over to him and his control panel. "Why? Why would we miss it? You do understand how important it is that we keep up with what is occurring there while we're gone, yes?"

Drendle swallowed hard. "Yes."

"Then why did we miss their call?"

Drendle shrugged. "We were greeting Gangleton."

Franc ground her teeth. "You never cease to let me down, do you, Drendle? You two, see to Gangleton," she snapped at Nylz and Lyken. "Ons, ring up Evanstide. I will not be left in the dark about whatever is going on there. Our mission is too precious."

Nylz and Lyken rushed to the elevator that would take them to the balcony while Ons worked in his booth. He pulled levers and twisted knobs as the orb's vibrancy faded a little more.

"Do you see? We need more energy. Go speak to these Gangletoners," Franc yelled to Nylz and Lyken just as they stepped onto the lift. "Have them fear the future. I want them afraid of their own shadows. Tell them disaster is drawing near." Her face spread into a wide, deceitful grin. "Have them prepare for the worst. After what we witnessed when we broke the surface, Gangleton will surely know what it's like to be at war soon enough."

The duo of Dignitaries paused in the elevator, speaking just loud enough for Drendle to overhear. He always enjoyed watching the two decide what was best.

"You lead," Nylz insisted.

"No, by all means you go first."

She shook her head. "You're the scary one, we all know that."

"Perhaps," he said, tenting his long, spindly fingers before his face. "But you have that commanding voice. I will concede on that point."

Nylz smirked. "You're right. Follow my lead, then." She pulled on the lever inside the lift, and they rushed up and up. "This should be quite fun, indeed."

They cackled darkly together as they prepared to instill fear in the masses.

Gahil whistled like a cardinal to his companions, hoping to bring a shift in their demeanor. Unfortunately, Metia, Dant, and Sphan did not share his optimism. They smiled for a moment before their attention returned to observe the submissive people toiling away in their yards. The group passed by a flourishing garden, its plants nearly reaching the boundaries of its fence, when the friends were confronted by Delebra, a perfectly kept and prideful woman.

"How dare you wander the streets during gardening hours when the Dignitaries are here?" she said sternly from the other side of her fence. "Why must you always bring shame upon our people?"

The youths continued on their way unperturbed.

"She's really riled up today," Sphan said with a wink. "We must be doing something right."

Metia piped up. "You'd think she'd just accept the reality by now."

Gahil stopped whistling. "The curse of expectations, I guess." They continued on their path to the cherry orchard, moving along the various garden gates which now appeared more and more like cages.

A loud horn spread a deep, ominous tone throughout the village.

Every face in Gangleton glanced at the Tower just as a dark mass of clouds moved in to block out the Sun. The friends looked to one another for an answer, for this was an unfamiliar sound.

Unlike the people, their ravens knew the call. At the second blast from the horn, the birds connected to each of the villagers began to unravel from their resting place under the hair of their human. The sound of wings flapping in unison spread through the air. Soon, the sky was filled with the ravens of Gangleton bringing every last man, woman, and child to the base of the Tower.

The only ones left behind were the group of friends, each grabbing their hats and pulling them down over the ravens. Their birds could not hear the beckoning call due to a spell that coated the hats and kept them from obeying the sounds from the Tower. The friends rushed to the outskirts of the village and the safety of the cherry orchard.

A high-pitched ringing crept upon the air, and Gahil stopped to fully cover his ears with his hands. He glanced at his companions for confirmation, and from their grimaces and the way they clutched their heads, they were all experiencing the sound. In the distance, the balcony doors were flung open, and the piercing ring was swallowed by the sound of the crowd cheering for the two Dignitaries standing high above them. Gahil slid on his goggles, and he could make out Nylz and Lyken with their hands raised in greeting. Then, Lyken waved his hands to quiet the excitement. Nylz stepped up to the microphone, resting her hand on the hilt of the sword always at her hip.

"Citizens of Gangleton," she said, voice booming through the speakers. "It is with a heavy heart that I come to you now. Unfortunately, this is not a time of celebration." The people glanced at each other nervously, their smiles slipping away one by one as she continued. "My dear people, though we tried to avoid it, I'm afraid that Evils have gained a foothold outside the safety of the dome."

She paused at the gasps spreading through the crowd, then Lyken bellowed, "We are at war!"

A chorus of cries went up from the crowd.

Metia caught Gahil's eye, the confused look on her face asking, "War?"

Before anyone could reply to Metia, Lyken's voice shot across the noise rising from the crowd. "We fear that the Tribe of Denton has turned against us."

"Our journey confirmed all our darkest fears," Nylz added. "We tried to establish peace, but we were too late to save them and make them see reason."

"They have been infected with Evils!" Lyken's long fingers curled around the railing of the balcony.

His announcement instilled even more panic in the crowd. They began to stagger away from the Tower, as if hoping this was all some horrible nightmare.

"They have no desire for our companionship," Nylz said. "I'm afraid negotiations failed. They are too far gone to ever listen to reason."

"They are planning to attack us."

Nylz raised her sword high over her head. "We will do all we can to defend you, the people of Gangleton, but I'm afraid I must ask you to prepare for the worst."

None of the people moved or spoke; they just stood there in terror, waiting for the Dignitaries to tell them what to do. Gahil couldn't understand what the Digs were up to, but there was something in their eyes and in the curl of their smiles that he found disconcerting.

Nylz leaned into the railing and shouted, "What are you waiting for? I said to prepare for the worst!"

"This is life or death! Get going!" Lyken jolted his arms out before him and fanned his fingers.

A horn upon the Tower blasted, igniting the crowd from their motionless assemblage. All at once, the people were carried away by their ravens. Some ran in the air or pushed off others to advance their progress through the crowd. These rash movements jostled the ravens' balance, causing them to collide with others.

Gahil glared at the two Dignitaries cackling to each other as they watched from above. They probably weren't expecting anyone to see them, but Gahil now understood there was definitely something deceptive happening within that Tower and in the minds of the Dignitaries.

A soft tug at Gahil's arm pulled his attention back to Metia. "We gotta get outta here. We have to consult our ancestors about this."

Gahil nodded, and they sprinted after Sphan and Dant, who were already racing up the hill in the cherry orchard to begin the ritual pyre.

CHAPTER 23

Finest Trickery

FRIDA, IN THE disguise of an alchemist, walked around the breadth of the throne room, holding a goose under each arm. Matik had finally stopped his squawks of protest, but continued to fidget about.

"Will you stop that?" Frida hissed. "Or I'll put you in the pot myself."

Matik let out another ear-piercing squawk, then something fell from his body and thumped to the floor. It rolled across the room, catching the flickering torchlight.

"I laid an egg," Matik said, though to anyone who was not Percilla or Frida, it simply sounded like he was back to honking. He ruffled his feathers as the sorceress hurried over to admire the egg. "Oh no," he mumbled. Another egg came out, then another. "Aw, stop that! Frida!"

"Stop what?" she asked with a bemused grin. "You're in no pain, correct?"

"Why isn't *she* laying eggs?" He twisted his long neck around to stare at Percilla.

Frida blinked twice. "Huh, good question. Why aren't you laying eggs?" She gave the other goose a bit of a jiggle. "We must be convincing."

Percilla honked in annoyance, then a golden egg struck the floor, followed by three more in quick succession.

"Oh, there we are," Frida said with a pleased grin.

Percilla considered biting the sorceress but stopped herself, remembering Frida's plots were always wild, yet somehow perfectly thought out in every way. However, she was still annoyed to be a goose. She'd been trying not to lay eggs, but now seemed unable to stop. "Why'd you have to jostle me about?"

"Authenticity," Frida replied, holding back her laughter. "Plus, it makes for great entertainment."

The door to the throne room opened. A beautiful woman walked in, but it was the sight of the man beside her that had Percilla honking louder than she had before.

Vahn. He was right there in front of her, but when she looked into his eyes, it wasn't her Vahn. Not anymore. If her vision hadn't made it clear to her, seeing him in the costume of the Dignitaries assured her of the worst. The Dignitaries had messed him up, dug their claws in, and she worried she'd never get her old friend back. Frida gave her a brief squeeze, and Percilla stopped making noise.

Vahn and Aurora were accompanied by Pith, the tall, older man who had let them into the palace. He bowed and took his leave, heading to the rear of the room.

The queen's ivory boot knocked one of the many golden eggs lying around the floor. A grin spread across her face as she walked toward her magical guests. "These are marvelous."

Frida was about to say something, but Percilla resumed her struggles, and Frida lost her grip. The goose spread her wings, and, just as Frida caught her again, Percilla laid a crystal egg. It plummeted to the floor, and Frida stuck out her foot, cradling the egg in the soft leather of her boot. Percilla returned to her roost under Frida's arm, shaking out her feathered crest.

"Don't want to break an egg," Frida commented in the deep voice of the man she appeared to be. "Especially not this one. Good day, Your Greats." She bowed, managing to balance the egg on her foot.

Aurora leaned down and picked up a golden egg. She rolled it over in her hands, looking the strange man up and down. "Greetings."

Vahn scoffed, nudging another egg with his foot. "So these be the golden egg-laying geese? They don't seem all that different from regular geese."

"Trust me, they are far from any ordinary ruffle-feathered geese." Frida readjusted them beneath her arms, and once she was sure the crystal egg wasn't going to fall off her foot and break, she squared her shoulders. "I am Malikai, the great alchemist of Bobentude. Though I must admit, I left many years ago and have since been traveling as an aide to all those who call my name."

Aurora glanced up from the golden egg in her hands. "Call your name? I'm afraid I don't follow. Did somebody in Evanstide call for you?"

Frida set down the geese and carefully picked up the crystal egg. She delicately cradled it in her hands, indicating the significance of its appearance. "It was you, my queen."

Percilla waddled over to Vahn and tried to send her thoughts to him through sheer will now that she couldn't speak.

"Me?" Aurora blinked in surprise. "But I don't think we've ever met. Nor do I have any idea who you are. How could I possibly call you?"

Frida's plan was unfurling quite well, and Percilla became less frustrated with her great-aunt. The wise sorceress had a way of convincing people—dismantle all sense of normal by presenting the curious.

"That is the mystery of the mind, my dear. Sometimes, we call for things without even knowing it's possible they may come. We call that a wish." She winked as she held up the crystal egg before the queen.

Aurora approached, entranced, until Vahn loudly cleared his throat. "Malikai, I must say, this is a bizarre occurrence. You were never called upon. Ever. Yet you try to confuse my queen with accusations, blaming her for bringing you to us. I do not like this, not one bit."

Percilla realized her efforts to reach his mind had failed and was irritated by his thick-headed intervention in their plan.

Frida shifted her regard to Vahn. Percilla flew up behind him, flapping her wings at his head while Matik left a rather unpleasant bit of droppings atop his boot. Vahn shielded himself from Percilla's rage with a grimace and shooed away Matik.

"Ah," Frida mused, "the brave king. It was before you arrived, when our sweet queen had many tears in her eyes." She held out the crystal egg to them, nodding to it. "Please, have a look for yourself, Your Greats."

Percilla waddled over to Matik and spoke, knowing he was the only one to decipher her honks. "Okay. Okay. Maybe her plan is worth it. They seem to be buying it."

Matik laughed. "Reminds me of something Symon would do."

Aurora leaned forward to look deep into the egg, and before Vahn could pull her away, her gaze became transfixed by whatever she saw inside. He found himself taken in by the sight too. An image of Aurora came to life within it. She was crying at the edge of the highest pool, staring at the Moon far overhead. The queen blessed herself with its waters, her lips moving over a silent prayer for help.

Aurora whispered in disbelief, "You heard me?"

"I did. That is why I came," Frida told her firmly.

Vahn scoffed. "I cannot help but wonder why you have been spying on the queen, for that is certainly what this means." He pointed accusingly. "You are nothing more than a spy."

Matik honked loudly, "We gotta get him outta here."

Percilla couldn't have agreed more. "If he weren't here, we could just tell Aurora the truth."

"Ha!" Frida exclaimed. "Spying? No, my great king. I do not spy, but when the kingdom of Rou speaks to me, I listen. And through the Moon, I heard her."

"So you brought *geese?*"

"Yes, they are my companions. Gold is a great exchange for many things." Frida shrugged. "What else would I have brought to honor such a great queen?"

"I want to know more about Rou," Aurora said. "What does it know of me? Why did they call upon my father?"

Frida offered the egg again. "This is what you seek," she said simply. When Aurora hesitated to take it, the sorceress took the queen's hand and rested the heavy item in it. "I cannot tell you what you need to know, for I am merely a messenger. It is up to you to understand your connection to Rou."

Aurora rolled the crystal egg over in her hands. When Vahn tried to take it from her, the queen moved out of his reach. Percilla put herself between the two and flew up before him, flapping her wings in his face.

Vahn swung his arms through the air to ward off Percilla. "We will not accept your magic egg. For all we know, you are an adversary," he insisted. "You have brought sorcery to our kingdom."

Percilla drove him into the corner of the room.

Frida clasped her hands behind her back. "You are wise to question me, King. But you are still short-sighted. Give me time, and I shall reveal my truth to you."

Percilla pushed Vahn toward the back of the room where Pith mischievously watched the meeting from behind a stone column. He may have been the queen's advisor, but the look in his eyes was dull, just like Vahn's. Something was off about him. He reached for a blazing blue gemstone on his ring and rubbed the stone.

She ceased her flight and waddled over as quietly as she could, hoping he'd not surmised she was indeed a human. And honestly, what human in their right mind would become a goose? Again, she hated to admit it, but her great-aunt's plan was indeed genius. Barely half a second after, a strange sound came from above. A black monkey dangled by its tail from the intricate stonework of the ceiling. When Pith looked up, the monkey let out a sharp bark, flipped over him, and aimed for the queen.

Pith shouted a warning, but the monkey was too fast. Using the ceiling and whatever else it could wrap its tail around, the tiny primate darted through the throne room. It swung over Frida and grabbed the crown atop Aurora's head, then scampered away with it.

"My crown!" Aurora panicked, clutching her head with one hand.

"Stop that monkey!" Vahn shouted. "Guards!" He rushed off after the pernicious primate, following a handful of confused guards who had already taken up the pursuit. Aurora's face swung between Vahn and her guests.

"Forgive me," she finally said, "but I don't think this is a good time."

Frida caught Aurora's arm when she tried to walk by. "I must warn you that Evils lurk in your kingdom."

"That's apparent. A monkey just ran off with my crown," she murmured, as if wondering if it was a joke or not.

Frida closed Aurora's other hand around the egg. "Please, accept this oracle. You are in danger. Rou will save you. If you wish for the purest voice to come through this egg, you must take it to the pool. Only then will all Evils be cleansed from you."

"Me?" Aurora said, alarmed. "You think *I'm* infected with Evils?"

"How dare you speak to my queen like that?" Pith shouted, rushing to stand between Frida and Aurora. He tried to shove the sorceress away, but Frida held her ground. Percilla was already back in the air, flapping her wings before him and honking.

"You evil man. This is all your fault!" she yelled, knowing he couldn't hear her.

"You misunderstand my words. Forgive me," Frida said with a low, sweeping bow. "You, my queen, are not evil. Those closest to you, however, I'd keep an eye on them." The sorceress snapped her fingers and was gone, leaving Percilla and Matik to stare at each other.

Pith glared at the spot where "Malikai" had been, then the advisor shook his head and spun around. "He is not to be trusted," he insisted. "Guards! Where are the guards?"

"Did I ask you to call the guards?" Aurora snapped.

He sputtered before finally finding the words. "He must be put on trial at once. You can't let him bring Evils to our people."

"Why are you talking as if you are in control?"

Percilla began to like Aurora more.

"My queen—"

She cut him off with a harsh swipe of her hand. "Enough, Pith."

He sucked in a breath and said in a rush, "The Dignitaries asked me to help watch over you."

Once the words were out, Aurora's facial expression hardened, and he gulped. Matik and Percilla looked at each other, then nodded. They both began pecking at his feet. Pith backed away from them and Aurora. He lifted his foot to kick Matik.

"Don't even think about it," Aurora commanded.

Aurora clutched the crystal egg in both hands. "The Dignitaries have no right to give orders in my kingdom. Do you hear me, Pith?"

Percilla and Matik returned to Aurora's side. "Looks like we are to protect her from here on?" Matik asked Percilla.

"That must be Frida's plan."

Pith began to move closer to the queen again, and Matik flew up into his face. "Where is your crown?" Pith asked, shielding himself from the newest feathery onslaught.

"What? Because I'm not wearing my crown, you do not see me as your queen? Is that what you're telling me?"

"No," he said quickly as Matik backed him into a corner. "I just didn't know you took it off."

Her eyes narrowed suspiciously. "Did you not just see a monkey steal it from my head? Where do you think Vahn and the guards have gone?"

"I was tending to other things," he said, wringing his hands.

Percilla followed the queen's gaze to Pith's fidgety fingers and his blue ring. "I suggest you pay attention to what your queen wants and not to these Dignitaries. They are outsiders, and I will not hear another word from you, not tonight."

Aurora turned around and headed for her chambers. Matik and Percilla waddled after her, both twisting their heads around to give one more indignant honk at the corrupted official that echoed off the stone walls.

CHAPTER 24

Message from Rou

SMOKE BILLOWED THROUGH the cherry orchard from the hilltop where Metia, Gahil, Dant, and Sphan gathered to offer their prayers to the ancient ones. Sphan placed the feather into his hat as he set the dish holding the sacred resin back over the ritual pyre.

Metia watched the wispy smoke spread around them, filling her lungs with its piney aroma and cleansing energy. She remembered the words Percilla spoke the night that changed their lives forevermore and knew the request must be the same this eve. "Ancestors, we ask you to gather with us, to show us the truth we need to receive."

As the last words slipped from her lips, Gahil stood. "Show us the Dignitaries' plot. I witnessed their lies. Please, bring us clarity. Please protect us from their deception." He spoke with an urgency that Metia had never heard from the usually happy-go-lucky man.

The smoke rose above the cherry orchard, veiling them in a dome of white haze. Fear arose in Metia, but the gentle touch of the air reminded her she was safe. A mushroom cloud puffed out from the resin on the ritual pyre, forming a luminescent orb before them. Metia sensed the ancient presence answering their call. They gathered closer, and an image of a person appeared in the orb.

"Percilla?" Sphan asked. The vision of their dearest friend walked across the barren earth. "She's alive."

"Are we sure? Ancestors, please tell us, is Percilla really alive?" Dant urgently called out to them.

Images pulsed in and out so fast, they overwhelmed Metia as the story unfolded. None of it made sense to her yet, but she felt joy at seeing her friend was safe and in the care of strong companions.

"She's alive!" Dant hugged Metia.

The four friends celebrated for a moment before the orb let out a blinding flash, calling their attention back to it. Percilla stood upon the barren earth once more, looking around for something. A green incandescence swelled behind her. As it grew larger, the swirling, gaseous orb moved closer and closer to Percilla, who was completely unaware of its presence. From inside the intoxicating mass, the five Dignitaries watched Percilla with nefarious eyes.

"Look out!" Metia shouted. "Why isn't she moving?"

Gahil stepped closer to the vision of his friend. "What are the Dignitaries doing?"

The image shifted to a mere reflection of those gathered around it. In the next moment, the image showed their feet, then passed through the ground like an elevator descending into the earth below them. The vision settled into sparkling blue stones gleaming across the walls of an otherwise dark cavern.

"I've seen this before," Dant said excitedly. "The ancestors showed me these caverns during another ritual and told me there was more for us to discover about Gangleton."

The image showed the Dignitaries exiting an elevator into the caverns. A breath later, the smoke from the resin dissolved, releasing the orb and spreading a wispy white vapor through the air.

"That's it?" Sphan asked, face taut with shock.

As the ritual concluded, the high-pitched ringing once again afflicted them. The friends clapped their hands over their ears and looked to each other for an answer. Before they had a chance to speak, the horn bellowed from the tower, followed by Lyken's eerie voice spreading across the orchard.

"Everyone must return to their homes. The enemy is approaching with their fires raging. I repeat, everyone, you must return to your homes."

After what she had just witnessed, doubt crept through Metia. "Is it just me, or was that a warning for us to fear the Dignitaries?"

Sphan looked around the orchard for any sign that they were in trouble. "What's that ringing?"

Dant spoke up. "Probably their new method of control."

"Do you think they know what we just found out?" Gahil asked with a quiver in his voice.

Inside the remnants of the mystical smoke, sparkles brilliantly flashed, catching the groups attention. While the colorful glimmers coalesced with the white haze, the face of a divine woman appeared from within it. She spoke with a voice as soft as the air. "You must not fear. Your work to save your home has only just begun. You must resist. Your people depend on you, as does the world. Percilla will return, and you must be ready to help her. You must be ready to guide her to where she needs to go." And with a bow of her head, the timeless beauty disappeared into thin air.

CHAPTER 25

Who Is in Control?

ONE OF THE wooden shutters of Dazell's house burst open, and the monkey from the throne room bounded in. Aurora's crown was held fast by its tail. The little primate snapped her fingers, and the home magically began shifting to its orderly state. Bouncing around the room, narrowly avoiding the enchanted objects organizing themselves, the monkey used their surfaces to navigate around the room. She halted in the center of the floor near a bubbling cauldron and waited, listening intently.

Vahn and the guards had given chase, but she had been too fast. The agility of her disguise had given them the slip, but Dazell wasn't about to shift back just yet. The seconds turned to minutes, and when no guards rushed into the house, the monkey shuddered. The little primate grew taller, and in its place stood Dazell. She held Aurora's crown in her hand, the blue crystals no longer glowing now that it was not atop the queen's head.

"All right then, let's see what's really going on with you, my queen," the sorceress murmured.

A flick of Dazell's wrist swept away the rug covering the trapdoor. Then, she tapped her foot in a sequence and the door opened to reveal a set of wide stairs leading down. Dazell hurried below, then knelt at the pool's edge and dipped the crown into the water. The crystals glowed so brightly, she had to squint to see them clearly. The pool took on a dark hue of blue until she removed the crown from it. The excess water created a puddle at her feet, but it wasn't the puddle that held her attention.

One after the other, symbols appeared on the blue gemstones of the crown.

"That's what you're up to," she whispered as they came into better focus. "And they claim they want to protect us. What a horrible, deceitful ploy."

She had wondered what had come over her dear queen, what sort of magic they were using that had made her so easily swayed by outsiders. Dazell had to get to the bottom of this mess before it was too late and Evanstide was lost.

A loud stomp, then a voice, echoed from above. Dazell peeked up through the trap door and spotted the alchemist. The man shook from head to toe, and the visage of the man faded away, revealing Frida, the sorceress with mischievous eyes and a bright smile.

"What is this? A trapdoor. Surely this wasn't here before," Frida pondered aloud.

Dazell blinked, gripping the crown tightly. Frida popped her head down into the opening.

"You...you were here before!" Dazell exclaimed

Frida scanned the pool behind her. "Yes, yes I was. Name's Frida. And you must be the Keeper?"

"What are you doing here?"

"You were the monkey?" Frida asked in return, staring at the crown in Dazell's clasp.

Dazell's eyes narrowed. "I said, what are you doing here? Who are you really?" Reclaiming her dominion, she stepped up onto the main level of her home.

"Isn't it obvious? I'm here to help."

"Is that so?"

"Yes," she stated firmly. "I'm doing the same thing you are." She nodded to the crown. "The Digs are up to no good like always. Trust me, you'll need me. Though I must admit, the primate act was quite good."

Dazell relaxed, seeing the truth in the woman's eyes and sensing nothing of Evils about her. "Thank you. I couldn't have pulled off the snatch as easily without your distraction."

"Ah yes, it wasn't just me."

"Your friends?"

"That they are. Well, at least one is. The other might never forgive me for turning him into a goose. He seems to be a bit put out by his new lot in life."

"And you left them there?"

Frida shrugged. "They have to protect the queen. As do we. That crown is quite the piece of work."

"I don't know how they were able to make their way into our kingdom. Our dome is supposed to protect us from any Evils."

Frida shook her head. "These aren't just *any* Evils. The Digs are not that powerful. This is Monzu."

"Impossible. That would mean they've managed to live on our planet. Let's test your theory." Dazell set the crown inside a vessel full of black sands. Upon contact, the crown melted. "You're right, but I still don't understand what you are doing here."

"Rou has sent us to unite the Keepers, and by the looks of where our portal brought us, I assume you are the Keeper?"

"Yes. It is time, then?"

Matik squawked as another golden egg dropped to the floor beneath him. Percilla had to laugh. Her great-aunt may be a powerful sorceress, but she also had a way of always keeping things entertaining. She nudged an egg out of her way and waddled closer to Matik, who finally broke into laughter with her.

"Does this madness run in the family?"

"I sure hope so. Because whatever is going on seems to be working."

The queen's chambers were quickly filling with eggs. Soon, there would be nowhere left to walk. Aurora paced slowly, the crystal egg in her hands. She barely noticed the two geese until she nearly stepped on Matik. He fluttered his wings to get out of the way. She playfully addressed them. "Are you going to follow me every-where now?"

Since they couldn't actually tell her yes, Matik and Percilla honked back.

"Very well, then. At least you two make better company than my own advisor these days."

Aurora crossed to the window. Percilla flew up to the windowsill beside the queen, and her spirits sank as she over-looked the monstrosity being built. "Matik, this is not good."

He flew up to the other side of Aurora, whose expression was filled with sorrow. Everything about her made Percilla's heart ache. This poor queen was being tricked, and she felt all alone. Percilla knew that feeling very well and sidled closer.

"Oh, Father," Aurora whispered, "what has happened to our kingdom? You left, and now I'm talking to geese." She laughed lightly. Percilla nudged her arm, and the queen touched her head gently, running her fingers over her feathered neck. "My crown was stolen by a monkey, and I'm going to bathe with a crystal egg to connect with Rou. This all sounds like a bad joke. If only you could be here now, Father. Your time on this Earth was far from over, and I fear...I fear I'm not ready to rule."

"I don't see the Digs anywhere. Do you?" Matik honked.

"No, but they've left their mark," Percilla squawked.

Aurora lowered herself onto a chaise lounge. "You two probably don't understand a word I'm saying," she mused. "That's all right. I appreciate the company all the same."

The door to her chambers opened, and Aurora sighed. Percilla admired the young queen. Even in the face of so much annoyance and grief, she managed to pull herself together. At least there was no longer the hazy look to her eyes from when they first arrived.

"What is it, Pith?" she asked roughly.

Matik waddled over to Pith and let out his goose droppings on the advisor's boots. Pith glowered at the goose as he hurried away, flapping his wings and squawking along with the other one. Aurora's lips twitched in a grin.

"My queen, would you like me to do away with these geese?"

"Whatever for?" she replied. "They are our guests and will be treated as such."

He shook out the boot now covered in goop. "Guests? You mean for dinner?"

"What?" Aurora exclaimed. "No, Pith, I mean as guests. I find I quite enjoy their company. And please clean up those droppings."

"My queen, they are geese. I know I have upset you, but you must not feel the need to turn to these...creatures for comfort."

"And who else should I turn to?"

"Your king of course," he said quietly.

Aurora scoffed. "Yes, well, he is currently chasing a monkey."

"Actually, the king has returned with the guards. They could not find this monkey, but he has ordered the men to be on the lookout for it and your crown."

"It's just a crown. It has no real power. That lies within me."

Pith's lips moved as if he was going to argue, but he bowed low instead and backed for the door. "The king wishes to speak with you when you have a chance, my queen."

"Thank you. Now if you please, just let me be for the rest of the day, and if either of these geese winds up in a cooking pot, you best hope you are very far from my sight indeed. They are not to be touched."

Pith bowed lower, then exited the chambers.

Percilla waddled her way to Matik as Aurora stood again and paced around the room. "I don't like that guy."

"Me neither," Matik replied.

"Think the Digs got to him?" Percilla asked, flapping her wings and stretching her neck as another egg rolled away from her webbed feet. "I wish Frida would magically stop this egg-laying thing now."

Matik's chuckle came out as a series of avian hisses. "Let's hope she can hear you."

"We have to stay with Aurora and make sure she doesn't get into trouble."

He glanced around at his tiny, feathered body. "And what exactly are we supposed to do if she *does* wind up in trouble?"

"Let's hope Frida gave us some warrior goose skills, I guess."

"These wings have been effective so far. At least we're not forced to march as circus monkeys." He tilted his head at her. "Never mind. Wait, where's she going?"

Aurora was at the door, but she waited for the geese as their webbed feet slapped against the floor. "Well, come along, then. Let's go find the king."

Percilla wasn't sure how to feel about being in Vahn's presence or the fact that he was here at all. And she had no idea what they could do to help the queen, but surely Frida was keeping an eye on them somehow. They'd come here to save Evanstide from the Digs, but all they'd managed to do so far was to lay a ridiculously large amount of golden eggs. Frida's disappearance did not help matters at all, but Percilla had faith that the sorceress's plan was still unfolding.

Percilla waddled around Aurora's feet, sticking close to her side. The queen moved through the halls, her head held high, growing more confident with each step. Whatever the Dignitaries had done to her, the effects seemed to be wearing off. Percilla hoped she could stay clear-headed for the sake of Evanstide.

They walked down one corridor, passing guards and servants alike. They all bowed with respect to their queen, but none of them stopped her. They eyed the geese, letting out surprised murmurs as they followed behind.

Percilla glanced over her shoulder. "You're not laying eggs anymore?"

"Doesn't look like you are either?"

"Let's hope that part of the plan is done, then."

They arrived at another set of double doors very similar to those outside the queen's chambers, and a guard bowed before opening them for Aurora. They found Vahn standing out on the balcony overlooking the last communal pool.

The monument rose out of the ground like some horrible beast coming to devour them all. Percilla hated it and squawked sharply when she and Matik reached the railing.

Vahn jumped and whirled around. "My queen," he said in a rush. "I did not hear you come in."

"Pith said you had returned."

"I apologize, your crown is still missing."

Aurora shrugged, her eyes fixed on the construction site. "It's only a crown. A new one can be made if necessary, but all here know who I am. I apologize for the state of the kingdom." She sighed heavily. "I've never experienced such a thing. Ever since my father was murdered, it's as if the world is turning against me. Against my people. I fear for them. Fear I won't be able to keep them safe."

"You will, Aurora, with help of course. Besides, it's not your fault this has all happened. There are Evils among us. I can sense it. I've seen it before."

Aurora nodded slowly, then stopped. "Evils. I've never seen them, only heard stories. What do they look like?"

Percilla let out a goosey scoff. All he'd have to do is describe what he saw in the mirror. Before Vahn had the chance to answer, Percilla pecked harshly at his foot. She did it again harder, hoping the queen might somehow understand what she was trying to convey.

"These geese, perhaps," he muttered, glaring at the offending birds as he shifted away from them.

Aurora laughed quietly. "They have been nothing but entertaining and comforting to me. Perhaps they are sensitive to the talk of Evils."

"Perhaps."

Percilla flapped her wings and charged at him, chasing him even farther away from Aurora. The queen giggled as Matik joined in the chase. Around and around the balcony Vahn went, until Percilla finally brought them to a stop.

The queen got her giggling under control. "I don't think it's the geese, though they have become very protective of me. It's sweet." She leaned on the railing, her smile fading. "No, there is something else in Evanstide. Something we can't see yet." She held up the crystal egg. "I'm going to the pool to cleanse myself, to see if I can't find some much-needed clarity. Will you join me?"

He cautiously stepped closer, the geese keeping a wary eye on him. "I'm afraid that I must see to the construction of the monument. And continue the search for your crown."

"There are more important things to tend to. The builders don't need you looking over their shoulders. And I wish you would let the crown go."

"How can I do that? A thief has stolen my gift to you, the symbol of our union." Vahn reached out for Aurora's hand. He glanced at the geese, but Percilla stopped herself from going after his feet again. "What kind of husband would I be if I didn't try to get it back for you?"

"One who understands there are more important things," she repeated, holding up the egg between their faces. "You've never been to the pools before, at least not to cleanse yourself. With these Evils running amok, you should come with me."

"I have not been tainted," he promised.

"The people would feel better if you were seen with me there. It would help them be more comfortable with someone not of Evanstide as their king. You do want to be their king, yes?"

"Of course I do."

"Then come with me, and show them that you are the same as they are."

Vahn took her free hand in his and kissed the back of it. A smile spread across his face, but it set Percilla on edge. She was tempted to go back to chasing him around the balcony, but stopped herself from giving in to temptation.

"Soon, they will love me for the power I can give them once the monument is complete. There is no need for me to do anything else." Aurora began to protest, and he went on. "However, if it will make you feel better, I will do the cleansing as soon as I am finished with this task."

Aurora's lips thinned, but she gave in. "Very well. At least once it's finished, my people will be safer."

"Our people," Vahn corrected softly. "And yes, they will be."

Together, they looked at the monument.

Percilla did the same and couldn't believe the monument was nearing its completion. This was bad, very bad indeed. Where was Frida? They had to put a stop to this before the Digs dug their claws in too deeply. She squawked with worry and noticed Vahn watching her closely.

Did he sense his old friend? Was the Vahn she knew still buried somewhere within this strange, horrifying version of him? Or was he lost to her forever?

CHAPTER 26

Illuding the Masterminds

FRANC TAPPED THE dimming gemstone on her ring. She glared at Ons, who was still meticulously pressing a myriad of buttons in an attempt to connect with Evanstide. The bulb on the phone apparatus in front of her was still lifeless. Her eyes darted back to the equally dull orb. "Ons! Why isn't this orb vividly alive?" she shouted. They needed to maintain a certain threshold of connection with Monzu in order to receive support, and the faint glow of the orb barely showed any real signs of power. She muttered under her breath, how pitiful Nylz and Lyken were at doing such a simple task.

The bulb flickered to life. "Evanstide is on the line," Ons informed her.

"Finally."

"And you can't expect me to activate the orb's harnesser while I'm transmitting. Be patient." Ons stomped out of his booth, shaming the impetuous woman.

"Unimpressed," she barked back to him before pressing the receiver to her ear. Pith appeared on a small screen upon the wall in front of her. "Well?"

Pith's voice came over the line, a bit out of breath. "Trouble."

"I assumed. What kind of trouble, Pith? And do be specific. I am in no mood to hear nonsense." Franc's irritation grew the more Pith elaborated the details recounting the events in Evanstide. "You aren't making sense."

"A monkey stole Aurora's crown!" He shouted so loudly that Franc had to tear the phone from her ear. "Just came in and snatched it right off her head. Vahn and the guards gave chase, but no luck so far. Please, you must return and set this right before the geese and their golden eggs infect my queen with Evils!"

Franc snapped, "Stop, you've gone mad."

"I've not. Evanstide is in trouble. Look." Pith lifted a golden egg for her to see.

She gripped the device so tightly, she was amazed it did not shatter. "Curious. We're making our way back now. Do your best to keep order." Franc slammed down the receiver, cutting off his mad babbling. Gazing at the faint pulse of the orb at the center of the tower, she seethed. "Are they doing anything at all up there? We must get back to Evanstide."

The words had barely left her mouth when a violet haze sifted through the walls of the Tower. It swirled around, then was sucked into the orb. There was a bright flash of light, and the haze became a thick fog. Franc raised her arms, reveling in the fear of Gangleton fortifying their power reserves.

"Now, that's more like it," she mused. The orb gave off a healthy glow that lit every inch of the Tower. "Drendle! Power up the 'pus. We're going to Evanstide."

By the time the Dignitaries were ready to depart, Gangleton was in the midst of a full-blown panic. Most people still had no real idea what they were supposed to be doing. A few of the men had taken up posts at their garden gates, holding shovels or pitchforks to defend against...well, they weren't entirely certain. They stared at each other tensely, not saying a word. Just waited. It was all they could do. Wait. Wait, and be afraid.

As the octopus maneuvered around the Tower, Franc cleared her throat, opened the domed bubble so the people could see her, and spoke into the large, brass megaphone. "People of Gangleton!"

All at once, faces turned to stare. Their ravens did not carry them to the Tower, but they didn't need to be close to hear.

"The enemy has come!"

She'd been ready to create an illusion to keep the people's fear feeding the orb. But a report had come in from the Barrens, saving her the trouble. She glanced back at Ons and nodded. It was time for the people to see what truly awaited them out in the Barrens.

For decades, the Dignitaries had hidden what truly lay beyond the force field in order to keep everyone happy, to keep them believing that outside Gangleton was a world overrun with danger and Evils. Ons pushed a large, red button, the illusion shimmered away, and what was left behind was a very disturbing sight. Screams erupted from the streets as those inside the force field stared in wide-eyed horror. There was truly an enemy at the gates of Gangleton.

The mass of Denton warriors were spread out across the vast wasteland. They had come for the Dignitaries, but all of the people of Gangleton cried out in terror. The leader of the Denton tribe stepped out of the ranks. The intimidating man could see in just as the people could see out. From the octopus, Franc sneered right back.

Fires burned, lighting the dusk with a triumphant glow. The captain shone like a god in the light of his torch. He blew into his conch shell, igniting the fire breathers to spit flames into the air that merged to form a phoenix. Fiercely narrowing his eyes on Franc, the leader pointed his torch directly at her.

"We're ready when you are, Digs!" he shouted. "Come out if you dare."

The people behind them screamed all the louder, and Franc smirked. "Your timing couldn't be better," Franc quietly assured herself. "Leave the illusion down. Let their fear feed our engines."

The Denton howled an incantation, the deep timbre of their collective voices shaking the very ground. They had certainly come for war. Franc's gaze shifted to the Tower. The longer the Denton remained, the more power the Dignitaries would gather. It wasn't as if the army could break through the dome. That would take time to decode the magic or immense power, neither of which Franc believed they had.

"Nylz, a speech if you please," Franc said over her shoulder. "Let the people know we stand with them always."

Franc fell back to prepare their route to Evanstide. Nylz stepped forward and held up her arms, but the panicked cries didn't cease. She gritted her teeth, then reached for the brass megaphone nearby.

"People of Gangleton!" They finally quieted as her voice reverberated around the village. "We are in grave danger. Do not leave your homes for any reason. You will be safe as long as the force field holds."

Everyone exchanged worried glances.

"We are going to fight for your protection," Nylz assured them and drew her sword. "Keep us in your prayers, for if we fall, you fall. Now, go to your homes. Stay inside, lock the doors, and whatever you do, do not attempt to flee. That will only lead to your deaths."

For a solid five seconds, no one moved an inch. No one spoke. No one even breathed. Then the Tower sounded, and all at once, the ravens lifted the people onto their rooftops to retreat back inside their homes. Shutters were closed and locked. Doors were barred. Soon, the streets that had been flooded with people became deserted. Though they were hiding inside their homes, the power of their pure essence seeped out as fear got the best of them, following the breeze. It wrapped around the Tower like a living being, bleeding through the walls to be dragged in by the orb and its powerful magnetism.

Franc checked the energy meter in the octopus; its needle hovered over the green line of high capacity. "Drendle, I hope you're ready to get us into the air," Franc said as the glass dome of their craft closed over the Dignitaries.

Drendle nodded eagerly. "We're good to launch."

"Good, then deploy the wings. Time to fly."

The tentacles curled in on themselves. The set of four wings clicked and locked into place. Ons turned a dial to the right, and the contraption drew power from the orb inside the Tower. The engine hummed to life, and soon they were lifted off the ground. Ons pressed another sequence of blinking buttons, and the octopus pressed through the top of the force field.

It shot up into the sky and took off across the Barrens. Franc stared down over the multitude of raging fires stretching from the gates of Gangleton in all directions.

"They'll be here when we return," Ons told her from his seat in the small control booth.

"I know."

"And? Do we have a plan?"

"One step at a time. We finish the monument in Evanstide, tap into their vortex, and then offer our loyalties to Monzu in exchange for the locations that we were promised." A dark grin twisted her lips now that her command was supported once again. They would ensure Aurora was truly on their side. They would deal with the Denton.

And then, they would deal with them all.

CHAPTER 27

Waters of Redemption

AURORA MEANDERED DOWN the pearl-lined streets, cradling the crystal egg in her hands with the esteemed geese waddling closely behind her. Fixated by the mystical gift from Rou, Aurora didn't want to miss anything it might bestow from within its colorful, glowing interior. She slowed her pace to gaze upon the images manifesting in its swirling haze.

For a moment the cacophony of the construction site burdened her mind, but then a sweet melody rode in on the breeze and caught her attention. A group of musicians had gathered in a circle near the pools, the hand-crafted instruments lightening the mood of the day. Aurora gestured to Patri, who was overlooking the pools from her watchtower. The woman bowed to the queen and blew into a conch shell, relieving all the workers from their duties. Within moments, the builders were clear of the area. The simple fact that construction of the monument had halted filled Aurora with joy.

She gazed into the depths of the mystic crystal. Her tears and silent wishes had not gone unheard. Rou, the sacred land of her people, which she'd never had the honor to see in person, sent a message directly to her. The crystal egg was sure to bring her some sort of clarity or divine guidance. "I am honored, Rou," she whispered.

Vahn rushed over to her. "Aurora!"

"You've come to join me." Aurora's spirit swelled as she spoke.

"Why has the construction stopped? Did you do this?" Vahn stood by her side, gaping at the scene in complete disbelief.

Aurora furrowed her brows. "This is my kingdom. And I am...we are going to receive the blessing that Rou has offered us before I signal for any construction to continue."

Vahn let out a heavy breath. Then, as if the word got out to the whole village, all the pathways surrounding the pools filled with people. She couldn't help but smile at the support of her community now standing all around her.

"They've come to connect with you, Vahn. You've not yet joined in one of our celebrations. Now is the time." She gently took his hand.

"I didn't realize we were having a celebration over this."

"Neither did I, but word travels fast here."

Aurora's faith in her kingdom grew stronger as she looked upon her loyal comrades' beaming faces. The pain from the events of the past week faded away in that moment. The children laughed and drew nearer to the geese, who donned headpieces of pearl and carnelian made especially for them.

"I don't think your vow to me alone is enough for our people to trust you." She rested her hand on his arm and leaned in closer. "Our people need hope more than anything. They need to understand and know in their hearts that their new, foreign king is looking out for their best interests." She sighed, and her hand started to slip away when Vahn reached out and caught it. She smiled softly up at him. "Join me in the waters. Just do this one thing for me? Look at all I've done for you."

Vahn looked her in the eyes and squeezed her hand tightly before kissing it. "For you, my queen, I will do anything. Let us not delay any longer." His lackluster reply clearly showed he was more concerned with the end of the ceremony than the actual event. Though the fact he was joining her was enough to bring warmth between them once again, so she kissed him.

"You have no idea what this will do for us, for all of us. These waters..."

"I know," Vahn said with a smile, clasping her palm over his heart.

They walked through the crowd gathered before them. However, Aurora's peaceful pace turned jarring with Vahn by her side. He held her by the elbow, shepherding her along. She responded by slowing even more in order to better greet her people. Vahn begrudgingly followed suit, each jovial salute a nuisance to him rather than an honor. Silently, she prayed that this crystal egg would change his connection with the people.

Vahn scanned the crowd as he limply set his hand out to be shaken by the next person along his route. To his surprise, it was tightly squeezed by a brawny man who stared at him with uneasiness in his eyes. The king nodded and flashed a smile. The man bowed, releasing his strong grip.

Vahn returned his attention to the only thing that concerned him: the construction. The obsidian slabs still lying on their sides, the crystal sphere still resting on the ground—the whole sight made him queasy. To top it all off, Aurora's crown, the sacred gift from the Dignitaries, was still missing. As he slowed his pace to match the queen's, he reminded himself that the project would be completed any day now. He only needed to hold on a bit longer, and the mission would be a success. The Dignitaries would be pleased and, hopefully, never know about any of this.

"Something wrong?" Aurora asked him as they neared the remaining pool.

He replied quietly so his new subjects couldn't overhear him. "Nothing, my queen. Just worrying about what's outside the borders of our kingdom. Such tragedy awaits our people if we can't find a way to save them."

Aurora gazed upon the people she loved so dearly, fright creeping into her eyes. Then, she squared her shoulders and gently tugged him aside.

One of the geese honked right by his foot. He jumped, then glowered at the foul beast. He'd gladly step on it if it wouldn't upset his queen so much. Why she found comfort in such horribly messy and noisy creatures was beyond him.

"Vahn," Aurora said, pulling his attention back to her. "Are you sure you're all right?"

"I *would* be if you would let me find a better use for these nuisances."

Aurora's lips thinned in displeasure. "As I told Pith, they are guests. Surely they can't annoy you that much. They're so innocent and sweet." The geese honked in unison. "Not to mention, they've brought us a special message from Rou and enough gold to create many wonderful things for all the citizens of Evanstide."

"If that's what you wish to do with the gold," Vahn said, then sidled closer. "Perhaps it would be wise to give this crystal egg to your subjects as well, make it a gift for the people."

"But that's not what I was instructed to do with it."

"You are queen, are you not?" he said harsher than he meant to. "I simply mean, why are you taking orders from a stranger who sees fit to gift you with geese?"

"If I hadn't seen something in the egg, then I might not, but with everything going on..." She lifted the crystal so it reflected the nearby torchlight in all its faceted edges. "I need answers to what's happening, Vahn. I need them, and I think you do too."

"It's why I'm joining you."

He glanced behind her at the massive stones ready to be assembled. It wasn't hard to see the uncertainty and distrust on the faces that gathered either. If he wanted them all to follow him without question, Aurora was right. He pressed his forehead to hers, and gently clasped her waist as he gazed into her eyes.

"I'm sorry I haven't been more appreciative of how welcoming you've been to me and my customs." Vahn kissed Aurora, wishing her to feel safe and supported.

Together they smiled, then turned toward the only remaining pool, hand in hand.

Even though the logic of going through the ceremony was clear, Vahn had to fight the urge to tug free and run. A voice in the back of his head said he shouldn't be doing this, but the crowd of people gathering around them stopped him from making a break for it. The geese didn't help either, honking and basically pushing his feet onward. The fine layer of algae on the smooth stones at its edge glistened with the same magic as the waters that gave it life. Vahn stifled his urgency to end this whole charade at the sight before him; something felt off.

Yet strangely, at the same time, he experienced a fervent urge to dive into the waters headfirst. The thought alone made him feel light, joyful even, but quickly his mind muddled with fear. The discordant thoughts swirled into a looming anxiety, filling him with a dizzying uncertainty. Then all at once the crowd quieted.

Aurora elevated the crystal egg. "People of Evanstide, we have been given a great gift this day," she announced. "A gift from Rou that will help guide us in the days to come. They seem dark, but this is a sign that there is always hope. There is always light."

The people cheered her on with the melodious enchantments of Evanstide. Vahn stood perfectly still, the smile frozen on his face. Aurora carefully stepped down into the pool. Her twinkling train spread out behind her and floated upon the water. Angelically, she glided through the pool until the waters came to her knees.

Vahn could only watch, impeded by a bizarre sense of uncertainty.

"Vahn," Aurora whispered. "Remove your boots."

He hesitated, but with so many eyes on him, he had no choice. His heart pounded, and his fingers quivered as he untied his laces. Slowly, he undressed his feet, then stepped down into the pool with bated breath. When all he felt was cool water rippling away from his legs, he relaxed. Perhaps his panic was for nothing.

He joined Aurora at the center of the pool. This time when he turned to face the crowd, their brilliant smiles and uplifting song made him proud to be their king. Aurora had been right. This was how he could get the people to trust him and believe in him.

Aurora held the crystal egg up above her head. "Today will mark the first time King Vahn is cleansed in the waters of our ancestors. May this day remind us all of our truth and devotion to Rou." She lowered the egg to the surface of the water. "May our waters be forever charged with the energy of Rou."

She let go. The sound of the crystal hitting the bottom should've been muffled by the water, but to Vahn it was like a cannon went off inside his head. He clutched at a stabbing pain in his chest, which worsened with every pulse of the crystal at their feet. The strobing light grew so bright he had to shield his eyes. Aurora's face was torn between shock and excitement as the crystal continued to work its magic in the sacred waters of her people. But something was wrong. Vahn couldn't stay there, he couldn't.

"These waters are now blessed," Aurora proclaimed, and her people sang even louder. She scooped up some water, and before Vahn could stop her, she let it fall over his head. She did it to herself next, then went to dump more over him. He subtly shook his head and bit his tongue to stop from bellowing in agony.

Each pulse of the crystal was in time with his racing heart, growing faster and faster until he was dizzy and staggered back a step. Aurora's happiness gave way to fear, and she reached out to steady Vahn.

"What is it? What's wrong?"

"Nothing," he gasped. "I'm fine, just fine."

"Vahn, your eyes," she whispered. "They're glowing. Vahn? Vahn!"

His muscles spasmed, and he collapsed into the pool, his arms and legs thrashing. Then his back arched as his entire body went rigid, a silent scream stuck in his throat.

"Dazell!" Aurora shouted and dropped to her knees to hold up Vahn's head. "Someone find Dazell, quickly!"

The pain that started in his chest coursed through his entire body. He couldn't see straight, couldn't hear anything except the thunderous boom of his heart and his own horrid gasping. He held up an arm and found that his veins were lit up. His skin lurched as if a creature were running inside.

Aurora and the two guards dragged him to the edge of the pool. Sucking in another breath, he reached for his neck and scratched at his agonizing, swollen veins. He had to get it out of him, whatever it was. Death surely awaited him if he didn't. His nails broke through skin, and he was dimly aware that Aurora was screaming.

His vision blurred and darkened.

All sound vanished.

There was only pain eating him alive.

He was going to die.

A chorus of shouts pierced the chaos swarming Vahn's mind, and his vision cleared long enough for him to see two women jumping into the pool. Presumably, one of them was Dazell. He thought he may have recognized one of them, and both had earnest looks about them. Deep down, he knew they were his only hope.

Aurora grabbed the arm of the woman holding a wand and spoke to her.

The woman cupped Aurora's hands as her lips moved. Vahn heard nothing but the churning tides of his inner world.

The sorceress placed the tip of her wand against his forehead. The other woman stood close by. She squeezed his shoulders and gave him a comforting smile.

A tinge of relief spread across Vahn's forehead where the wand touched.

Immediately, his body stilled, and everything turned to blackness.

Vahn had gone so still, Aurora feared he had died. A cry escaped her lips, and she dropped her forehead into her palms to cover her eyes.

"What have I done?" she whispered.

"You have done nothing wrong," Dazell told her firmly, resting her fingertips on Aurora's neck. The sorceress' caress released Aurora's mind from the memory of Vahn's distress. No longer in despair, Aurora straightened up. Dazell continued. "Frida and I must take him. We will do all we can to save him. I promise, I will explain it all to you when there is time."

Dazell's eyes narrowed as they focused on someone at the edge of the crowd.

Pith stood there, wringing his hands and looking for all the world like he feared for his life. Why was he so afraid? Was it because of what happened to Vahn?

"Aurora," Dazell murmured, drawing the queen's attention. "We must take him. You need to get to the palace."

Aurora wasn't certain she should go. Frida climbed back into the pool to stand beside Aurora.

"You need to return to the palace," she said sternly. "It is the only way we can help you."

"Help me how?"

"Trust me, you'll know it when you see it. You're not alone, Your Majesty." The woman winked. Then she leaned over and whispered something to the geese waiting at the pool's edge. When she stepped away, a gold band was wrapped around each goose's leg. It was odd, but Aurora was too caught up in the moment to question what this woman had given the geese or why.

The sentries holding Vahn waited for Aurora to give them permission, then they carried Vahn away, following the sorceress and this foreign Frida woman.

Aurora took the wrist of another guard and stepped out of the pool. She turned to grab the crystal egg resting on the bottom, but for some reason she knew it had to stay there. It was not just for her, it was for her people just like Vahn said it should be.

"Your Majesty?" the guardsman asked.

"I'll return to the palace now." Not bothering with her slippers, she walked through the streets barefoot, unable to give any words of comfort to the people she passed. How could she when she wasn't even certain about what occurred?

The geese, to no surprise, followed right behind her. Through the whole ordeal, they had remained silent. Even now, they didn't let out so much as a honk, just waddled alongside

Aurora as if they too were part of her guard detail. Some of the bystanders reached out and gave her sympathetic looks. Most, however, had retreated and returned to their homes after the spectacle. Aurora didn't blame them. She hurried back to a palace that no longer felt as if it could give her sanctuary.

CHAPTER 28

All in the Action

F RANC STEPPED OUT of the octopus contraption and onto the glistening sea-stone ground. She didn't have to look long to know something was more than just amiss in Evanstide. People rushed back to their homes in clusters, whispering with their heads close together. The rest of the Dignitaries climbed out behind her and stood at attention, waiting for orders.

"Well?" Ons asked after a while.

Franc breathed in deeply, then charged forward. The rest followed and flanked her. "Spread out. Find them."

"Which 'them'?" Lyken asked, tilting his head and squinting at the crowd.

"Vahn, Dazell, and the man Pith mentioned, the man with the geese. Find them all and bring them to me." When no one moved quickly enough for her liking, Franc clenched her fists and turned to confront them with a heavy stomp of each foot. "Go! Now!"

Nylz and Lyken took off in one direction, Ons and Drendle went in another. Franc's eyes followed the main path through Evanstide right to the front doors of the palace.

Her lips twitched into an evil smirk. "I think I'll have goose for dinner tonight. Let's see just what you're up to, Dazell."

Water dripped from Aurora's gown, leaving small puddles wherever she went as she feverishly paced about the throne room. What was happening to her kingdom? To her king? That morning, she had a direction, she knew what she was doing. Now, she wasn't sure which way was up. It was like the dome around her kingdom had collapsed and she was drowning.

"Leave me," she muttered to her sentries. They exchanged a long look and when they made no move to do so, she sighed. "Please, I'll be fine, I promise. I just need room to breathe."

The guards bowed and exited the throne room. Aurora sank to the floor in a heap, and the second she was alone, she rested her forehead on her knees. She was an awful ruler. She was failing her people, and the worst part was she couldn't even remember how it came to this. What changed? As she tried to think back over the last few days, the doors opened, and the one man she did not wish to see strode inside.

"Pith," she gritted. "Do you need something?"

"I have come to warn you, my queen. To be your voice of reason as I have always been."

She scoffed. The geese honked along with her, like they also recognized his blatant lie. Lately, she sensed her advisor was against her more than there to support her. "What is it you want to tell me?"

"The incident with Vahn in the pool, we cannot ignore it."

"I'm not ignoring it. I'm thinking," she countered. "Can't you see that I just need time to think?"

Vahn. She had to return her attention to Vahn and what she had witnessed. The crystal egg had blessed the waters in ways she'd never seen before. It was meant to soothe and heal...

Aurora gasped and clambered to her feet.

"My queen?" Pith asked in alarm.

"Evils," she muttered. "They warned me that Evils lurked outside our kingdom, but they were already *here*, already *in* Evanstide...or they came with Vahn. He must be possessed. It's why he reacted so badly, why the waters did that to him. They were trying to heal him." She pressed her fingertips together before her lips, recalling the sight of Vahn's suffering. "I did that to him. I made him feel so much pain. But it will save him, it must."

"No, my queen." Pith hurried toward her. When she backed away, the two geese rushed to get in between them, squawking and flapping their wings. The advisor, impeded from any close encounter, joltily outstretched his arms. "My queen, please be at ease. I'm going to look out for you. I always have. I'm here to serve you."

"Evils, Pith, here in Evanstide," she repeated. "He was possessed by Evils. How can this be?"

"No, he was not," Pith barked, and Aurora leveled her chin to stare at him. He had never raised his voice to her, not like this. And he'd certainly never done so to her father when he was king. "You are being deceived by sorcery."

"Sorcery? Who is the sorcerer?"

"Dazell and that new woman. I've never seen her before. She's a wicked sorceress, just like Dazell is."

Aurora asked sharply, "They're doing this to Vahn?"

"They've placed a spell upon him. Don't you see? They're going to harm him. You need to send the guards to Dazell's home and bring all three of them in."

"What evidence do you have that they are behind this horrible incident?"

Pith licked his lips nervously. When he tried to approach her again, the geese flapped their wings and honked even louder. "I just know, Your Majesty. Dazell is after something, and it has to do with Vahn."

Aurora frowned. "Speak plainly. I have no time to try and decipher your babble."

"Dazell is threatened by Vahn."

Aurora smirked, then laughed. "Threatened? Why would she be threatened by him?"

"It's not him exactly. It's her control over the vortex. When the monument is completed, it will be taken from her. Please believe me, Your Majesty. The witch has nothing but ill intentions. Her true colors are starting to show, they have been since Vahn stepped foot in your kingdom."

"But why?" she demanded. "We do not fight over the power of the vortex. It's for everyone. Dazell more than anyone else here understands this."

"Yes, she does, but it has *not* been for everyone, not in a long while. Dazell is working against you. She is trying to bring down our great kingdom. She wants you off the throne," he insisted. "She will be your downfall."

"Enough," Aurora said, but her voice was weak. Her head spun with Pith's accusations and the events of the last couple of weeks.

"My sweet queen, you are too innocent to see the deception right in front of you. You are too young to understand the complexities of what's happening here. You don't see what I do. You can't possibly comprehend—"

"How dare you speak to me like that!" Aurora roared, silencing him. "I am not blind to what passes within my own kingdom. I know exactly what is happening here, Pith. If Dazell is hungry for power, she is not the only one. You have been rather eager of late, and don't you dare deny it. We're only in this situation because *you* pushed for it. Am I wrong?"

He backed away a step and bowed. "I never said you were blind," he replied, not answering her question. "I am only speaking the truth that times are not as innocent as they have been. There are dangers lurking everywhere. If we turn our backs on our new allies for the sake of those we once called friends, it will doom us all."

"Out," Aurora retorted, pointing at the door. "I said go! Leave me!"

Pith bowed lower just as the doors to the throne room were thrown open and her guardsmen hurried in. "As you wish," Pith conceded, then rushed out, shoving past the sentries on his way.

Aurora fumed and motioned to her guards to leave her again. They hesitated even longer this time, but gave in. The sound of the doors thudding closed echoed around the room, and she staggered back until she sank onto the steps leading to her throne.

"What am I going to do?" she whispered. "I have no allies now."

The geese waddled to the bottom of the steps, flapping their wings gently and honking.

"What? You two? As much as I appreciate your company, what can you two possibly do for me?"

She expected them to start laying eggs again, or squawk and chase each other about. Instead, they each held up the leg with the gold band and shook it. A gentle chiming sound echoed off the walls. It steadily increased in volume, then the geese shuddered. Two puffs of white smoke burst from the floor, engulfing them.

A bee buzzed around, clearing the haze and revealing two people around Aurora's age. One was a woman wearing a maroon top hat, which the bee had landed on. The other was a man holding the golden hilt of a sword at his side.

Aurora rubbed her eyes to dispel what had to be a hallucination. But when she opened them again, the strangers were still there.

"Good, no more laying eggs," the man muttered and shook out his arms.

The woman nodded as she patted her body, checking for things hidden in her pockets. "I still feel as if I have webbed feet." She glanced around, then stared at Aurora. "Oh, right, hello there."

"You...you're human?" Aurora murmured.

"Yes, we are. Sorry for the deception, but it was the only way we could get to you and help you out of this mess." She stepped forward and curtsied somewhat gracefully. "My name is Percilla, and this is Matik. We came with Frida to aid you. We were sent by Rou."

"Rou? But you...you and the eggs. The crystal one, it hurt Vahn. It's threatening his life. *You're* threatening his life." Aurora hurried to get to her feet. "I don't understand. You came here to harm my king?"

"What? Oh no," Percilla said quickly. "The egg was meant to help, we promise you that."

"But you gave me the egg to use, and that man, he told me to take it to the pool."

"Ah, that man was actually Frida," Matik explained. "The woman who's helping Dazell."

"Pith was right. You were summoned by Dazell to bring Evils into the kingdom." Aurora thought she was dizzy before. Now, all she wanted to do was lie down and pray this was all some crazy dream. "Vahn was fine until he entered the pool with the egg."

"Not by a long shot." Matik grimaced. "Your king is possessed by the Dignitaries and has been for a long while, we think."

"What?"

"And he isn't the only one. Tell me, how do you feel without your crown?"

"My crown?" Aurora reached up to feel her head. In the chaos of the afternoon, she'd nearly forgotten a monkey had snatched it earlier in the day. She grew light-headed and wobbled on her feet. Her two new guests rushed forward and helped her sit on the throne. "What does any of this have to do with my crown?"

"The Dignitaries have been controlling you with it." Matik crouched before her. "Once it was gone, did you feel different? Less fuzzy in the head maybe? Can you think a bit clearer?"

Aurora tried to remember the past days, but everything was a blur. She recalled the moment the Dignitaries arrived, but all the moments since her wedding were foggy until the most recent events. "How did I let this happen? Are you certain?"

"Yes, I'm afraid we are," Percilla replied. "I come from Gangleton."

"Vahn's kingdom?"

Percilla laughed, but Aurora failed to see what was so amusing.

"Gangleton is not a kingdom," she clarified. "It's just a village under a dome in the middle of the Barrens. We don't have nobles, and we certainly don't have princes or kings. Your King Vahn is not a prince, Aurora. He never was." She took a deep breath and her eyes darkened with sadness, followed by anger. "He was once my best friend. A renegade, just like me."

"And you're what, here to rescue him?"

"Not exactly. I'm the Keeper of Gangleton's Eye of Rou, and I'm here to let your Keeper know the time has come to unite."

Aurora gazed into Percilla's eyes, and the light inside of them brought a relief to her that she hadn't felt in some time. She sat back into her throne. "I believe you."

"That's good, because we can't exactly just bolt out of here."

"She's right," Matik said. "Not until you take care of something first. The vortex, you have to make sure it doesn't get utilized by the Dignitaries."

"The vortex." Aurora was on her feet in an instant and sprinted into her chambers. She only stopped running when she reached the balcony, clutching at the stone railing until her hands cramped. The monument was nearing completion. It might already be done for all she knew; she wasn't sure exactly what it was meant to be. "What have I done?" she whispered, horrified.

"You aren't the only person to be tricked by them," Percilla told her.

Matik pointed to Pith stealthily exiting the palace. "Yeah, your buddy. They definitely have him under something."

Aurora could do nothing but nod in agreement. Pith had been acting strangely for a while now. To think, he'd been under the control of such Evils this whole time. When had she become so blind? She should've seen this, should've known her advisor was no longer a man she could trust. The monument she let them build, it would take away control of the vortex and give it to these outsiders, these Dignitaries.

"It's not too late," Percilla said. "You can fix it. You can."

"How? Everything I've done is destroying my kingdom. Everything."

"Well, you did one thing right."

"Yes? Please, tell me what exactly that might be." Aurora didn't mean to sound so harsh, but she was so angry with herself for being led into this trap. She was backed into a corner with no clear way out.

"Vahn is an amazing person," Percilla said with a slight smile. "When he's not under the Digs' control, probably one of the most king-worthy people I know. He really is a good guy. And you, well, I actually think you started him on the path to salvation today by dragging him into that pool with you."

"He seemed so against it. I guess now I understand why."

A commotion from the throne room drew their attention. Aurora hurried to the door of her chambers, but before she could pull it open all the way, Matik and Percilla were there. They shook their heads and whispered for her to wait.

"Trust us," Percilla said.

Aurora nodded and stopped herself from flinging open the door. They cracked it open barely an inch and pressed their ears to the opening.

"Pith! Bring me Pith!" Franc shouted.

"Oh no," Percilla whispered. "Franc's here, which means we're running out of time."

Aurora's heart plummeted. This wasn't what she wanted for her people or her life. She thought everything had been fine, and now she was in more danger than ever before. They all were.

"We need to go," Matik urged. He shut the door on Franc's shouting and the sounds of guards rushing to and fro to follow her orders. "Aurora, is there another way out of here?"

"No, the only way out is through the throne room." She swallowed hard as fear gripped her. "We're trapped."

"No, not trapped." Percilla peeked around the door again. "Franc's left. You are the queen, Aurora. Nobody has more power in your kingdom than you. Please stay strong, and don't let Franc find Vahn. She can't."

"What are we going to do?"

Percilla shrugged, and then shared a hopeful grin with Matik. "Hope for the best. Franc will be back. Time to put on a show, Your Majesty."

CHAPTER 29

Release the Evils

DAZELL SIFTED THROUGH the vials of liquid in her apothecary. Annoyed by the eyes of the guards staring at her every move, she snatched up two full-face, long-nosed masks. Frida gladly accepted one, and together they strapped them on, followed by heavy aprons and gloves.

She shouted to the guardsmen, her voice muffled by the mask. "Whatever your king suffers from might be contagious. I would go if I were you. Things might get nasty."

The two men exchanged a quick look, then practically tripped over one another to get out of the house. Dazell nodded firmly to Frida, who didn't waste another second and shut the door. She ensured it was locked, then bolted and sealed every point of access into her home. They tore off the costumes and went to work. Frida used her wand to open the trapdoor beneath the rug while Dazell collected the vials and jars. She passed them down to the other sorceress, who prepared everything alongside the hidden, underground pool.

Frida poked her head through the hole a minute later. "Ready."

Vahn groaned on the floor between them, his legs twitching and eyelids fluttering open. "Where...where am I? What's going on?"

"Oh dear, he's waking up!" Frida exclaimed.

"Then we mustn't delay. *Lavantus Aquapanus*," Dazell recited, and Vahn levitated into the air.

He was guided down through the trapdoor by the motions of Dazell's wand. Frida helped ease Vahn through the opening from below. They laid Vahn on his back in the shallow pool. The twitching morphed into shudders that had his body quaking and creating ripples in the water. Dazell carefully poured the sparkling contents from a jar into the pool, followed by a bright red liquid, two black feathers, and a large pearl. Dazell made circular motions with her wand and recited a spell to finalize her enchantment.

The water turned a bright white, and sparkling flakes

appeared, fully surrounding Vahn in a perfect geometric pattern. The particles encased his body in gold, which made him jerk even more. Frida tried to soothe him, but his eyes shot wide open.

"What's going on? Who are you?"

"Hush now, let us help you," Frida said tranquilly.

Vahn tensed again. His groan of pain turned into a yelp so sharp, it was as if someone had stabbed him. The flakes moved over his body, pulled to his veins like magnets.

"It's in his blood," Dazell said dismally. It was the worst possible result.

Frida pulled an optic apparatus from inside her purse to inspect the flakes more closely. "It most certainly is. I'd hoped it hadn't gotten to this, but I honestly would expect nothing less."

Vahn's veins began to throb intensely. The muscles in his neck strained as he twisted and turned to escape the pain. The only way to get rid of it would be to expel the Evils possessing him.

"We'll have to do a full blood cleanse. What do you think?"

"We're running out of time here. We need to save his life. That's the only option we have."

Dazell darted back upstairs, Vahn's anguished screams following her. A small part of her considered letting this man die. After all, he came here with the Dignitaries. He worked with them, helped erect that horrible monument. He should be in pain. He should suffer for all the harm he'd caused. Another shout from Frida had Dazell dismissing the horrible thought and rushing to grab what she needed to save him.

If he was possessed by Evils, then all he'd done since coming to Evanstide was not of his doing. She wasn't going to say he was completely innocent, not yet, but she wasn't an executioner. She certainly wasn't going to watch this boy die a horrible and painful death. With the necessary supplies in hand, she rushed back down the steps and fell to her knees at the edge of the pool. Vahn's muscles twitched and pulsed faster, like a beast wriggling around inside a bag.

"Hurry," Frida urged. "I'll have to hold him while you do the cleansing."

"Prepare him for me, then. I need to prepare the potion."

Frida nodded. Resting one hand under his back and pressing her other flat to his chest, she closed her eyes to focus her intention. When she opened her eyes, there was an aura surrounding Vahn. Her lips parted and she whispered a spell.

Vahn's body calmed, and his eyes closed. He wouldn't be out for long, but his body would be more open to accepting the potion.

"I'm surprised that worked," Frida mused.

"Don't hold your breath. We still have to give him the full treatment." Dazell poured the substances from both vials into the jar, screwed the lid on tight, then gently shook it three times. She dipped the tip of her wand into the jar, and the teal liquid was absorbed through into the instrument. When the vessel was drained, she tossed it aside and climbed into the pool.

"Ready when you are," Frida murmured, her eyes fixed on Vahn.

"This could get a bit messy," Dazell warned, but there was no turning back now. She pressed the tip of her crystal wand against Vahn's forearm. His body convulsed, fighting against the magic meant to save him. The Evils were resisting, and Dazell hadn't even started the cleanse yet. "Are we sure this is going to work?"

"No choice. Do it, Dazell. Now."

Dazell let out a breath, then shoved the tip of her crystal wand into Vahn's arm. At first, nothing happened. She pressed harder, burying the tip of the wand under the skin. He gasped, and his eyes shot open, the irises ignited by a sickly, green sheen. As the potion fed into Vahn's body, he screamed and pleaded for the pain to stop. Frida held him as he twitched, and Dazell worked not to let the wand come out of Vahn's arm or tear his skin.

"Just a bit longer," Dazell told him over his screaming.

"Help," Vahn whimpered, his movements slowing. "Please, just get it out of me. Get it out."

"You'll be okay," Frida assured him. "You will. I knew you were still in there, Vahn. This creature, you mustn't feed it your energy. Do not fear. Not now. Remember love, only the love."

The sickly radiance from Vahn's eyes began to fade. Dazell removed the tip of her wand from his right arm and gently inserted it into his left. He winced, but Frida kept talking to him, calming him down.

"It's eating me from the inside out," Vahn moaned. "Just make it stop. I just want it to stop." He started to say something else, but it was cut off by a shuddering gasp. His body arched violently. "What's happening to me?"

Dazell feared the worst as she withdrew her wand, but then a liquid, the same eerie green of his eyes, shot out its end. The poison gushed into the pool, but when it touched the blessed water, it sizzled and burned away. Frida continued to soothe Vahn until his breathing slowed and his eyes shut.

"Have you ever seen anything like it?" Dazell asked.

Frida's lips thinned. "No, and I hate to say it, but I don't think this is the last time we will."

Both sorceresses watched the poison continue to spill out of Vahn's body until every single drop was taken from his veins and burned away in the pool.

CHAPTER 30

One Queen

EXTERNALLY, AURORA MAY have appeared still, but internally she was a raging storm. Her heart pounded, her cheeks hot with the blood rushing to her face. Frozen on her throne, she waited for Franc to burst into the room. Any second now, she'd come through those doors, and Aurora would have to stare her down. Unable to bear the anticipation, she rose and paced around her dais, taking deep breaths that calmed her ever so slightly.

The muffled sound of Franc's voice seeped through the closed doors. The Dignitary screamed at the guards to find Pith like she owned the place. As the voice came nearer, Aurora returned to her throne. This was her kingdom. She was queen. No one told the queen what to do, and certainly not this Franc woman.

Aurora elevated her chin when the doors flew open. Golden eggs were cast across the room by the heavy force of the distasteful woman's intrusive entry. She hesitated to enter further when her eyes locked onto Aurora's. Removing her top hat in one swift motion, Franc dipped into a grandiose, sweeping bow. When she straightened, she held a golden egg in her hand, and the sneer that stretched across her face appeared unnaturally large. It made Aurora's skin crawl, but she did her best to hide her discomfort. Franc's attention went to the egg. She silently tossed it between her hands, raising the tension in the room. Aurora wondered what this dreadful woman was plotting now; her games were unpredictable.

But Aurora was queen. No one else. This was her home, and this woman threatened it. She threatened every single life in Evanstide. Her father would never let such an enemy stand. Aurora was no different.

Franc met Aurora's gaze once again. The queen squared her shoulders and sat up straighter, meeting Franc's sneer with the calmest expression she could muster. It worked better than she expected, because Franc's eyes darkened, and her smile shifted into an annoyed frown.

"I did not expect you to return so soon," Aurora said when the other woman seemed unwilling to speak first. "And must you really barge around my home shouting at the top of your lungs? It's quite rude."

"Apologies, Your Majesty," Franc said with another bow. "I had urgent news for Pith."

"For him and not for me?" Aurora's anger bolstered her courage. "He is not in charge here, Franc. I am. Or did you forget that in your short time away?"

"Not at all. I just didn't wish to trouble you with such trifling matters."

"I will decide which matters concern me."

Franc strode forward a few steps, kicking the golden eggs out of her way with the toe of her boot. Thankfully, her fixation on the eggs kept Franc from seeing Matik and Percilla hidden among the stone columns that lined the room. It took everything Aurora had not to glance over and give their position away. From what little Percilla had been able to tell Aurora, Franc was quite keen to get her hands on them.

Aurora would not let this come to pass. They came here to help. She narrowed her gaze and tapped her fingers on the arms of her throne. It was something her father used to do when visitors to the throne room wasted his time.

"Well? Are you going to answer me or not?" Aurora demanded.

"I would rather wait until Pith is here, if it's all the same to you, Your Majesty. I hate delivering information twice. Don't you?"

Aurora stopped her tapping and nearly peeked at Percilla and Matik for guidance. She stopped herself at the last second. "Very well, then, though I must tell you, I have not been getting on with Pith today. The man has become a great annoyance. I have quite the headache thanks to his insufferableness."

"Is that so? I'm sorry to hear it." Franc took another step closer. "It's hard to find those we can truly trust and who understand us, is it not?"

"Yes, quite."

"I hear you had a mysterious visitor while we were away." Franc tilted her head as she studied the egg intently. "Tell me about him."

Aurora bit her cheek instead of asking Franc how she'd come to know about it. Pith. He must've been feeding information to Franc. What else did the Dignitaries know? What about Vahn? Were they here because of her visitor, or were they here because they knew what Aurora had done to Vahn? Her courage faltered under Franc's glare, but she reminded herself what was at stake and forced herself to remain steadfast.

"Yes," she replied. "He brought me a gift. Two geese. The egg you are holding is one of their many offerings."

"Interesting. And where might these geese be now?"

"You know, I'm not quite certain. They've been sort of roaming about the palace. I'm sure my guards are sick of them laying eggs everywhere. For all I know, they might be in a pot by now getting cooked for dinner." She smiled, but Franc didn't even attempt to return it. "It's a shame you missed them."

"Something tells me I'll be seeing them soon enough."

Aurora tensed at the threat behind her words, though she had no time to ponder it. The Queen's Doorway burst open for a second time, and Pith hustled inside. Sweat covered his brow, and he went rigid at the sight of Franc.

"Ah, Pith," Aurora said, and his gaze flicked to hers. "Good of you to join us. Now then, Franc, Pith is here. What is this news that's so urgent you had to come all the way back to Evanstide to deliver it?"

Franc's eyes never left Pith. "I would love to, Your Majesty, but I'm afraid we must wait yet again. Where might King Vahn be? This news involves him as well."

"Him and Pith, but not me."

Franc turned slowly and subtly lowered her head. "With all due respect, it has to do with Gangleton."

"I'm a part of Gangleton now, just as Vahn is a part of Evanstide."

"Even so," Franc said and whipped back to Pith. "Where is King Vahn?"

Pith sucked in a deep breath. "The king—"

"—is indisposed," Aurora said, cutting him off sharply.

"Indisposed?" Franc shifted so she could look from Aurora to Pith and back again. Her gaze darted to the top of Aurora's head, clearly making note of the absence of her crown.

"A lot has occurred today, and he's quite exhausted. He hasn't been injured or anything, simply feeling a little sick. Thank you for reminding me, Pith."

Pith frowned, then glanced to the right at the set of stone columns. Aurora shot to her feet, prepared to yell for her guards to remove him, but Franc was moving forward again, a predator about to pounce on its prey. Aurora's pulse thundered away in her ears.

"What do you mean by sick?" Franc asked. "How sick is he? With what exactly?"

"He's been treated by our finest healers," Aurora blurted, fumbling over her words. "He, uh, he'll be fine by morning, I'm sure of it. If you'd like to wait until then to speak with him, he'll be in much better spirits—"

"Intruders!" Pith shouted.

Aurora had been so fixated on Franc, she hadn't noticed Pith had shifted to the right side of the room. Though Aurora attempted to silence him, he shouted for the sentries again. Percilla and Matik charged out from behind the columns, hands outstretched as if they could grab Aurora and somehow miraculously make it out of the throne room.

They had nearly reached her when Franc shouted a hex. An echoing snap of the woman's fingers reverberated throughout the room, plunging it into darkness.

Aurora's mind became a swirly mess as she stumbled, tripping over an egg and tumbling to the floor. She yelled for her guards, but she couldn't know if they heard her through the surging winds and loud howls accompanying Franc's curse. She tried crawling, but the darkness was so thick, it was like she was pushing through mud. The winds battered and disoriented her, and she could no longer remember the layout of her own throne room. The air stopped blowing but became so heavy her lungs felt compressed. Blanketed in the blackness, a sparkle in her mind's eye stole her attention from the chaos. Resting her eyelids to receive the vision, a glimmer floated out from the center of a twinkling nebulous. Divinu. His spirit illuminating with the same warm glow of the many gems in the cavern under Evanstide.

"Thank you, Father." She exhaled before taking a slow, full breath and rose to her feet.

The murkiness ominously parted, and Franc stood in the center of it. The Dignitary held up her hand, and two bodies were yanked from the shadows. Percilla and Matik struggled against the snake-like tendrils of smoke coiling around their bodies, holding their arms and legs tight. The deadly fumes climbed higher, wrapping around their necks. They gasped and sputtered.

"Stop this," Aurora demanded. When she tried to storm Franc, she was shoved back by an invisible force. Her head knocked against the back of her throne. She attempted to stand, but black coils strapped her in. "Franc, you will release them."

"And you will be silent." Franc turned her back on Aurora. "Percilla, funny running into you here. Tell me child, why did you run away from your family?"

Percilla's eyes closed as her lips moved. A burst of white light ripped through the black tendrils holding her, and she landed firmly on her feet. Matik followed seconds later.

Franc swept her hand through the air, rapidly lifting and cracking the gemstone floor. Fast, but not fast enough, for

Percilla had already placed an enchanted wall before her, stopping and splintering Franc's magic, which now oozed demonic vapors. Franc sneered, then raised her arm, slowly spinning her fingertip around the face of her wrist apparatus.

A piercing sound blasted through the room, and all but Franc slapped their hands over their ears. Aurora shouted, and though she couldn't hear her own words, Franc's glare said that her voice was not fully silenced.

Franc prowled toward her other captives. With a snap of her fingers, black tendrils cast out from the shadows, latching onto Matik and Percilla once again.

Aurora dropped her hands experimentally, and the noise level remained unchanged. The ringing was somehow coming from inside of her head. Blocking her ears would not save her. Aurora closed her eyes and willed her attention away from the sound that had taken over her mind.

She called upon her inner light, the thing inside of her that had given her strength through all the tragedies she'd endured. As she realigned with her truth, the screeching began to fade away. Summoning the strength of her ancestors, she willed Percilla and Matik to hold on. She had the power of her people flowing through her kingdom and the power of her ancestors in her veins, and it melted away the magic binding her to her throne.

Franc snapped her fingers again, and the tendrils lifted Percilla and Matik high into the air. "You should have joined our team, Percilla. You and Vahn would have been quite a duo. But instead, you chose the pitiful circus boy." Franc laughed and slammed their backs together. The tendrils bound them into an endless knot.

Aurora closed her eyes, forcing herself to focus on the light. She inhaled deeply, and her breath passed all the way through her body and into the ground below her. Her mind's eye became engulfed in a brilliant, amber light. The mystic wellspring surrounded her entire body, nearly lifting her off the throne.

The floor shook, and the walls trembled. The life force energy of the vortex and all her people flowed through her blazing eyes. The quaking intensified until Franc threw her arms out to keep her balance. The ghastly tendrils vanished, and Percilla and Matik fell to the floor, clinging to one another.

"What is this?" Franc snarled. She charged, ready to lash out at Aurora, but the queen just smiled confidently as the malicious Dignitary moved closer.

Geysers shot through the quaking floor. Franc lost her footing and crashed to the ground. The force of the water cut her forehead, and a mixture of liquids dripped down her red cheeks. Rage boiled out of her eyes like scorpions ready to strike.

Percilla grabbed Aurora's hand to pull her out of the room, but she didn't budge. As their eyes locked, she knew at that moment the other woman understood. Percilla started to shake her head, but Aurora shifted her gaze back to Franc. She was a queen, and she protected her people. That included her allies.

"Aurora!" Franc stalked over on unsteady legs. "I demand you stop!"

"You do not demand anything from a queen," Aurora replied, lifting her palms up. Crabs morphed from the rising waters and scuttled over Franc's entire body. "You bow."

The crabs clamped onto Franc, manipulating her movements and lessening her strength. The geysers threw her body into the air, sending her crashing to the ground time after time, but her defiant snarl never left her face.

"Run!" Aurora shouted to Percilla. "Go, get out of here!"

Percilla hesitated for a moment, then she and Matik bowed before rushing out the door.

CHAPTER 31

The Art of Fearmongering

LYKEN AND NYLZ charged through the thin layer of water glistening upon the azure streets, shoving through pedestrians. Lyken clasped his knotty fingers upon a woman's shoulder and turned her to face him. Nylz did the same to a brawny young man. They looked to each other for second opinions, then released their intrusive grasps on the startled citizens. People hurried to get out of the way of the two Dignitaries in mad pursuit, but their panic only bolstered the inquisitors' spirits.

Nylz stopped in front of the door of a rundown home near the edge of the dome. In one swift motion, her spinning kick lifted her off the ground, and she grunted fiercely. The door flew clear off its hinges. She prowled through the doorway. There was nothing. Nylz gripped the hilt of her sword and turned her glare back to the people in the streets.

Lyken was a few yards behind her, questioning the locals. His long and spindly fingers stretched out in full to the people in question. He darted his head forward, his slimy hair nearly slapping the villagers. The woman and her husband in question merely stared at him, more shocked than afraid, and covered their noses. He sneered at them and strode away. Nylz nodded at another street that twisted and turned until it neared the palace. It was one of the few they hadn't traversed yet, so they took off for it.

They were nearing the palace when Nylz came to a skidding stop and threw her arms into the air in frustration. Lyken arrived moments later, wheezing slightly. He put his hands on his knees to support himself while he caught his breath.

"This is pointless," Nylz snapped. "Do you even know who we're looking for?"

Lyken replied on a short exhale. "Geese."

"Geese? Then why are we stopping people?"

Lyken held up a thin finger, and Nylz tapped her foot impatiently. Finally, he wheezed, "Geese...that aren't geese...but are."

"Nothing about this makes any sense."

Lyken opened his mouth to rebuke her, then stopped. "You have a point," he muttered. "Maybe we should check in with Ons and Drendle to see if they had better luck?"

"Absolutely not. Those two are most likely playing in the puddles. We will find the culprits ourselves." Nylz nodded up the road and charged forward.

Lyken followed. He roughly grabbed a man by the arm and pushed him to the side, yelling, "Move out of the way! Dignitaries on official business. Move, I say!"

"There's an intruder in your community!" Nylz scanned the area, searching for any hint of feathers. "Run to your houses!"

But unlike in Gangleton, where the people were prone to believe every word the Dignitaries said, the people here just gave each other curious glances. They grouped together, whispering quietly and pointing at the Dignitaries.

Upon Lyken's impertinent approach, one man spoke up. "We don't take orders from you. Whatever business you have is your own. We only listen to the queen."

"We speak for your king," Lyken said, standing to his full height.

The man simply crossed his arms, glaring right back. "*Your* king maybe, but not ours. Who knows what he is, or what you've brought to our homes?"

"No matter who you listen to," Nylz said, stepping between them, "there is an intruder in your midst, and it would be safer if you all were to return to your homes. Now."

"Who is this so-called intruder?" the man challenged.

"One who bewitched your king and has ensnared the mind of your queen," Nylz replied. "A man of great power who has come here to do you all harm. Do you have any idea what lies beyond the borders of Evanstide? What Evils are just waiting to find a foothold here? We have come to save you, or have you forgotten so soon?" She spotted a flat boulder nearby and jumped on top. "I have seen horrors out there in the world. Men who have lost their minds torching whole villages! Burning people alive!"

Several bystanders gasped, and parents held their children close. Lyken's lips curled into a grimace of delight as Nylz went on.

"There is darkness out there, like writhing snakes ready to devour each and every one of you." She paused for dramatic effect, undulating her body like a prowling snake. "They rise up out of the ground, snatching innocents as they pass." More people gathered closer to see the spectacle. Taking pride, she enlivened her performance with grander gestures. She darted her finger at the crowd, and she squatted in a skulking, hunched-over posture. "The one who came here has unleashed a terrible curse upon your new king, a king who was more than willing to become a part of your people. Now, in his hour of need, you turn against him? Against us?"

"You all and your king are the only Evils here," the man argued.

Still caught in the depths of her performance and intent on gripping the souls of those before her, Nylz directed her growling face at the man. Without hesitation, she hopped off the boulder to stand toe to toe with the dissenter. If only they were in Gangleton and this man had ravens she could control.

"We don't want you here," he went on. Nylz placed her hand upon the hilt of her sword, but he pressed on. "You and the rest of your lot should go and leave our queen be."

Nylz dismissed the nuisance by slowly turning away from him and back to the frightened subjects. "Don't you understand? If your king is in danger, then so is your queen."

Whispers grew louder in the crowd, and Nylz sensed their mood shifting ever so slightly. All she had to do was get them to fear, get them to believe the situation was dire indeed.

Nylz slammed her palm over her heart. "After she returned to the palace, your queen took ill just as the king did. Whatever is happening within Evanstide, it's coming for everyone." Nylz pulled her hands together, tightening them into fists before her chest and shaking them as if she could not contain her emotion. "We are the only ones who can stop it, but you must listen to us. We have to find these intruders and stop them before your home is nothing but a bunch of ruins at the bottom of the sea."

She collapsed to the ground, scooping up the azure pebbles. Rising ever so slowly, she opened her hands to show them to the group. She moved around the circle, eyes pleading. "Please, don't make me witness another tragic ending to a Rou community. Do you wish to be like so many other forgotten peoples? Do you?" She dashed the rocks upon the ground at her final word. The enraptured audience watched the tiny, blue stones scatter.

As if on cue, the deep sound of a bell cut through the air. The crowd turned their attention to the palace. From its gates, royal guards dispersed through the streets.

"See? There's your sign. The intruder must have reached the palace!" Nylz's hand went to the hilt of her sword once more. "You must return to your homes. Quickly now!" Her voice was so urgent, one might even believe she was about to dart to the palace in a fury to protect the kingdom.

More people rushed away, following the orders of the guards over Nylz and Lyken's words, but it worked all the same. Between what she told them, the events of the afternoon, and now the ringing of the warning bell, the air was rife with the people's fear. Nylz breathed it in deep and spread her arms wide once she and Lyken were alone in the street.

Lyken clapped slowly, offering a slight bow of approval to his companion. "That was by far your best performance." He chuckled. "It's too bad we don't have our vortex apparatus installed."

"Yes, the intimacy of the setting really helped me feel engaged. Their energy fed my performance. They wanted more, so I gave it! I can still feel their fear seeping from their worthless beings. Can't you?"

"Hm, yes. Don't mean to rain on your parade, but the alarms really nailed the coffin, if you will. I'd say you were the warm-up act. Good, but you wouldn't have had that urgency if it weren't for the alarm and the guards. The guards really pulled through for the grand finale."

Nylz scowled and unsheathed her sword several inches.

"That'll never work. You know that," Lyken said with a cackle. "Come. Let's take your act to new audiences and see if you can do better."

Nylz ignited with delight to see their plan unfold and nodded eagerly. They started down the street at a much faster pace now that it was empty. They were almost to the palace when two figures darted out of a side door, their hands clasped together. They stopped and seemed to be discussing something.

"You there!" Nylz wasn't one hundred percent certain, but at her yell, the pair looked directly at her, and all her doubts disappeared. The two figures bolted, and she followed.

"Is that who I think it is?" Lyken asked, rushing to keep up with her.

"Percilla. Yes, it is. And that circus boy."

Lyken swiped his hand across a metallic pin on his jacket. "Sounding Franc. We can't lose them."

"Don't you think I know that?" The face of the man she had dueled upon the hot air balloon was sharp in her mind. More eager than ever to take down her opponent once and for all, she dug deep and sprinted onward.

CHAPTER 32

Healing Bonds

FRIDA WHISKED HER wand over Vahn, wishing one of her spells or methods would revive him. He lay motionless in the pool, floating with her help. His color was dull, and his breathing was labored, as if he fought against a weight on his chest. She and Dazell had done all they could for him.

"His energy is lower than I expected," Frida murmured. "He needs time to recover. A safe place to get his strength back. They'll be on the lookout for him."

"My home is well protected magically, and I have a few tricks up my sleeve."

"When are they expected to return?"

"You tell me." Dazell started for the stairs. "You know them, yes?"

"Unfortunately. I'm surprised they even left at all. They'll be back soon. To get what they came for." Frida sighed.

"Then we'll just have to show them they won't get it anytime soon. Come on, let's get him upstairs. I can hide him."

Frida shook her head. "He's safer down here, isn't he?"

Dazell winked. "Trust me."

Frida let Vahn go, and the other sorceress hoisted his body gently from the water with a flick of her wand. Drops fell from his soaking wet clothes and trailed down his fingertips while he floated up through the trap door. Frida climbed up last and closed it behind her, stepping ever so gracefully around Vahn, who lay next to the opening.

Dazell nodded at the far wall, where a painting of a ship on calm waters hung. "What do you think of my painting?"

Frida reached into her bottomless purse and pulled out her magical spy glass. She curiously walked over to the painting, scrutinizing through the lens all the while. Brushing her fingertips along the frame, a jolt of magic shot through Frida, illuminating her body like a lantern. "It is a lovely painting. You think it'll work? I suppose anyone who touches it will be easy for you to follow."

Dazell giggled. "Indeed. I've never tried that spell before. Looks like it works."

"Yes, it's a good one. You can turn it off now," Frida replied, not one to enjoy being the subject for another's shenanigans. She heard a sound behind her, then dashed to the young man's side.

Vahn grunted and shielded his face from the glow. "Where... where am I?" His eyes fluttered open. "What happened?"

Frida knelt beside him and smiled. "You're in Evanstide, darling. Everything's going to be all right, though. You'll see."

"Evanstide?" Vahn struggled upright with Frida's help, then he scrambled to get on his feet. "What happened to my house? How did I get here? I never left Gangleton. I don't understand." He spun wildly, on the verge of panic.

"Much has happened, but it's important for you to stay calm," Frida assured him. She pulled out a vial of sparkling, aqua liquid and handed it over. "Here, drink this."

"Wait, why do you look familiar?" Vahn asked. "Have we met?" He shook his head and blinked his eyes open as wide as they could go. "Why is your skin glowing?"

"Something like that," Frida replied to his first question, knowing he was probably recognizing bits of Percilla the longer he stared at the sorceress. She offered him the vial again. "I'm enlightened, darling. Trust me."

Vahn took the vial and drained it. "Whoa. What is that?" he blurted out, energetically more perked up now.

"Very good magic." Frida tucked the empty vial away.

"Can you explain how I got here? And who is she?" he asked, pointing to Dazell. "This must all be a dream, right?" A nervous laugh slipped through his lips. "The last thing I remember is... well, I was talking to my friend...I think I'd better get home now. My mind is so fuzzy."

"All in good time," Frida told him with a gentle smile. "But for now, we need to get you somewhere safe so you can rest."

"Safe? Why do I need to be somewhere safe?"

Frida laid a comforting hand on Vahn's back behind his heart. She didn't wish to worry him further by explaining the whole awful series of events he'd endured and settled on saying, "You left Gangleton a long time ago. The Dignitaries, you remember them?"

Vahn's body grew rigid, and he scowled at the floor. "They had me in a dungeon."

"They had you doing more than sitting in a cell, I'm afraid, but we were able to cleanse your blood. I'm Frida, and this is Dazell." She pointed at the other sorceress, who waited by the painting. "I was worried we weren't going to get to you in time, but you seem to be doing well."

The door burst open, and Percilla, followed by Matik, rushed inside, out of breath. They slammed the door behind them. Matik pressed his back to it, then slid to the floor, sweat covering his brow. Percilla collapsed beside him.

"What happened to you two?" Frida asked, alarmed.

Between sucking in gulps of much needed air, Percilla gasped, "They're...here."

It took Percilla a moment before she could register that it was Vahn right before her now. Catching her breath, she locked eyes with him. It wasn't just his body this time; the look in his eyes told her it was really her friend.

"Vahn!" Percilla dashed over, wrapping her arms around him as tears built up in her eyes. "I thought I'd lost you."

Vahn took a deep breath, then blew it out. "I don't even know what happened. Dazell and Frida just told me I was with the Dignitaries." He went silent for a moment, as if catching a glimpse of his real life. He looked deep into her eyes. "How did you get here?"

They exchanged a smile. "I made it to Rou!"

Vahn pulled Percilla back into his arms, squeezing her. "Thank you for saving me."

"You are most certainly welcome," Frida interjected. "I do apologize, though, we haven't any time to waste."

Percilla leaned away and laid a hand on his cheek. "You can come with me now."

Dazell walked over to them with her wand in hand. "I'm sorry, dear, but he is not well enough. He has just had a full blood cleansing."

"And Aurora needs help," Matik blurted.

Unspoken disappointment shone in his eyes. She knew he was right, but her magnetism to Vahn tightened the clasp around her long lost friend. How could she let him go again?

"Is she hurt?" Dazell demanded.

Matik stood, his hand at his sword. "She was holding her own against Franc and told us to leave. But Franc...I've never seen her like that. Her wrath..."

"Time to go, my queen needs me."

"Where, uh, where am I going, then?" Vahn asked.

Percilla squeezed Vahn's wrist, but she knew in her heart that he needed to recover, and he couldn't do it on her quest.

"I'll come for you again, Vahn. We'll be in Rou together soon."
They exchanged a final smile and embrace.

Frida gently rested her palm between his shoulder blades to guide him. "Think of it as a mini-vacation."

Dazell softly pressed the tip of her wand against Vahn's forehead and whispered, *"Gilgam Tins."*

Vahn instantly shrank to the size of a bee.

Dazell flicked her wand at the painting, enlivening the sea inside the frame. The boat rocked, and the sails billowed in a strong breeze. The sorceress lifted Vahn with a tap of her wand and directed him into the painting. "You'll be perfectly safe. Get some sun, enjoy the sea breeze."

Vahn was set down upon the ship's deck. He hesitantly gazed around at his new setting, then waved a final goodbye before his attention was drawn to something in the distance. The women admired their handiwork as the waves came to a stop and the ship remained fixed in the center of the frame.

"I'm glad you are all safe, but I'm afraid you must go," Dazell told them. "You have a long journey ahead of you."

"Go?" Percilla interjected. "We can't go yet. I have to make sure the Keeper knows what to do."

Dazell cupped Percilla's cheek. "I know, child. My name is Dazell, and I am the Keeper of Evanstide's Eye of Rou. This is the moment every Keeper has been prepared for."

"You know what to do when the color hits the sky?" Percilla asked.

Dazell nodded, fanning open her fingers. A small, golden pyramid appeared, then opened like a flower to reveal the orange Eye of Rou floating in its center. "We open the Eye to signal the alignment of the planets to restart Time. The Moon will once again cast its protective shield around Evanstide, just like it did for our ancestors. I'm sorry to see it's come to this," she said quietly, then closed the pyramid. "Now go, continue calling the Keepers to arms. I must save my queen, but I will be ready when the time comes."

"You're going alone?" Matik asked. "Franc is powered by Monzu. You should have help."

"They might have power where you're from, but here they are weaker. The power of our vortex still belongs to us. Now please, be well." She gave them all quick hugs, then patted Matik on the shoulder. "Trust me, brave warrior, I can handle myself."

Dazell stepped back from them, her wand surging with the force of her vortex. Fire sparked at its tip, then she tapped the top of her head. A flash of flames had Frida, Percilla, and Matik shielding their eyes. While they squinted against the brightness of the fire, a phoenix twisted into shape. She spread her wings wide, and, with a piercing call, she soared through the window, shattering the wooden shutters. Percilla made it over in time to see Dazell fly in the direction of the palace, shimmering particles falling from her flaming wings.

"Good luck," she whispered, then refocused on their next step. "Right then, Keeper three. Time to get a move on."

Frida reached to her neck and lifted up the chain with the third key. The yellow gem shone brightly against her skin. She squinted through it to locate the portal. The pyramid materialized when the key moved closer.

Frida inserted the key into the lock, and the door opened, beckoning them forward into the portal and onward to their next destination.

CHAPTER 33

Idle Pursuits

LYKEN STOOD BESIDE Nylz, watching the flaming phoenix that had just burst through the window. Nylz slowly drew her sword, then skulked toward the house. Percilla must be inside. Franc had given them clear instructions to wait for her arrival before they made a move. But Nylz wasn't one for waiting around when her quarry was right inside that door.

"That phoenix isn't Percilla."

"Can't be too certain," Lyken replied, eyes fixed on the soaring creature.

Nylz gritted her teeth. "That little girl wouldn't have that sort of power. I'm going in."

She lunged at the door like a caged beast, but Lyken slid in between her and her target. He glared from the doorway. "I'm not going to deal with Franc's wrath on your behalf." His words were accompanied by a ghastly stench that sent Nylz reeling back.

Nylz's anger churned inside her. She took her sword from her scabbard and charged at her companion. The weapon's tip stopped a hair's breadth away from his pointy nose. "Move."

Lyken, unfazed by her threat, used the metal band on his wrist to push the sword away. "No."

Nylz spun around and drove her sword over the top of his head, cleanly slicing the feather right off his top hat. As the feather descended, she cut it in half and stopped her swing directly at the skin of his neck. "I said, move."

Lyken lifted his long, scrawny leg, put the toe of his boot to her chest, and pushed her back. "No." He leaned down to collect the fallen feather.

Nylz grunted in annoyance, then kicked Lyken square in the rear. He fell forward, landing sprawled out on the wet ground. Nylz smiled and let out a subtle laugh before turning her attention back to her prey. A sudden jolt at the back of her knees sent her crashing to the ground. Lyken dragged her back and tossed her away from the door while she cursed and thrashed.

"Playing games while the rest of us work hard," Ons said as he and Drendle arrived on a steam-powered chariot. "Why am I not surprised?"

Ons gallantly stopped the chariot in front of them, it took all of Nylz's self control not to whack him over the head with his own cane. They weren't out of breath, covered in dirt, or sweaty. Ons most likely had only run far enough to get out of Franc's sights, then told Drendle to search for geese. Idiot that he was, he'd probably found a whole flock of ordinary geese while Ons made this stupid contraption that he so proudly rode in.

Ons dismounted. "Why are you playing games outside? Shouldn't you have her bound by now?"

Nylz ground her teeth harder. "Lyken's set on obeying Franc's orders to wait for her."

"Well, I am second-in-command, so let's go in." Ons strode over to the doorway.

"Second-in-command? Pretty sure I am. I think we can all agree. Right, guys?" Nylz glared over at Drendle and Lyken.

"I'm pretty sure I am," the buffoon Drendle insisted.

Ons took no heed of the conversation. He proudly set a circular apparatus on the door, then pressed a series of buttons on a remote device.

All of this foolishness made Nylz fume. With a running start, Nylz yelled to Ons, "Move!" She let loose a furious kick to the door, but it only shook in its hinges, and she dropped to the ground.

"Second-in-command." Ons laughed as he pressed a button on his remote.

The front door burst into a shower of wooden shards, revealing the interior. Nylz scrambled to her feet and sprinted forward with the other Dignitaries following. A portal swirled at the center of the room.

"No you don't!" Ons snapped as he opened a pocket watch. Black, shadowy snakes exploded from inside, then slithered for the glimmering ring. They smashed into it and pushed their way through. "Get in there, Second!" Ons yelled.

Nylz bolted for the portal. "You're not getting away from me that easily, Percilla."

Percilla tumbled out of the door onto solid, dusty earth alongside Matik and Frida. Her attention pulled toward the illuminated dome in the distance. She frowned at the sight of the familiar structure. Beneath her was the dry dirt of the Barrens, but that dome, that was Gangleton.

"Why are we here?" she asked Frida in a panic. "We weren't supposed to come to Gangleton."

"I didn't use the key for Gangleton." Frida's eyes widened, and she whistled. "Well, *that* certainly isn't Gangleton."

Percilla wasn't sure what she meant until her great-aunt grabbed her by the shoulder and spun her around. "Oh my, no, that is not."

"Who are they?" Matik asked, squinting through the darkness. "Do they...do they look like they're moving closer to anyone else, or is that just me?"

It was hard to tell what was going on at first, but a chorus of war howls erupted from a line of lights growing brighter every moment. "They're headed this way!" Percilla shouted. "Back to the portal. Frida, key four!" She turned back to rush to the door, then spotted the dark tendrils slithering through the opening and gasped. "It's still open!

Frida and Matik charged back to the portal at Percilla's alarmed shout.

"Stand back," Frida ordered. She flicked her wand, and a surge of magic pushed against the door. Her eyes lit with fury, and the strain of fighting against Monzu's magic showed on her face. "I can't hold them forever!"

Percilla glanced over her shoulder at the mass of armored people charging straight for them. Their yelling grew louder, and the ground shook with the weight of their advance. She was able to make out majestic rams pulling chariots at the head of the army. Percilla spun back to warn Frida, and the sorceress was about to topple over from all the energy she exerted. Worse, the chain for the yellow key slipped back into the void, back to Evanstide.

Nylz forced her head and arms through from the other side. "I've got you now." She struggled to get through, but Frida's magic held her at bay. Only her hands were free to rummage around the keyhole.

"No!" Percilla lunged for the key. The shadowy snakes all around Nylz's arm lashed out, swarming over each other and fighting to get to their prey. The key was too important to let go, so she threw herself at the door. A bellow rose up from behind them.

Matik's strong arms yanked her backward. To Percilla's horror, the key was torn from the keyhole and disappeared with the snakes into the void.

"Frida, behind you!" Matik yelled.

The sorceress counted under her breath, then she snapped her fingers and cast a spell. The three of them were lifted into the air just as the first chariot charged into the invisible door, slamming it closed. Percilla struggled against Matik's grip, but he held onto her. More chariots rumbled beneath their hovering feet.

"The key!" Percilla pushed against Matik, then she escaped out of Frida's magical hold. She hit the ground with a grunt, but was right back up again.

Frida and Matik reached the ground with a bit more grace.

"I need the key to Evanstide." Percilla grabbed for the orange key around Matik's neck.

"Percilla, you can't go back there," Matik replied, clutching the chain for the key to Evanstide. "They'll be waiting for you."

"I don't care!" The warriors halted their chariots and climbed out, circling around the portal. Their leader stepped forward, waving his hand through the empty air where his ram had crashed to a halt a moment before. He faced the trio, studying Percilla, Frida, and Matik. Beyond him, the fires burned and the war cries, chants, and songs continued as if they were the very air these people needed to survive.

"Did you say Evanstide? What have you been doing there?" the robust man asked, his voice a deep timbre.

"Yes," Percilla snapped, more concerned with the key than politeness. She darted over to Frida, pleading, "We have to go back."

"We can't," Frida replied. "We have a mission. And we can't let them get you."

"I know a few folks who recently went to Evanstide. Who's on the other side of that door?" the man asked with an air of authority. "I suggest you answer my question quickly. I don't have time for games."

Percilla had no idea who this man was, and though he was certainly intimidating, he wasn't nearly as sinister as the Dignitaries. She squared her shoulders and looked him right in the eye. "The Dignitaries."

The man smirked. "That's who you're working with?" He turned around to face his army and bellowed, "Looks like we found the portal to the Dignitaries! Make ready your weapons. They won't get away from us now."

A chorus of shouts and howls went up throughout the ranks, but Percilla shook her head and tapped on his shoulder until he faced her again. His gold armor gleamed in the torchlight, and she took a split second to admire the detailing on his chest-piece. It was quite magnificent, but now wasn't a time for admiring armor.

"The door doesn't just lead to the Digs. They just currently happen to be on the other side of it. We use the portal to reach the Eyes of Rou."

The man gave them a suspicious look. "What are they doing with an Eye of Rou?"

Percilla snubbed his remark all together. "Matik, I need the key to Evanstide."

The man stepped between Matik and Percilla. He lowered his head so his narrowed eyes were level with hers. "What are the Digs doing with an Eye of Rou? Answer me."

Percilla threw her hands up in frustration. She didn't have time for his questions; she had too many questions of her own. Where was the next Keeper? Why was she outside of Gangleton? Why was there an army surrounding it?

She stabbed her finger into his breastplate and demanded, "Yeah? And who are you? What do you want with those people anyway? They're not fighters."

"It's not *them* we want." He tilted his head, then subtly nodded. "I am Maz. This is the community of Denton, and we have come for the Digs. You will not stand in our way, and you will tell me why they have an Eye of Rou."

Percilla opened her mouth to reply, but Frida wheeled her way between them. "They don't. They just took a key that leads to a Keeper of an Eye. But they may be able to use it to find the Eye, and we want to stop them."

"Let me get this straight," Maz said. "That portal you all just walked through, that leads to the Keeper of the Eye for...you said Evanstide?"

"Yes, to all of the Keepers."

"Right. And this key..." Maz reached over and snatched the key from Matik. He lunged to get it back, but two men moved in to flank him. Matik muttered under his breath but backed off. Maz continued, "And this key leads to another Eye of Rou?"

"Yes, it does," Matik replied, his jaw clenched. "Look through its end and see for yourself."

Maz turned the key one way, then the other, its light shimmering like a beacon in the night. He peered through the gemstone end and nodded slightly. "If that is true, then the key you used to get here is ours." He closed his hand around the key. "And thanks to you, they can get to us now. Clearly, you three are working with the Digs to stop our attack."

Percilla groaned, ready to tear her hair out. "We are *not* working with the Digs! Those would be the last people we'd team up with. We were sent by Rou to unite the Keepers and call them to arms."

Maz didn't appear convinced. He reached for a large conch shell that hung from a leather strap at his waist. He blew into it, and the deep sound of the horn echoed across the Barrens. The army crowded in, cutting off any chance of escape. Percilla wanted to smack the large man upside the head, but she was fairly certain that would be a terrible idea.

"Please," she tried again. "We have to go back."

Maz snapped his fingers, then a booming, female voice asked people to step aside. A tough woman appeared in the torchlit circle. She slid her goggles atop the green helm covering her long, white braids entwined with metal beads and precious stones. The woman saluted Maz.

"Zimbella, have you seen this door before?" He handed the key to her. She looked through the gemstone end and moved toward the portal.

Zimbella reached for the goggles and pulled them over her eyes. She tapped the metal frame and something mechanical dropped into place. She stared at the front of the door, then scanned from top to bottom and side to side before circling it three times. All the while, she whispered under her breath, but the words were too quiet for Percilla to hear. Zimbella finally shrugged, removing her goggles.

"Never seen the door, but that right there," she said, pointing to a symbol in the upper point of the door and handing the key to Maz to see for himself. "That's Rou's sigil. And this here, this lock and that key are connected by an energy of some sort."

"That's what we've been trying to tell you," Percilla said, exasperated. "We have the keys because we're trying to unite the Keepers. Please, just listen to us. They have a key to the portal, and we need to get it back."

Maz crossed his muscled arms over his burly chest. "You are not from Rou. Where are you from?"

Percilla hesitated. She knew the news would not be received well. "Gangleton."

Maz laughed briefly. "And that just seals the deal, doesn't it? I don't trust anyone from Gangleton."

Frida interrupted. "Can you honestly stand there and tell me you think we work for the Digs?"

"The Evils of this world wear many faces, especially when the Digs are involved."

"You imbecile, don't you see you are confusing yourself with false accusations?" Frida charged at him with her wand raised. "If you weren't one of us, I'd do away with you right this instant. Now, resolve this nonsense before I *make* you resolve it!" She aimed her wand at the sky. A bolt of lightning crashed to the earth behind Maz. Frida stumbled forward and steadied herself against the warrior. "Your idiocy has exhausted me," she said, pushing herself away from him.

The man's brow arched, but he did not seem at all worried about Frida's show of power. "Feisty sorceress. There is a way to ensure you are not possessed by Evils." Maz turned to Zimbella. "Fetch me Filp and Chancy. I think it's time for the test."

"Test? What test?" Percilla glanced around, wondering who Maz summoned now.

Zimbella took off, darting through the crowd of Denton. Neither Filp nor Chancy sounded as if they would be too hard to deal with, but this test had her worried.

Percilla stepped closer to Matik and Frida, whispering, "Do we try to get out of here? We don't have time for this."

Frida patted her on the shoulder. "It's the only way. We need to speak with their keeper. Plus I've always been superlative at tests. This should be good."

There had been several times on this new adventure of theirs that Percilla questioned her great-aunt's sanity. One moment, she was ready to leave by using any magic she could, then the next she was excited for an obstacle. Ultimately, she was right. They needed to unite with the Denton's Keeper, but this blockhead was getting in the way of their entire urgent expedition. Percilla crossed her arms and glowered at Maz. The crowd parted, and a pair of Denton stepped forward.

"About time," Maz said. "We need a scan."

CHAPTER 34

Tenacious Affinity

FRANC STROKED THE blazing green gemstone on her ring. An energetic form leaped out of her like a wild animal, then snapped back into Franc's body. Now powered by a force not of her own, Franc got to her feet. The crabs dissolved into giant drops of water and became puddles around her.

Aurora stood before her throne, generating barriers of the sacred waters rising to protect her. She knew this wicked sorceress would not be able to harm her inside the shield, but for how long was uncertain. One moment of fear from Aurora could destroy her defenses and bring about her own death. She needed more than a barrier to rid her kingdom of the Dignitary.

Franc paced on the other side of the liquid shield, shoving the wet hair from her face and revealing her incandescent eyes. Though blood now streamed from both her forehead and her nose, she had never looked stronger. She stopped pacing and gathered the black shadows around her. A dark fog swarmed over the ground, rising under Franc's control as she lifted her hands. With a flick of Franc's wrists, a crack of green light dispersed like a web inside of the darkness. Demonic shapes twisted and churned around Aurora's shield, slamming into and shaking it.

Aurora recalled the tale of her father's death and was now certain the woman standing before her was the culprit. She closed her eyes, summoning a force deep inside the Earth below her kingdom, a guardian that had long been an ally to her people.

A brilliant flash burst into the room, and Aurora opened her eyes. The energy closed in upon Franc, caging her like the wild beast she was. A phoenix hovered at the peak of the fiery prison.

But Aurora hadn't summoned a phoenix, or so she thought. However, the energy radiating from this mystical being was certainly of Evanstide. Franc rubbed her ring again, but the darkness surrounding her with its malicious flashes was being diminished.

Aurora stepped closer to the dome of flames and held Franc in her regal gaze. "You will leave my kingdom."

Franc's lips curled into the most sadistic of smiles. She fanned out her fingers.

Pain shot into Aurora's back. She turned around to seek the source and was met with the charged, virescent eyes of Pith. He clenched his raised hand, and pain shot up and down her body, making her collapse. The queen looked to the phoenix for help, but she knew in the same moment that the being was already doing all it could just to cage Franc. This battle with Pith was her own. Her trusted advisor was now her adversary, just as her new allies had warned.

Upon the ground but not out of strength, Aurora closed her eyes. She placed her hands flat upon the earth, summoning the Moon goddess Irita and the power of Rou to give her strength. A force spread up through her hands, recharging her body and banishing the pain. Aurora rose to her knees, pulling water through the stone floor to shoot from her hands.

Pith careened back under the force and smacked against a column. Aurora hated to see him in pain, but she knew it wasn't him any longer. She bound him to the stone pillar with enchanted chains made of water. With him neutralized, she could focus on her main threat.

Franc was completely engulfed in the malicious smoke. An instant later, the darkness sucked in on itself and vanished, leaving nothing behind.

The fiery cage disappeared as the phoenix descended. The mystic creature morphed in midair, revealing its true identity, Dazell.

Aurora's heart and spirits were renewed. Finally, someone in her close circle proved to be loyal. The Keeper was someone she could trust and most certainly the best person to unite with against these Evils called the Dignitaries.

CHAPTER 35

Temerarious Empowerment

FRANC ARRIVED TO Dazell's home at the same moment Nylz pulled herself from the portal. The magical gateway swirled in on itself behind Nylz, who gripped a golden key. Halted in the doorway and seething at the sight, the leader of the Dignitaries barked, "Someone tell me what's going on!" Drendle began to open his mouth, but she cut him off. "Not you."

"Nylz pulled the key from the portal that Percilla escaped through," Ons blurted.

"It was Ons's idea that we go against your orders and chase after her," Nylz whined.

Franc ripped the key from Nylz's hands. The yellow gemstone flickered. "Why am I holding a key and not Percilla?"

"They seem to have closed the portal from the other side."

"That still does not explain why I don't see Percilla bound and gagged at my feet."

"She...escaped."

Franc ground her teeth. "How? How did this pitiful little girl escape?"

Green tendrils slipped out of her gemstone ring and slithered all about the key in her hand. The energy on her ring pulsed back to life, and the tendrils slithered back inside. Stashing the key in her breast pocket, Franc spun around and marched out of Dazell's home. The other Dignitaries followed behind, waiting for her command.

"It's time we take control of our new vortex." With a quick whirl of her hand, Franc signaled at them to charge forward.

Nylz was the first to take off after Franc. Lyken squeezed his lanky body onto the chariot with Ons and Drendle. Franc paused long enough to press the buttons on her boots and was lifted from the ground, gliding forward faster and faster.

She reached the monument in no time and looked all about for signs of its readiness. Ons, Lyken, and Drendle arrived on the chariot a moment later.

"I need to use that vortex now! Get it up and running," Franc ordered.

"The monument...is...complex," Ons replied, pressing a series of buttons on his handheld apparatus. "We won't be able to use it for at least another day."

Franc whipped around, pinning him to the spot with a fierce glare. "I do not care what the plans are. Make it work *now*. Monzu will not reinforce us if we don't supply them."

"Franc..." Ons said. "What's that sound?"

Franc craned her neck, listening to the rumbling sound echoing through Evanstide. At first, she swore it was thunder, but there were no storms beneath the sea. When it grew louder, she cursed.

Geysers shot up through the solid earth, forming a dense wall of water. Nylz was thrown to the ground, and the other Dignitaries were now separated by the piping hot water blasting upward, trapping them each in their own cage.

Above the tumult, Aurora walked on a shimmering, fluid pathway, illuminated with an orange aura. She calmly strode into the gathering area, barefoot and possessing an air of confidence Franc had never before witnessed in the young queen. She had donned her ancestral crown, and the gemstones set into it pulsed with the energy of her vortex. Her eyes glowed their natural color of purple, and she was the very image of a queen surrounded by the power of her people. With the barest motion of her hands, she created a pathway for the Dignitaries.

"Leave my kingdom," Aurora commanded, no longer the timid woman weighed down by grief as she had been when the Dignitaries first arrived in her home.

"Your magic is far stronger than I gave you credit for," Franc replied, unfazed. A pulse of energy shot into her being.

Aurora's eyes narrowed. "You've only begun to see my wrath."

"And you mine, sweetheart."

Franc removed her top hat and swept it across the stones in a low bow. The same moment she straightened, the gemstone on her finger glimmered. She thrust her right hand out, and a surge of energy shot from the ring and slammed into Aurora. She sailed back and landed upon the walkway. The geysers continued to reinforce the watery walls all around them, but now Franc had her moment to rise.

A green luster surrounded her, and the energy carried her high above the churning water. Monzu fed her power, protecting her from the heat of the geysers. Franc furiously shoved her soaking wet hair out of her face. When she could finally see clearly, a single wave of her hand forced the geysers caging the Dignitaries down, dismantling the surging traps.

When she realized the queen had disappeared somewhere in the mayhem of the ever-shifting geysers, she roared, "You're going to run away, are you? It won't do you any good!" Franc swooped down to the other cowering Dignitaries. "I want the vortex, and I want it yesterday. Get it up and running, and do it fast, understand?"

The Dignitaries all bowed, then took off at a run toward the octopus contraption, leaving Franc to storm after Aurora.

"Come here, my little queen." She pushed her way through the tumultuous geysers. "Come out and play."

This should have been a day to celebrate a victory for the Dignitaries, and instead she was chasing down a queen who didn't understand when she'd lost. She glared across the drained pools and through the dense, watery walls until she spotted Aurora. Standing in the center of the last pool, her eyes locked on Franc.

The Dignitary approached, cackling. "You do not have the power of the vortex. That is all mine now, thanks to you."

Aurora didn't move an inch, but Franc wasn't going to give her a chance to attack first. She raised her right hand and uttered a hex. A blast of energy struck Aurora, but she held her ground.

Franc's fury amplified, and she shouted the curse a second time, then a third. Each time, Aurora managed to stay on her feet.

The water around the queen's legs swirled and flowed over the stones at its boundary. "This is my kingdom. And this is Evanstide's fury."

A new geyser burst up in front of Aurora, and she manipulated its force, shooting it forward. Franc created a new barrier. It held, but she had to strain to keep it up. She lifted her left hand, and the barrier turned into an orb surrounding and protecting Franc from the angry water ready to destroy her.

Aurora stood atop a shimmering pillar of sacred water, and a crystal egg flashed a blinding light at the Dignitary from within it. The queen raised her hands, and the water concentrated around Franc.

But the Dignitary wasn't giving in, not yet. She dropped her left hand to the ground. The barrier weakened but held long enough for her to summon a dark, malevolent force from beneath her feet. It let out a high-pitched shriek as its monstrous scorpion body emerged. Its electrified green and black form burst through the barrier and penetrated the walls.

Franc snarled, "Our monument, our power. You lose."

Inexplicably, Aurora lowered herself to the ground before the pool and parted the protective barrier of water. The scorpion now had a clear path to her. Franc grinned, ready to watch this troublesome queen meet her end.

The demon scuttled forward, but just as it was about to strike Aurora, she threw her hands forward. What had once been merely water spun, turning into a beam of pure moonlight. It crashed into the demon, shredding it like paper.

Franc's jaw dropped. "You...you can't."

"But I can. You'll remember this day, Franc. You'll remember it for a very long time. Evanstide does not belong to you. It never will."

The ground rumbled, and the largest geyser Franc had ever seen shot out of the pool behind Aurora. As it rose, it coalesced

into the giant, elegant form of the elemental dragon from Evanstide's caverns. Flames churned within its very being, and the dragon loosed a torrent of fire from its maw.

Franc barely got her hand up in time to block the attack. She yelled out a spell, but nothing happened. She checked her ring, and the glow had faded. Her augmented power had finally run out.

Her lip twitched, and as the dragon made ready for a second attack, she snapped her fingers and vanished in a puff of black smoke.

CHAPTER 36

Fires of Freedom

THE FLAMING TORCHES of the Denton warriors parted, making way for the two men offering the test. The first man sputtered like an idle engine as he entered the circle, riveted by the fire he held. He appeared to be made of solid muscle. His braids were haphazardly tied back with a wild assortment of beads, shells, and metal woven into them, lending his counterpart the air of a perfectly manicured garden by contrast. The second appeared astute and hardly made any gesture or sound at all. He gently placed his monocle inside of one of the many pouches on his bandolier. Nothing about him was out of place, not even a single curl. He bowed and nudged the zealous man beside him, who beamed with fervor and jabbered to the flames like they were alive.

"If that is what you wish, then a scan you shall have," the poised man said to his commander. He beckoned to the wild man. "Come, Chancy, bring the fire, but don't light it yet."

"Fire," Chancy murmured. "The fire is ready to test them." He shoved two stones into his mouth and shuffled them around with his tongue.

"Excuse me, what?" Percilla grabbed hold of Matik's arm. "What does he mean?"

Instead of answering, Filp flicked his palm to the crowd, and they backed away. He opened one of the pouches at the center of the bandolier and grabbed a handful of some sort of black powder. He walked in a circle around Percilla and her companions, sprinkling it on the ground. Then, he crouched low and dug symbols into the dirt with a knife. Each one glowed a subtle yellow. As he completed the last one and stepped back, he nodded to Chancy.

"Now, if you please."

Chancy squatted, put the torch in front of his mouth, and blew. Fire spewed from his mouth, and he never paused for breath as he raced around the circle seven times. The powder ignited, and the yellow symbols disappeared into towering walls of fire. If Percilla and her friends weren't trapped before, they were now. The flames were warm but, confusingly, not uncomfortably hot.

Maz was visible through the shifting flames. He watched them closely, then he spread his arms wide. "Who's first to walk?"

"You want us to walk through the fire?" Matik asked.

Maz bowed. "Yes, that is the test."

"To walk through fire? What good will that do?" Percilla demanded.

"The flames will check you for Evils. If you are free of them, then you will be unharmed. If you are possessed by the Digs, the fire will know, and you will no longer be our problem." Maz waved to the flames impatiently. "Now, if you please. You can't stay in there forever."

Percilla couldn't believe this was happening, especially on the borders of Gangleton. A strange pang of homesickness hit her. She'd never believed she would miss a place ruled by the Digs, but in truth, part of her just wanted to go home and forget all about her grand mission.

Matik and Frida each took a hand, reminding her of their collective strength and togetherness. The world needed their help. This was her task, and as a team they would see it through.

"Right, through the fire," Percilla mused. Tibs flew in front of her face, then buzzed through the fire. From the other side of the wispy flames, a little twinkle of light met Percilla's gaze. "Does that mean she is safe?"

Frida lifted their clasped hands. "Together. Think of Rou, and you'll be fine." She winked.

Percilla squeezed Frida's and Matik's hands and set them in motion. The three stepped toward the flames, which licked at their skin, but there was no pain. Their clothes didn't catch fire. The heat was intense, but they came out the other side unscathed. Percilla let out a heavy sigh of relief. The symbols from Valti glowed on the foreheads of her allies, reminding her of the protection offered by Rou.

Filp hurried forward and held up a single, small lens to his eye. He searched them from head to toe, then finally straightened and turned to Maz. "They're clear. No Evils here. These sigils are of Rou," he said, tapping Percilla's forehead with his finger. Chancy raced around the circle, stomping out the flames with his heavy, leather boots.

Maz seemed relieved by the pronouncement, and he let his arms fall to his sides. "Thank you. You may return to the others now."

Filp and Chancy bowed and stepped back into the throng of their people. Chancy blew into the torch in his hand, and the flames formed a symbol of Rou. The pair disappeared into the sea of cheering warriors.

Maz rubbed his hands down the front of his armor, then rested them on his hips and stared at the three travelers. "I am sorry for the test, but we had to be certain. We've faced many dark days out here in the Barrens. I will not risk my people."

"We understand," Frida said with a soft smile. "We, too, have seen immense darkness since we started our quest."

"I'm still not certain that *I* understand. Who are you people? And what is your connection to Rou?"

Percilla cleared her throat. "We were sent by Rou to unite all the Keepers. That's how we found you, and that's why we must recover your key and save you."

Maz tilted his head as his eyes narrowed. "Save us? We have never feared the Digs."

"And you never should, but this is bad. They'll be able to find you now, or, even worse, they may be able to find Rou."

Maz went still and held up his hand to silence her. "Hold on, there's a message coming through."

Percilla wasn't sure to whom he was speaking but simply watched him nod slowly.

"If that's what you want," he said and waited a beat. "Very well, then."

Maz reached to the engraved metal disc covering his solar plexus. He rotated it, then removed it completely from his breastplate, revealing a brilliant glow.

Percilla and her friends stumbled away from the blinding light. When it receded enough that Percilla could open her eyes, her jaw dropped at the sight before her. Inside of Maz's armor was a miniature woman, a warrior much like the other Denton but with a royal appearance unlike any of them.

The lady leveled her regal gaze at Percilla from inside the breastplate. In every way, she was the divine feminine complement to Maz's robust masculinity. Under her golden armor, soft, white leather and silk covered her muscled form. She was powerful yet serene as she regarded those before her throne. A pair of white lions lay attentively beside her throne. The woman placed her hand atop the male lion's head, silencing her roaring guardian. He responded with a gentle nuzzle.

The divine warrior stood from her throne, her body surrounded by a radiant halo of purity. For an instant, she dissolved into the aura before growing into a full-sized woman. She smiled at Percilla and spoke in a mesmerizing voice tinged with power. "Blessings. It's an honor to be visited. I am Inanna, Keeper of the Eye of the Denton people, Priestess to the planet Mars."

Frida bowed, and Percilla and Matik followed her lead. "The honor is all ours," Frida replied.

Percilla wanted to fall over in relief that they'd found her. "You know what to do when the color hits the sky?"

Inanna's smile faded. "We open the Eye, upholding our solemn vow to offer our vortex to Mars. Time must be reset. I can't say we didn't see this coming. Too many people have fallen to Evils. And as the planets align to where Time begins, we will pray to unite with you once again under better circumstances."

Percilla's heart sank at her words, and tears began to fill her eyes.

"Child, we will be safe. Mars will provide protection inside the safety of the caverns. We will meet you inside the Earth." Inanna touched the Rou symbol on Percilla's forehead. A calm spread throughout her mind.

"I'm so sorry that we were unable to protect the key that leads to you."

"As are we for interfering in your doing so." Inanna turned a stern gaze to Maz before continuing. "It is my sworn purpose to protect our Eye. But Franc and the other Dignitaries have great Evils inside of them. They are an enemy of the people of Rou, and you cannot let your guilt weigh you down. Instead, you must keep moving forward, and we must lock that door eternally or face dire consequences."

"We can't!" Percilla yelped, louder than she should have, but she was at her wit's end. "That door is our only way to find the other Keepers. We have vowed to unite them, and we need that door to do it."

"We must close it. I am sorry. The Dignitaries mustn't have access to that portal."

"But what if they find a way to use the key to find Rou?"

Inanna smiled. "Rou cannot be entered by Evils. Even if they tried to get in, only their purest form would enter."

Matik stepped forward eagerly. "Then let them in. It'll end them for good."

"Sadly, that is not our choice to make. We can only live out our purpose."

Percilla fell to her knees before the Keeper. She reached for the woman, and Inanna held her hands firmly in hers. "And mine is to unite all the Keepers. To do that, we need the door. Please, I don't want to fail. We can't fulfill our mission without that door."

"Percilla." Inanna sighed and pulled the young woman back to her feet. "You don't need the door. We can help you. Trust me."

"How?"

Inanna glanced to the sky. "You'll see soon enough."

Maz removed a spyglass from his chariot and handed it to Matik. "Take a look."

Matik scoured the sky. "What am I looking for?" he asked, then froze. Percilla worried it was the Digs or some worse storm of Evils coming to hurt them. Then, Matik let out a whoop of excitement and grinned from ear to ear. "Panya and Dawookrunk!"

Matik handed her the spyglass, and sure enough, there in the sky was the ornate and colorful array of airships headed straight for them. Just beyond the ships, circus tents she would know anywhere followed. She lowered the spyglass and handed it back to Matik, who put it right back to his eye.

"We travel together," Inanna told her. "As I said, we can help you."

Maz's eyes took on a faraway look, as if he was remembering something he'd rather forget. "We burn the Digs down; it's what we've been doing for years. Panya builds and plants, then Dawookrunk brings in the lost people to start a community. One free of the Digs' influence and Evils."

"That's incredible," Frida said in awe.

"It's our way of keeping the Digs in line. Chase, destroy, burn, and plant our villages in their place."

"You abandoned your vortex?"

Maz laughed, spreading his arms wide to take in the collective of warriors surrounding them. "Do you see our power? We use it all right."

"Secret to all," Inanna chimed in. "I knew the Evils would come eventually, so we never built our village atop the vortex.

We built it close enough to remain connected, but far enough never to reveal it."

Maz's voice became wistful. "Our city was the greatest sight to behold, powerful beyond belief. Right inside the stone arches of Mars, our hand-carved buildings spiraled around the innermost plaza. The fountain at its very center held the most pristine waters charged with the citrine from our vortex. Every night as a tribe we gathered there to hold bonfires and celebrate." He paused for a moment, his eyes closed in remembrance.

Frida's brow furrowed. Looking to Matik and Percilla, she said, "That was your village? We received an omen from Vincent there, but the whole area...it looked like it had been attacked. Burned to the ground."

"It was." Maz rubbed a hand down his chest, suddenly exhausted. "I'm sure you've heard this story. The same tragic story retold in numerous ways. We were accused of stealing Gangleton's Eye. They said we were a danger, the Digs, and threatened war."

"Is that why you became nomadic?" Percilla asked.

His face darkened. "In a roundabout way, yes. We thrived for as long as we could until the Digs came and threatened our way of life, threatened everything we had."

Percilla could tell he was no longer seeing them or his people. He was reliving the very words he spoke to them.

"What happened?"

"They came to us, called a meeting. Tried to drive us to fear like so many others. Thing is, I don't believe in fear. None of us do. It's not our way. We left them in the plaza, then we set the place on fire." His darkened gaze latched onto Percilla's as he added, "I don't like threats. Unfortunately, they escaped the fire. But we'd already gathered our chariots and our rams, more than ready for a fight. Like true cowards, they fled in that elephant contraption of theirs while our home burned to nothing but ash and charred stone."

"You burnt your own village," Percilla whispered.

Inanna went to Maz and caressed the back of his head. "It was us or them."

"Freedom is more important than fear. They would have come back, no doubt with more Evils, and we needed to show them that we, the people, have the power." Maz slowly took Inanna's hand.

"I'm humbled by your bravery. Your story is my favorite yet," Frida told them. "If only everyone could be as brave as you are."

"I don't want to ask you to return to a place of so much pain," Percilla said. "But seeing as Rou is calling on the Keepers to do their duty..."

"There is no pain, only memories," Inanna said when Percilla couldn't find the words. "It's time we go to the land of our vortex and make our real home."

"Home?" Maz asked.

Inanna nodded. "The time has come, Maz. We must prepare for the new life of our people and whatever else might come our way."

Illusion of Power

ONS WAS RARELY a mess or disorderly; just the sight of him so out of sorts made Drendle sink into his seat. Watching Ons wheeze while he frantically turned dials had Drendle humming to block out the chaos. Franc's demand was certainly outrageous, but no one wanted to tell her no. Drendle was trying to shake the idea of Franc's terrifying wrath from his mind when Ons yelled to him, gasping for air in between words.

"Drendle...are you...going to start this 'pus...or am I going to...have to do this...all myself?" He shook so much he had to lean against the wall.

Drendle spun his chair around to face the control panel. He flicked a series of switches, spun a dial, and pushed the glowing button, then pulled down a ring hanging from the ceiling. The engines ignited and pistons churned, illuminating the interior. The urge to put this 'pus in drive and get as far from Franc and Evanstide as possible nearly had him doing just that, but it was impossible. She would find him, and the other Dignitaries would certainly put him in some sort of violent captivity. No, it was best to just abide by the orders of Franc, for she was the one with the real plan. Drendle paused for a moment, face scrunched in fear as he wondered if she or any of the others could hear his thoughts. He turned toward his fellow Dignitaries to be certain.

Ons had rendered the monument and the vortex below it into a hologram. Its control panel was also a projection directly next to it. Nothing seemed too impressive when it came to the levels of energy the monument was channeling. From what Drendle could tell, the vortex was fully activated, but not even a tiny amount of that energy was being harnessed by the monument.

Ons handed Nylz two cone-shaped mechanisms while Lyken held a quartz pyramid. Had Ons found a way to make the vortex work, or was it on the verge of killing everyone? By the looks of the sweat dripping down his face and his panicked wheezing, the inventor was sure they were all going to die.

Drendle sank back into his chair, then spun around to the control panel to stroke the buttons, probably for the last time. The sound of Franc's voice snapped him to attention. He rotated right into the last wisps of black smoke that accompanied her return. A furious, red-faced Franc stood before him, brushing what looked like ash from her shoulders. Her top hat held in her other hand showcased melted blobs of metal instead of pins. She muttered under her breath until her head shot up, and she glared at the Dignitaries who stifled any maneuvers at her arrival.

"What are you all waiting for?" She placed her damaged top hat back on her head. "Drendle, get us out of here!"

Caught off-guard, yet relieved to hear the order, Drendle's word shot from his mouth without thought. "Now?"

Franc's fury slammed into him like a punch in the gut. "Yes, now," she seethed, then shouted at the top of her lungs. "Now! Now! Must I always say 'now' to get you moving? *Now*, Drendle, before I throw you out of this contraption and let the dragon eat you."

He fumbled over the controls. "Dragon?"

"Now!" Franc slammed her hand to the back of his neck, pressing his face flat upon the window and holding him there. "You see that massive, watery beast charging right for us? Tell me, Drendle, would you like to be swallowed whole today? Or burnt to a crisp? Because that can be arranged."

Though he whined and tried to push away, she held him in place, forcing him to witness the twisting and turning shape of a dragon completely formed of water. It stormed down the street right for them, leaving puddles in its wake. Wings of shimmering mist spread from its back, and it threw its head into the air as fire spewed from its powerful jaws, fire that Drendle could easily imagine burning him down to the bones. He was not going to die in Evanstide, be it in a torrent of vortex energy, at the hands of Franc, or in a pillar of fire.

Franc removed her hold on the back of his neck, and Drendle went right to work. Franc stood beside him, her attention fixed on the beast charging through the streets. She slammed her hands down on the screen next to the control panel, which slowly pulsed with a blue light. The Monzu ring on her finger looked duller than usual, and nothing happened when she furiously rubbed it. They had so little power now, Drendle had no idea if they would even be able to leave. The icy tendrils of utter fear crept up his spine.

"Everyone, take your stations," Franc commanded. The octopus rose on its eight legs. "We are under attack, and I will not be brought down by this pathetic queen and her pet."

Ons pounded the buttons on the control panel a bit harder than was necessary. Drendle cranked the gears, and the octopus rushed through the gates of Evanstide. Nylz reached the telescopic apparatus she used for navigation and flicked a switch. A giant circle shone upon the magically sealed dome.

"Charge!" Franc shouted.

Smoke and steam billowed out of the contraption as it picked up speed. They pushed through the dome and into the water surrounding it.

Drendle let out a quiet breath of relief.

The feeling only lasted until the dragon tucked its wings against its back and dove right through the force field to follow them.

"Faster," Franc muttered, then her voice echoed off the metal hull. "We have to go faster! Move it!"

A bubbling undercurrent exploded to their right, rocking the contraption. Drendle gripped the steering mechanism tighter as a second explosion burst overhead. He tried to look behind him, but all he managed to see was Franc's face set in a furious scowl. He whipped around and pulled back on the controls to send them into a steep ascent. When they broke free of the surface, they caused a tidal wave across the sea, and the dragon followed them into the air.

Franc stomped toward the porthole windows. The dragon let loose a fireball, and the surface of the sea roiled. Its misty wings spread wide as it soared after them. It circled once, then held its position and took aim.

"Brace yourselves!" Franc yelled.

The force of the blast rocked the octopus and nearly sent it tumbling out of the sky. Drendle and Lyken worked to steady the hulking metal beast, and then they were soaring away. The dragon did not follow.

After a deep, relieved breath, Drendle glanced over his shoulder. "Where to?"

"Where do you think?" Franc uttered darkly. "Gangleton."

CHAPTER 38

Prideful Bargains

ONS DABBED HIS forehead with a hanky and downed a concoction to open his bronchi. Breathing in a full breath, he turned to the window. The golden aura of Gangleton's dome now softly beckoned them home, setting him at ease. The long, frantic night was coming to an end. Soon, more energy would be powering their engines, and their connection to Monzu would be renewed. Right beyond Gangleton, however, another light source blazed—the fires of Denton.

Franc craned her neck to take in the whole scene. "Prepare to attack!" she screeched. Her eyes set aflame, she faced the Dignitaries.

Drendle piped up from behind her. "We don't have enough power."

By the look of Franc's clenched fists and furious gaze, Ons knew this would now be his problem. Franc turned her attention to Nylz and Lyken, and Ons searched his database for a way to give them power.

"I could take the pterodactyl to Gangleton and get us more energy," he proposed.

"Brilliant. I want Gangleton to ooze fear into our engines," Franc said. "Nylz, Lyken, get moving!"

The two Dignitaries had scurried up the ladder leading to the flying contraption by the time Franc finished her command. Ons envied them in that moment, perhaps the only time he ever would. They'd be out of the range of Franc's fury.

The gauges that measured energy levels were low, very low. Next to that, the screen and its usual pulsing green light was still blank. Ons watched the pterodactyl whiz across the sky toward Gangleton. He took a deep breath, readying himself for the furious woman now storming toward him.

"We need more power," Franc snarled, touching the lifeless screen. "Why have they abandoned us?"

"You used it. Remember? Monzu only offers assistance if we provide." Ons peered at her with his peripheral vision so he could continue working. She needed to realize this wasn't his fault, after all. He was the savior here, working tirelessly so she could battle whomever she pleased.

"Are you saying *I* pushed them away?"

"Is that what *you're* saying?" Ons retorted.

Franc snapped her fingers and set a fire inside her palm. It caught Ons's attention, his pupils widening as it ensnared him. Before it went any further, he clicked two lenses directly in front of his eyes to block out Franc's silent magic as if to say, *Don't even think about it.*

"Do not give me excuses." She dug into the pocket of her coat and pulled out the gemstone key with the symbol of Rou on it. "Try this."

Ons snatched the key from her palm. Spinning it in his fingertips and peering through the yellow stone, he concluded, "The gemstone is sanctified by Rou, so that's worthless. But the gold. That'll bring support."

Franc's glare turned into a slight smile, then she retrieved a golden egg from her holster and tossed it to Ons. "Don't let me down." She patted his back, her confidence restored. Franc strode to her post in the center of the room.

Drendle called over his shoulder. "Um, Franc, you want me to take another route?"

"Why?"

"You might just want to come see for yourself."

"What scares you now, Drendle?" She snatched the spyglass from him. Franc must not have liked what she saw because she began doing her usual array of angry movements—fingers coiling, body swaying, and then, the final two-foot, sturdy stomp. This wasn't good.

"Percilla is with the Denton! Attack!"

"No!" Ons yelled. "I'm still connecting."

"We need to end this. They will not delay our advances ever again."

"Why don't we wait for Nylz and Lyken?" Drendle suggested. "They've just arrived."

Ons nodded along with his words. "We need to fill our reserves."

Franc silently looked upon each of them, then back toward the window. "We don't have time. We need to attack before they do. I will not be knocked out of the sky by those barbarians." She squinted through the spyglass.

Ons wondered what sort of magic Percilla must be using. What sort of portal had they gone through with this key? What did it all mean? And what was she doing with the Denton? In front of him, the golden egg and key from Rou slowly dissolved into particles, and with the touch of a button, the particles disappeared. The screen came to life and pulsed with faint green light, illuminating his face. "We have power. Not much, but enough for now."

Metia slammed her hands over her ears to stifle the blaring bells from the Cuckoo Clock Tower. A flying contraption zoomed toward the village center, its lights flashing across the sky.

"Things must be getting worse out there!" Dant struggled to stand without taking his hands away from his head.

"How can they get any worse? We just had an army of fire warriors breathing down our dome." Metia looked out into the empty lands. "The Digs need to stay away. Those people are probably after them."

Sphan stood next to Dant. "None of this makes sense. Nobody in Gangleton ever leaves besides the Digs, so why threaten us?"

Lyken's voice blasted from the loud speakers of the contraption hovering before the Tower. "People of Gangleton, we have come to warn you! The enemy has located the secret entrance to our village. We are doing all we can to stop them from killing every last one of you. Please, stay in your homes until we come with news." At his last words, the alarms grew louder and sirens rang across the dome. If the people weren't scared stiff in their homes already, they were now.

"Secret entrance?" Gahil shouted as he finally stood from his deep meditation. "Do you think that's how Percilla escaped?"

Sphan waved everyone in. The group circled up shoulder to shoulder to hear him out. "We need a plan. These Digs are clearly doing something that is putting all of us in danger."

CHAPTER 39

Eternally Bound

ENTON'S FIRES EXPLODED into the air, commemo-
rating the communion with their new companions. Maz
stepped onto his chariot and held up his hands. All fell silent.
"The time has come, my family. We have done our part to unite
many lost souls and destroyed the attempts by the Digs to
build communities of fear. It has been a long journey since we
burned our village in the name of freedom."

The Denton let out howls and hollers. They waved their
torches, and the bonfires danced with the same excitement of
the people.

Maz smiled broadly and lifted his voice to be heard above
their boisterous noise. "Now, however, we must protect our
vortex. Create a new home. The time for the end draws near,
and if we are to survive, if we are to win out the day, we must
do this and with all our might protect what is rightfully ours.

We must keep it from the Dignitaries and their Evils!" The howling grew louder. "Together we are strong, and together we will thrive!"

Percilla and Matik exchanged a look of utter amazement to hear so many voices raised as one. She had never seen so many people united in their true strength and devoted to one cause for the greater good. It wasn't like Gangleton, where people were devoted to the Dignitaries and lived in fear of losing their protection, even though it wasn't true. None of it had ever been true.

But just as the thought raced through her mind, the familiar figure of Zimbella burst through the tribe. She sprinted up to Maz and pointed to the sky. "We have company and not the good kind."

Everyone turned to scan the sky. The octopus contraption of the Digs soared toward them from the opposite direction of their allies. Percilla slipped her hand into Matik's, and he squeezed it. They were never going to be rid of them. Not until they managed to do as the Sages of Rou told them and unite the Keepers.

"It looks like they finally want war." Maz rolled his shoulders and nodded firmly. "Then let us give them war." He raised the conch and blew two short bursts followed by a long one.

In seconds, the chaotic atmosphere of the Denton became orderly as they rushed to form ranks and fell back into lines. Those commanding the chariots grabbed the reins and directed the rams to the front. Weapons were drawn, fires were stoked, and soon Percilla, Matik, and Frida were left standing alone beside Inanna and Maz. Percilla locked eyes with the Keeper, then she bowed her head.

"I'm sorry." Inanna stepped forward. "But I must lock the door. Go to Panya; they will help you."

"I understand." Percilla started to turn away when the priestess rushed forward and wrapped her in a tight embrace. Warmth and hope flooded Percilla, and she hugged the woman back. "Thank you."

"We send you with our blessings. Blessings to all of you."

Inanna released Percilla, then hurried toward the door. She lifted her hands and shut her eyes. Gold light broke free of her aura and floated toward the portal, solidifying into a golden chain. It wrapped itself tightly around the door, binding it forever. As the final link fell into place, it shone vibrantly in the night, then faded. Inanna lowered her hands and gave Percilla one more encouraging smile before her aura obscured her. The light condensed into an orb and zoomed back into Maz's breastplate.

He replaced the disc and faced the others. "Either you all are going to stay and fight, or you have to leave. This is war."

Frida's hand fell on Percilla's shoulder. "You have our blessings."

"Please, keep Inanna safe," Percilla said.

Maz bowed and rested his hand on the disc. "With my life. Good luck to you on your quest. I hope we meet again."

The leader of the Denton stood tall upon his chariot. He picked up the reins in one hand, steadying the rams eager to join their brethren. He raised the conch horn to his lips and

let out a fierce bellow that echoed across the Barrens and resonated deep within Percilla's core.

"We have to go," Frida urged. She dug into her bag
and tossed them each a vial. "Drink this."

"I'm not taking another one of your concoctions,
Frida," Matik said, eyeing the vial suspiciously.

"There's no time to argue." Frida downed her potion.
Just as she removed the vial from her lips, she levitated
into the air. Frida impatiently called down to them,
"Come on you two!"

Percilla looked toward the vibrantly illuminated
airships in the distance and nodded to Matik, knowing
whatever her great-aunt had in mind would certainly help
them. Together, they drank their potions and rose alongside
Frida. The wise sorceress smiled and took their hands, and they
soared into the sky.

They zipped away from the Denton and the approaching
Dignitaries. Percilla glanced back, longing to witness what
would be an amazing sight, but knowing full well it was nothing
she wanted to be a part of.

Percilla could now see Dawookrunk on the ground beyond
Panya even without the aid of a spyglass. Frida's potion had
them gaining fast when a violent flash of lightning struck right
before them. The shockwave crashed into them with a force that
stunned Percilla and sent them all careening to the ground.
The earth began to rumble, shaking violently and disorienting
them even further. Percilla sat up, pain throbbing throughout
her body. Her head was spinning, and dust blurred her vision.

Matik was already running toward her. The ground between them thrust open, throwing him back. At that same instant, a green dome coalesced all around them. Black fumes seeped up from its depths, then shot through the bedrock, shattering its surface like glass.

A malefic bolt struck Matik in the back, bulldozing him flat to the ground. He scrambled to get to his feet, but he fell time and time again.

Percilla held her hands together and concentrated. A white haze spread before her to form a pathway. The shadow demons swarmed to fill the area under the dome and soon had swallowed the meager light. The darkness was so stifling that Percilla couldn't see anything, but she felt the tiny legs of Tibs landing on her nose. When the bee took off, Percilla followed her twinkling companion and charged into the void with all her might.

Lightning crackled throughout the black brume as it began to churn with life. The sand-loaded winds whipped Percilla. She hunched herself into a ball to protect her face from being thrashed. Fear seeped into her mind, chasing away her brief moment of focus. She felt helpless and pulled herself into a tighter ball.

"Please, Rou, help me. Rou, please, somebody help me."

Squirming her way through Percilla's cover, Tibs buzzed on the young woman's forehead. The sensation sent a gentle vibration inside Percilla's head that rippled throughout her brain, clearing her mind the longer the bee buzzed between her brows.

Percilla opened her eyes. "Thank you, Tibs. Thank you, Rou," she whispered, then recited a spell. A light reappeared inside her clasped hands. She stretched them out in front of her and spread the light over her body from head to toe. Lifting her head slowly, she was relieved to see the white merkaba structure forming around her.

With the spell in place, Percilla could see through the blackness to locate her companions. She spotted Frida hovering in the air with her palms open and casting a vibrant light through the darkness. When Frida caught a glimpse of Percilla, she flew down to her. Another lightning bolt crashed between them, sending Frida flying back to slam against the wall of the electrified dome. She fell to the ground and limply lay there. Percilla yelled out to her, but if Frida heard her, she didn't respond. She had to save her, but what about Matik? Where was he? She looked all around again for the warrior and found him by chance when the wicked creature perching over him moved its head at the sensation of her light.

Percilla reached inside her jacket for the Eye of Rou, the only thing she knew could stop Evils. She cast its brilliant light into the face of the entity, and it burst into nothingness. Percilla hid the Eye safely inside her jacket as she raced over to Matik, but something wrapped painfully tight around her arms, yanking her down to the ground. Her limbs were bound, and her body was surrounded by black snakes made of smoke. They hissed and coiled around her legs, dragging her to the edge of the cracked land.

This was it. They'd lost. Percilla had nothing else to give, no more magic to save them.

As she gave in to despair, a crimson cobra slithered up from the earth, breaking the infernal snakes' hold. The shriek of a train whistle pierced the sounds of chaos. A red light burst through the darkness, and white, billowing steam stood as a mystical beacon of hope breaking through the Evils. Another whistle reverberated through the area, cracking the diabolical shell surrounding them.

With all sounds but murmurs in her ears, a red light surrounded Percilla. She floated upward, and her energy slowly returned. Frida and Matik were also being lifted by a force on either side of her. San and the Hazan stood around the trio, offering their prayers as they performed a ritual to aid them. The rhino engine of the Wonkt Train roared to a halt. Inside a glass dome atop the train, Deena furiously pulled a lever to release another burst of sound.

She spoke into a mic next to her, and her voice projected out into the Barrens. "Best y'all get outta here. Blessed ventures. Go to Panya."

Percilla felt alive again. She looked at Matik and Frida, and she breathed a sigh of relief to see them flying toward her. Frida's lips were moving, then something touched Percilla's back and fitted itself to her. She glanced over her shoulder to see a set of wings fluttering to get her out of harm's way. Matik and Frida also soared through the sky on their own sets of wings.

Matik's relieved expression fell. "Beneath you!"

Percilla had just enough time to scream when the clawed hand of a monstrous beast lunged out of the abyss. It caught her by the foot and cast its infernal energy around her. A stinging sensation paralyzed her body. Her eyes filled with a haze, and she could only see the fuming maw nearing her. A burst of red blasted through the demon from below, then there was nothing but space.

Her head drooped. Her whole being felt limp and numb, as if her inner light were nothing more than a tenuous spark clinging to life. Then, a warm embrace she would know anywhere wrapped around her.

"I've got you," Matik said, gripping her firmly. "I've got you. You're safe."

Percilla clung to him, her greatest warrior.

CHAPTER 40

End of Times

MAZ BLEW INTO his conch shell, igniting the spirit of the Denton as they blasted fire into the air. Watching his new companions escape safely made him proud of the loyal people of Rou.

Flashes of crimson light came from the ground before him. Out of the numerous runes, cobras rose and morphed into the Hazan. San stepped up to Maz.

"You did well, Brother," Maz said as he hugged the chieftain.

"Thank you. It wasn't all us, though."

The Wonkt Train howled its way toward them. It flew across the Barrens in a churning mass of white light and steam, nearing within seconds. As the train circled the tribes, it left a trail of luminous, violet runes behind it.

Deena popped up in the glass dome, waving. "Blessed be, everyone. Hate to spoil y'all's reunion, but we gotta move fast." She pointed at the octopus contraption charging forward with an accretion of malevolence surrounding it.

Lightning cracked through the darkness, and the metal beast ramped up its speed. The Denton stood in several circles, their edges marked with mystic symbols carved into the earth. The ground pulsed with Denton magic, enhanced by the Wonkt community.

San signaled for his people to begin a new ritual. The earth below them ignited with their energized, scarlet glyphs. The frequency of the three communities aligning together emitted a powerful shockwave that extended all around them. They created a new force of life, nothing Maz had experienced before. The energy of a thousand people thrumming together made his body, mind, and spirit feel more alive than ever.

Maz jumped onto his chariot and snatched a burning torch from its rest. He held it up and roared through the entire Denton community. They all extended their torches as he passed, readying their breath. Tempestuous winds surged around them. Darkness fell.

The Wonkt Train chugged around the gathering, and the white smoke billowed from its exhaust, clearing the gloom. The sacred glyphs below the train beamed violet brilliance high up into the sky, forcing the demons that were formed of shadow to recoil.

The Dignitaries barreled toward the Rou communities. A thundering stampede of malicious creatures extended from their contraption. A wail pierced the air.

San and his people lifted their chests skyward. The crimson light of Hazan flashed up against the force pressing down like a weight upon them. The beam crashed into the hex hovering above them and held there for a moment. San waved his staff over the earth, carving runes into it.

The land rumbled. An elemental garnet dragon burst out of the earth. The majestic creature soared through the siege, splitting it in two and casting a blaze of red across the sky. The shrill tone ceased as the Hazan dragon broke through the barrier of Evils above them.

The Dignitaries were now within range, and Maz let his hand fall.

The yellow symbols of Denton came to life as fire breathers set them alight. Each circle created a bonfire that stretched into the sky. The flames twisted into the air until one massive orb of fire hovered over the Denton. It expanded and took shape. The thunderous roar of a dragon made of flame boomed across the empty lands of the Barrens. It reared, spreading its blazing wings inside the fire. The dragon grew to its full size, covering the entire community that it had taken to form it. Maz blew into his conch shell, and the mystical creature shot toward the metal octopus.

"Just hold still," Maz whispered.

The blazing dragon unleashed its wrath. The octopus was consumed by the inferno, turning its hull alight before

it vanished within the flames. The dragon held the octopus captive, and with the help of his spyglass, Maz saw the contraption smoldering and the shield around it melting.

When he shifted his gaze to the remaining malevolence ahead, the plumes of black churned forward to form a mighty beast. The scorpion's eyes were teeming with the malice of

Monzu. It heaved its stinger high into the air and raged into the gathering of tribes.

Maz charged through the Denton, the blare of his conch alerting them to take a defensive formation. The tribe moved to encircle the Hazan and protect them from the ensuing Evils. The beast plunged its stinger into their ranks, but not fast enough to hit the Hazan as they shifted into their cobra bodies. The Wonkt Train howled louder, infuriating the demon and overwhelming it with magical plumes of smoke and driving it straight into the center of the collective. The Hazan fanned out to join the Denton in their three-ring formation around the thrashing creature. The cobras morphed back into humans, and each tribe performed their respective rituals.

Crimson, yellow, and violet forces swirled together as they shot at the scorpion, piercing it with a magnitude of power beyond what Monzu possessed. The entire area was set ablaze, and the demon burst into nothing.

Maz shifted his attention back at the sky. The octopus remained intact but was falling fast, a billow of smoke trailing behind it. Though it headed for Gangleton, Maz doubted they would make it that far. As much as he wanted to go after them and ensure their demise, the quiet voice of Inanna whispered through his mind.

Their time will come. For now, we have work to do. They have been wounded. Let that be enough. Guide our people home.

He placed his hand on his breastplate. "As you wish."

Maz blew into his conch, eliciting celebratory cries from the gathered tribes. The Wonkt Train howled, and white smoke billowed out into the land, cleansing the area of any last Evils. Spirited music erupted from the Wonkt exiting the train to offer refreshments to the Hazan and Denton. San bowed his head to Maz and together they thrummed their chest. Deena hollered along, joyfully offering them both a sparkling, purple concoction.

"Blessed be, fellas, blessed be. Can ya give a lady a boost?" She grinned. San and Maz lifted her to their shoulders. "Blessed be!" she hollered over the joyous voices, calling their attention. "May y'all remember today as the end of times and the beginning of times. Today, by our duty and honor to Rou, to our tribes, to our freedom, we aligned as many in body, and as one in mind. We defeated Monzu and the Digs. Blessed be Rou. Blessed be the Reckless united." She lifted her glass to the crowd. Together, they all lifted their glasses and united their voices.

"Blessed be Rou. Blessed be the Reckless united!" they said with one breath, then downed the sparkling concoction.

Deena jumped down to face them, and Maz smiled at the other leaders. "Denton will be heading back to our vortex. Percilla, the Keeper of Gangleton's Eye has spoken. The time has come to unite."

"The omen has come to Hazan as well, and we are prepared."

"Well, fellas, ya'll better get on along then. We'll be doing as we've always done till the Nevuk vortex calls us home."

San bowed to both of them, then he waved his staff in the air. The people of Hazan morphed into cobras and vanished into the crimson glyphs on the ground.

Maz squeezed Deena in his arms, then blew into his conch shell and mounted his chariot. "We will not be chasing the Digs any longer, but know we have wounded them severely this day. Please, do not let your spirits fall. We...we are going home."

Dead silence met his words, then one after the other, the Denton shouted in triumph. They spit fire into the sky and turned toward a home they had been away from for far too long. Maz threw his head back and spit fire into the sky with them, venting his frustration and celebrating their return. One day soon, the Digs would get what was coming to them.

Maz just had to be patient and hope they had enough time.

CHAPTER 41

Forgiven Treachery

EVANSTIDE'S DRAGON FLEW over the kingdom, blessing the people with shimmering droplets of sacred waters. Aurora stretched her arms up to the dragon and knew the Evils would finally be expelled from within their dome. She no longer had to worry about the Dignitaries' devious maneuvers to take over.

That thought was cut short when Pith appeared from behind the monument, his eyes still alight with malicious intent. After what he'd done to her, she should banish him from Evanstide. But in looking at him, she felt sorry for her dear friend and advisor. He had been deceived just like her, just like Vahn, just like everyone in her kingdom, and he deserved to be saved. There was much cleaning up to do to purify their home. The megalithic blemish upon her beautiful city still needed to be destroyed.

"You've done well, my queen," Dazell called out behind her.

Aurora turned to the sorceress with a smile. "I'm afraid we aren't fully rid of the Evils yet." Her shifting glance directed Dazell to Pith.

"My goodness, poor guy, he's so muddled. Well, let me just change that for him. And as for your concern over this hideous thing..." She spun and pointed toward the monument. "I'll make sure that gets taken care of while you reconcile with this lovely man." She moved out of the way so Aurora could see Vahn standing alone, awkwardly waving a greeting.

The sorceress left Aurora to go help Pith just as the dragon flew down to the monument. It released a stream of fire and melted the hateful structure. The dragon stood on its hind legs, then as it charged forward, it shifted into a wave. The water bashed into what remained standing until the horrid monument was nothing but a pile of stones. Where the geysers had broken through the earth, there were now pools once again, filled with the sacred waters. The last of the original pools stood at the center of them all, extending the blessed liquids to trickle down from it.

Vahn slowly approached Aurora. His brow was furrowed, and his face carried an immense worry. Although he was in much better shape than when he was dragged away from the pools, Aurora hesitated for a second, unsure of who this man really was. She knew him when he was under the control of the Dignitaries, but now that he was free, she didn't even know if he remembered her. Then she recalled what Percilla had told her and felt excited to meet the real Vahn, the good-hearted man who was devoted to truth and Rou.

He held his chest high and straightened up his appearance the closer he came to her. She laughed a little at his fidgeting; he knew exactly who she was, or he wouldn't be so nervous.

When he neared Aurora, he bowed. "Aurora—I mean, er, Queen Aurora," he sputtered. He gently took her hand as he dropped to his knees. "I'm so sorry for everything. If I had any idea of what I was doing, I would've stopped this, all of it. I'm sorry I wasn't strong enough. I'm sorry I was involved with them at all. I'll go if you want me to, or if you'd rather lock me up, I'll understand that too."

Aurora smiled wider. "Vahn, you weren't the only one." She tugged on his hand, pulling him to his feet. "They've tricked many people, including me." Relief shone in his eyes as she assured him, "I know who you really are. Your dear friend Percilla told me how loyal you are to Rou."

His shoulders slumped. "I can't believe I wasn't there to help her. We were going to set out together when...when the Dignitaries took me captive. I've failed my best friend and brought harm to your kingdom." He looked at the rubble of the monument. "I don't know what I can do to fix this, to help Rou."

"Will you stay by my side? Continue to be my king?" She pulled him closer, then turned him to face the people entering the area. "*Their* king? I'll need you in the days to come."

Vahn stood taller and squeezed her hand. "I will, my queen, but I don't think I deserve to be a king."

"Let me be the judge of that." She peered deep into his eyes, then pressed her lips to his. They smiled at each other and stepped forward to face the community. Aurora raised her hand to gain the attention of her people. "Today will mark the day we defeated Evils in our kingdom."

The crowd let out a shout of celebration. The sacred pools glowed the vibrant orange of their vortex. It mirrored the determined spirit growing inside Aurora. When she saw Dazell taking Pith toward the pool, she knew all the Evils that had been brought into Evanstide would never return to her kingdom. She had new allies and stronger bonds with those she had known for so long. There was surely nothing that could stop them now.

"Tonight will be the night we redeem our strength as we nourish our energy in the pools. Your king has battled the Evils from within, and his strength makes us all stronger. I stand with him. Will you?" Aurora held her breath, worried she'd asked too much of her people.

A man stepped forward, then a woman. Every person moved closer to their queen and king. A chorus of shouts and hollers went up, and soon Evanstide was filled with them.

"I never imagined I would find a place where people lived in such harmony," Vahn murmured. "I am humbled now and forever to be your king." Once again, he sank to his knees and bowed his head. "I promise to protect you and your kingdom. I swear it on my life."

Aurora reached down and tilted his face up so he could see how much those words meant to her. "With Rou in our hearts and love in our veins, we are all in this together. We are all one."

CHAPTER 42

Allegiance to Rou

SEEING THE PILLARS of violet light encircling the fires of Denton and the glowing garnet runes of Hazan ignited Percilla's spirit. The strength that came from the united communities of Rou ensured her mission was worth everything she endured. On top of that, the Dignitaries' flaming octopus contraption plunging toward the ground was truly a sign that their mission had gone better than she could have imagined.

Matik broke the silence. "Finally, they've met their destruction."

"Temporarily, yes," Frida muttered. "Something tells me this is not their end."

"I can only hope you're wrong," Percilla sighed.

"I don't understand," Matik said as their wings fluttered in unison, propelling them once more toward Panya. "Why don't we just bring them to Rou? Inanna said only their purest selves would enter."

Frida spun around to face Matik and Percilla. "They know that. It's why they brainwash people into following them. If everyone remembered their connection to Rou and embraced their own power, who would serve the Dignitaries? They wouldn't have people to feed on. You have to remember, the Dignitaries haven't always been the same people. They themselves were brainwashed by those before them. It is a cycle of Evils that has continued to find a home in people for some time. Remember what Valti said. The Sages have seen humankind fall time and time again, but with each growth cycle humankind does evolve. Remember the hell at the gates? That's what they..." She trailed off and stared in the direction of Panya's airships with a curious look in her eyes. "Speaking of hells."

Percilla wasn't sure what she meant until she too spotted the bicycle contraption coming toward them. Whoever was riding it waved furiously in greeting. As he drew closer, Percilla's eyes widened in disbelief. "Is that who I think it is?"

"Hey! Where ya ladies been?" Shru yelled, adjusting his goggles.

Frida barked, "Shru, go away. Shoo, leave, fly, don't bother us. We have work to do."

"Aww, come on, Frida love. Have I ever done ya wrong?"

Matik and Percilla fell back as Frida and Shru bantered the rest of the way to Panya. Percilla slid her fingers between Matik's and securely clasped their hands together. She was filled with restored hope after giving the message to yet another Keeper and uniting another community of Rou. She was learning on this journey that the Sages of Rou had their own way of revealing the truth to her. It seemed each Keeper she called to arms would reveal a little bit more to her every time. The Keepers of the Eye needed to unite their people over their vortexes and prepare for when the ruling planet of each community aligned to draw the power of the vortexes up. Then, the colors would reach the sky, and the people would go inside the caverns of the Earth. The planets would go into alignment to begin the cycle of Time once again. And then Inanna said they would be protected. From...

She wasn't sure exactly what would occur next. But as she admired the numerous Denton, Hazan, and Wonkt celebrating behind her, then turned forward to see Panya and Dawookrunk approaching, she knew the people of Rou would thrive again.

Someday, as long as they kept uniting their strength and remained devoted to Rou, anything was possible.

Epilogue

ALARMS BLARED INSIDE the octopus as it shook violently. Drendle struggled to keep it flying.

"We need more energy!" Ons looked at the fading green glow upon the screen. He cursed Monzu and reclaimed his handheld apparatus, formulating a new plan.

"They were right there," Franc muttered. She rubbed her forehead, then tossed her top hat to the floor with a shout of rage. "Why is it whenever I need energy, we don't have it? Where did Monzu go? Could somebody speak up and give me hope that I'm not traveling with a bunch of idiots?"

Ons slid his hand over his tablet. He eyed the blueprints on his screen. "I have an idea."

"You'd better," Franc snapped.

As Ons motioned for Franc to join him at the small, round table in the center of the space, Nylz poked Lyken in the side. "Why do you look so scared?"

"I'm not scared. You're scared," he replied.

Nylz laughed. "You're the one clenching your whole body."

"No laughing!" Franc shouted, and they both stilled. "Why are you even laughing to begin with?"

Nylz and Lyken glanced at each other, then shrugged.

"We have a plan," Ons informed them. "Get over here." He waited until everyone but Drendle joined him at the table. The map of the world was projected on it from his device. "These illuminated spots are the vortexes we know of. This is how we can get Monzu more resources. And *this* is how we can amplify our own energy supplies from them while keeping Monzu better connected to Earth." He zoomed in to a specific location on the map, then overlaid it with an impressively rendered design, one that none but Ons truly understood.

Franc's eyes narrowed with greed, and her lips curled into a wicked smile. "We're not out of the game just yet."

Ons grinned. "No, no we're not."

Kaiva Rose is a Storyteller, Astrologer, Intuitive, Reiki Master and Instructor. Her passion for writing fantasy began as a means to create eccentric characters, though quickly turned into a means to mirror society in an alternate reality. Inspired by writers of antiquity, Kaiva creates pieces of writing that are meant to stand the test of time.

Join the "Rou Odyssey" Community!

Connect with us, write us a letter, check out the Rou Odyssey website!
We would love to hear from you!
www.RouOdyssey.com

Follow us on social media for the latest updates and offers!

CPSIA information can be obtained
at www.ICGtesting.com
Printed in the USA
BVHW011729150321
602576BV00001B/2